T0285284

Praise for the earlier novels by Thérèse:

India's Summer:

"*India's Summer* is a furious, fast-paced, fun romp through the excesses of life in the Hollywood fast lane, with some thought-provoking wisdom interspersed throughout."
- Jane Green, *New York Times* bestselling author

"A book has an energy field all of its own and *India's Summer* has a really great one."
- Ekhart Tolle, spiritual leader and *New York Times* bestselling author

"India's fascinating character is what makes *India's Summer* a compelling read. She is trying to make a big shift in her life, in her career, in the choices she's making. She's funny, clever and vulnerable and you are rooting for her every step of the way."
- Goldie Hawn

Letter from Paris:

"What a wonderful book, a dramatization of an authentic way of being and the journey that India, the main character, takes to get there."
- Beverly Donofrio, author of *Riding In Cars With Boys* and *Astonished*

"I am delighted that PARISIAN CHIC inspired India to explore Paris. Thérèse must have been French in another life."
- Inès de la Fressange, author of *Parisian Chic*

Let it Shine

Let It Shine

Thérèse

The Story Plant
1270 Caroline Street
Suite D120-381
Atlanta, GA 30307

Copyright © 2023 by Thérèse
The Library of Congress Cataloguing-in-Publication Data is available upon request.

Story Plant hardcover ISBN-13: 978-1-61188-369-5
Story Plant e-book ISBN-13: 978-1-61188-381-7

Visit our website at www.TheStoryPlant.com

First Story Plant Printing: September 2023

Printed in the United States of America
0 9 8 7 6 5 4 3 2 1

"What is the new horizon in you that wants to be seen?"
- John O' Donohue

"Hold fast to dreams, for if dreams die, life is a broken-winged bird that cannot fly."
- Langston Hughes

For Adeline, whose light shines so brightly.

DEIRDRE

The sun had dropped behind the mountain, leaving an expanse of streaked indigo sky. Deirdre stepped out through her kitchen door into the fading light. Shivering from the sudden chill, she pulled down her sleeves, tightened her cardigan, and wandered to the end of the garden. She gazed out across the darkening fields with an intense longing. A sliver of moon appeared from behind the clouds, and she looked up.

"Where are you?" She choked, "Where have you gone? Where? Where?... Where?"

An upsurge of grief enveloped her. Powerless to fight it, she clung onto the fence and wept. As the waves passed, she straightened up, pressed her eyes hard with the heels of her hands and turned back to the house. Closing the door, she pulled across the sitting room curtains and flopped into an armchair by the fire.

"It's time for change." She told the empty chair opposite. "I can't carry on like this for much longer. It's putting years on me, and I don't know what to do with myself. I don't know what I'm for anymore."

Reaching over to throw on a log, she sank deeper into the cushions and wrapped a throw around her shoulders.

"Did I tell you I've signed up with a life coach, Niall? I bet that'd surprise you...me admitting I need help, but I can't make my way out of a paper hat these days, or is it a paper bag? You'd be able to tell me, wouldn't you? You'd be laughing now, wouldn't you... Are you laughing? Are you watching? Are you listening? Are you?"

She swallowed hard.

"Thing is..." She managed after a while. "I need to get on, but I don't know what to get on with... I've signed up with this woman Caroline knows. We're going to Zoom. Yes. I Zoom Niall, you'd be amazed."

The silence reverberated

"According to all the books, I'm supposed to see this widow business as an opportunity for growth and do all the things I couldn't do while you were alive. Whoever's writing them didn't have a marriage like ours, did they? You weren't keeping me from doing anything, so I don't know what it is I'm supposed to be doing. I've no interest in seeing the Taj Mahal or the pyramids without you. I don't have a bucket list. Time..." She sighed, glancing up at the mantel clock.

"Time...I have too much time on my hands. Turns out I spent a lot of it making our dinner and doing the laundry. Who'd have thought I'd miss washing your socks?"

She smiled, remembering his penchant for polka dots.

"That's how pathetic I've got; I even miss your underwear. I don't want this. I don't want a new life without you, but I've no choice, do I? I have to find a reason to get out of bed in the mornings. Can you help me? Can you show me what I'm supposed to be doing?"

A log shifted in the grate.

"Is that the best you can do by way of a sign?" She shrugged, heaving herself from the chair and poking the last of the embers. Lifting a silver frame from the mantelpiece, she ran a finger over her wedding photograph.

"I love you sweetheart." She whispered. "I love you so very much. "I got through another day. How many more will I have without you?"

Resting it down gently, she switched off the light, dragged upstairs to the bedroom, and pulled back the covers on one side of the bed.

Deirdre's phone buzzed as she was washing the breakfast dishes the next morning. Pushing a strand of hair from her forehead, she shook the suds from her hands and picked up.

"Hang on Caroline, while I turn down the radio. Okay. I have you on speaker. What did you say?"

"I saw Father Rafferty just now. He said to call him if you need anything before the Anniversary Mass on Tuesday."

"Ah! Thanks. It's unbelievable it's a year, isn't it? A whole year. I don't remember much of it, to tell the God's honest truth."

"It's nothing to the forty-four you had with him."

"That's so true."

Deirdre shook out a dishcloth and swept it across the draining board.

"You got me through it. What would I ever do without you?"

"Hopefully you'll never have to find out." Caroline laughed. "It's as well we don't know what's in front of us, isn't it?

"It is. I feel so old these days."

"Hauld on, missus! We're not buying into that one. I saw an interview with Clint Eastwood; he's ninety-two. They asked him what keeps him working."

"What did he say?"

"He said 'I don't let the old man in.' Isn't that just brilliant?! We're nowhere near his age and we're not going quietly. Look at your woman: Jane Fonda, Goldie Hawn...Maya Angelou."

"Maya Angelou's dead." Deirdre offered.

"Well, if you're going to be a stickler for detail." Her friend laughed. "Next you'll be telling me Elvis is dead, too."

"Never."

"Ha! But you're right. It's all about energy isn't it. Some days it feels like it's coming back, and then I'll have a day like yesterday when the waves hit me like a tsunami. I could hardly get out of the chair. I was in bed by eight o'clock."

"Well, you did get through it, and it's a new one today. You're doing great. One day at a time. It's all any of us has."

"It is."

"I've the call with Sally in a few minutes."

"Ah! Great. Let me know how it goes. I think you two will get on great."

"Will do. I'll call you later."

"Okay. Talk soon."

Deirdre quickly checked her reflection, ran a hand through her hair and pulled out a chair at the kitchen table. She fired up her laptop, angled the screen and waited to join the meeting.

Sally greeted her with an open smile.

"Hello Deirdre. Lovely to meet you."

" You too Sally. Can you see me okay?"

"I can."

"That's good." Deirdre said. " It's my first time using Zoom. Caroline showed me the ropes the other day.

"She said you've known each other a long time."

"A very long time. We were at school together from the age of four."

"Were you really? I was one of her lodgers when she lived in London."

"I know. She told me you were an absolute delight to have around."

"How sweet of her. I remember these great suppers. She's an amazing cook - taught me all about wine. I think of her every time I have a glass of Chablis."

"She certainly likes her Chablis." Deirdre laughed.

"I've been meaning to get over to Ireland to see her."

"Well, you must. She'll make you very welcome. I'm glad she came back home, though. I'd never have got through this year without her. She's been an absolute rock."

"I can believe that. I'm so sorry for your loss." Sally said, dropping her voice. "How do you think I can support you moving forward?"

"Thank you. It's been a rough ride, that's for sure, but it's time to make some changes, and I need some help to figure things out." She looked over her shoulder. "I'm sorry, could you just bear with me a moment?

5

There's someone at the door. Wouldn't you just know it."

"Sorry Sally. That was a neighbor checking in about the Anniversary Mass next week." She said, coming back to the screen. "There'll be people here at the house afterwards; she wanted to know if she should make some vegetarian sandwiches but..." She threw her head back and laughed. "She wasn't sure what a vegetarian sandwich consists of or how many to make."

"So what did you suggest?" Sally asked.

"I said I'd make them myself. I don't want to send her in search of avocados. You can get them at Tesco's, but I doubt she was planning on going that far. So, where were we?"

"I was asking how I might support you. Maybe you could tell me a little about yourself so we can get to know each other?"

"Ah! Yes. That was it. Where to start? How much time do we have?"

"Plenty, almost an hour."

There was a long pause.

"I don't know where to begin."

" Would you prefer me to ask some questions to get us started?"

"Maybe." Deirdre nodded thoughtfully. "I suppose I'd find it easier to tell you about myself if I knew who I was anymore." She sighed. "I feel like I've lost my sense of identity."

"In what way?"

"Most of my life I've been the other half of a couple. Some part of me doesn't know how to function on my own now that Niall's gone... it's still so hard to believe.

You'd think it'd have sunk in by now. I was in grief therapy for months. I've prayed, meditated, scoured every book on grief I could lay my hands on. I've climbed up the side of that mountain so often, there's a track where I walk."

She gestured towards the window and shook her head.

"I'm exhausted, absolutely wiped. I'm worn out trying to manage this pain every minute of the day and night."

'I can only imagine. I'm so sorry."

"Thank you..."

Aware that she was sounding more intense than she intended, and that Sally's brow had furrowed, she changed tack.

"I've been journaling. Here look."

She pulled across a large cardboard box file.

"This is full of letters I've written to Niall every day, every single day. You've no idea how angry I get in some of them. So angry he had to leave me. It doesn't make any sense. Nothing makes any sense."

She paused again, a catch in her voice.

"Some days I'd just write what I was doing or think-ing. You know, all the little things you never realized you just told someone you live with, like who I bumped into down the road, or that I had a paper cut or what I was having for my tea. Nobody cares what I have for my tea anymore...and most days neither do I."

"It sounds like you've shown a lot of strength in how you're handling this." Sally said quietly.

"I'm doing the very best I can, but I'm going round in circles. I need to move forward, but I don't know how. I understand that coaching can help someone to get focused and set goals. That's what I need."

"Personal development work is exhausting even when we aren't in the depths of grief. You've made enormous progress. Just look at what you've achieved - you're still positive, you're a fighter, you're not playing the victim. Don't be hard on yourself. It may be a cliché, but this is a journey and it's sometimes helpful to think of it as just that."

"I'm sorry. Do I sound shrill?"

"Not at all."

"If I do, it's only frustration."

"You don't. You sound very self-aware."

"I need guidance. I've lost all sense of direction."

Sally paused.

"Okay. How does this sound? I'll ask different questions. I'll ask you what you love doing, how you like to spend your time, what films you watch, what books you read. We'll build up a picture of Deirdre Macardle together. We'll look at what you value, what you believe in, where you feel confident, where you feel scared. Then when you're ready, we'll begin to work towards a vision of your future."

Deirdre took a deep breath and heaved a sigh of relief.

"That sounds incredible. Thank you," she said. "That's exactly what I need."

"Great. So, let's start to get to know each other a little. What kind of films do you enjoy?"

Deirdre relaxed into the conversation and closed out of the session with a vague sense of optimism. 'A vision of my future.' She thought. 'And only when I'm ready to face it.'

She sat for a while. The future was still a terrifying prospect. Getting through today had been a challenge.

If she looked ahead to Christmas, she panicked. If she thought about money, she had an anxiety attack. The idea of a night out filled her with dread. Clichés had real meaning now; "butterflies in the stomach, weak at the knees, breaking into a cold sweat, frozen in the headlights, overwhelmed by grief." 'Yes.' She thought with a wry smile, 'I can feel fearful, lost, abandoned, and desolate all in the space of a few minutes. It's like a whole new talent.'

Standing up and stretching her arms above her head, she reached down and rested her hands flat on the floor. Grief, she had determined, could do many things, but it would not immobilize her. From the very first days, she had known that she had to keep moving. Unexpectedly, getting out of bed and getting dressed had been the easy part. It was ingrained from childhood; she did that on automatic pilot.

Slowly lifting up, she inhaled deeply. She would go up the mountain as far as the "Holy Well" and tell Niall about the conversation, how she was planning on beginning a new chapter. Niall was the only person whose voice she wanted to hear, and she could hear it best in the silence of the mountain by the shrine where they had picnicked together so many times. Pulling on an old pair of boots and grabbing a water bottle and snack, she stepped out into the late morning sunshine. A farmer greeted her down the lane.

"Good morning, Deirdre. Fine day for it," he said, brandishing a stick back and forth to guide a cow that was wandering into a blackberry hedge. "How're you doing?"

"Ah! Not so bad Peter." She smiled. "How's your mum getting along?"

"The auld knee's still bothering her, but she's driving again. You can't keep that woman indoors; she'll see us all out."

"How old is she now, Peter?"

"Ninety-three coming next month and still winning at Whist! Must be off; these creatures'll be the death of me," he said, herding the last of the heifers through the gate.

"All the best now."

As Deirdre turned onto the narrow road leading up to the mountain, she was struck by an alarming thought. 'Ninety-three! She's thirty years older than me. What if I've another thirty years left? Thirty years on my own? It's unthinkable.'

Reaching the ancient churchyard, she levered the heavy chains from the gates and stepped through the overgrown grass past crumbling tombs to stop at a granite headstone. She perched on the edge of the grave.

"Hello Mammy." She whispered, "Not staying long, just couldn't walk by without saying 'Hello.' I ran into Pete McGuinness on the road just now, and he told me Kathleen's ninety-three, I was thinking you'd have been that same age. You were at school together, weren't you? It's such a funny old business, this life thing, isn't it? I wonder how long I've got. Some days I just want to climb right in there next to you, but I can hear you giving out to me, telling me to wise up and get on with living. So that's what I'm trying to do."

She stopped speaking as a circle of crows flew through the lintel of a doorway into the ruins of the church.

"Okay, then," she said, once the cacophony had stopped. "I'll drop by on Tuesday after mass. I'm going to read my favorite Yeats. You remember the one, *When You are Old*. I know that's what Niall would have picked."

Yanking out at a clump of dandelions from the stonework, she knocked the soil from her hands and stood up.

"Well, I'll be going now. Bye Mam. I love you." She murmured, making her way back to the gate. Determinedly fighting back tears, she turned up an over-grown path at the side of the graveyard. The fastest way to the well was across the fields.

In recent years, the mountain had been named an "Area of Outstanding Natural Beauty." Hiking trails had been carved out for visitors to reach the shrine, and there were roads to the lake at the summit. Deirdre had mixed feelings about it. It was progress in the context of the years of sectarian violence she had lived through, but she felt a protective ownership of this mountain where generations of her family lay buried.

Further up the incline, she negotiated the pebbles across a stream and paused to catch her breath. Then, pushing back brambles from a hawthorn bush, she opened the gate to a derelict cottage that had belonged to her mother's friend Winifred many years before. Taking out her phone, she snapped a few pictures of cow parsley set against a dry-stone wall, and, clambering over a stile, continued climbing until she reached the well. Lifting a bottle of water from her bag, she tore open a packet of crisps and sat on a flat rock.

"I had a great old chat with the life coach, Niall," she said, "She used to be a psychologist or a psychiatrist; you'd be able to tell me the difference. I'll have to look it up now."

She twisted the top of the flask.

"Here's the thing, Niall. It's been almost a year and I can't get you out of my head. I go to bed and there's this big empty space. I make our coffee, then pour half the pot away. I look to you to finish my sentences. I can't tell a decent story; you'd always come in with the punchline. But this has got to stop. I can't spend my days walking endlessly like this and talking out loud like I'm unhinged."

She finished the last of the crisps and lay down on the grass, relishing the sun on her face, She closed her eyes and listened to the water gushing over the rocks, drifting off for a while then jolting up with a shiver. The sky was darkening rapidly. Pushing the empty bottle and wrapper into her bag, she began making her way down the slope.

"You'd have told me to wear my Mac, wouldn't you Niall?" she said. "I've nobody looking after me any-more... Nobody."

Feeling increasingly desolate, she reached Win-ifred's cottage. As she wrestled with the iron gate, a tree branch sprang back and whipped across her face. Outraged by the sting, a mounting fury swelled in her throat. She let out a ferocious scream, then another and another, her primal howls echoing across the hillside as the pain ripped through her. Kicking open the gate, she tore through the fields, running until her knees buckled. Doubling over, she clutched her chest waiting for her heart to stop pounding. Then, steady-ing her breath, she continued down the mountain.

A car horn honked as she reached the lane. There would be no way of avoiding the neighbor waving to her. She knocked some grass off her sweater and walked across to the car.

"Deirdre. Just the woman I wanted to see. The missus and I were wondering if you'd be up for a bite of dinner on Saturday night? She was going to call you

"You know Peter. I'd like that," she said, after a moment's hesitation."Thank you."

"Grand. Come over 'round eight. Can I give you a lift?"

"No thanks. I need the exercise."

"Fair game to you." He grinned. "All the best now."

Deirdre watched the car disappear down the road, then walked on. The rain was hitting her shoulders, but she didn't care. Her screams had been cathartic. Something had shifted. A weight had been lifted. She would walk until this feeling had settled into her bones.

"So how are you, Deirdre? "Sally began their call the following week. "I know you had the Anniversary Mass the other day."

"I'm okay, thanks. So many people came out to remember Niall. I was so grateful for it. I do seem to be stronger than I was a year ago," she said, thinking back to how she had chosen the blue silk dress Niall loved to see her in, and made an effort with her hair and makeup. At the tea reception afterwards, there had even been fleeting moments when she'd forgotten why they were all there. It had felt good to have the house full of friends again.

"I'd been dreading the anniversary, and now it's behind me."

"It's the benefit of having a community, isn't it?

"It really is."

"That's a beautiful flower arrangement, Deirdre."

Deirdre pushed the vase across the table a little closer to the screen.

"Peonies. Yes, aren't they beautiful, such a gorgeous shade of pink. Our daughter Somhairlin sent them. She wanted to come home for the anniversary, but I told her I'd be fine. She just started a new job a few months ago, and her dad would have never wanted her missing work."

"What a lovely name."

It's Irish for Samantha."

"How old is she?'

"Just turned thirty-two. She has her whole of her life in front of her, but she's still lost without her dad. They were so close."

"It must be so hard for her too."

"Yes."

"So Deirdre..." Sally said after a pause. "I was wondering what you did when you left school. Did you go to university?"

Deirdre welcomed the change of topic. Her heart was sore for Somhairlin, and even though she'd insisted she'd be fine, she had missed her at the service.

"Ah! No, Sally I didn't do well at school at all," she said. "The careers teacher pointed me to hairdressing. It was soul-destroying, all those horrible perms and standing on your feet all day long listening to people drone on about the weather. I hated it. Of course, nowadays you can earn a fortune and travel the world, but there weren't the opportunities you have now. It was all rollers and hairspray. I'm that old."

"So, let's go back a bit. Tell me what you enjoyed doing when you were younger.

"Let me think. Oh yes!"

Her face lit up.

"I loved dressing up," she said. "I just had a flash-back of shuffling around in my mother's high heels with a long head scarf twisted around my neck like Sophia Loren. Like this..." She gestured, twirling her arms around her head.

"Oh! And something else... I had an aunt who lived in England. She arrived over one Christmas wearing a gold lamé suit. It had a cowl necktie and covered buttons down the back and a pencil skirt. I'd never seen anything like it. I asked her if she would leave it to me when she died! Can you imagine! I think I was about nine at the time."

"That's priceless," Sally spluttered.

"Anyway, a few weeks later a parcel arrived, and in it was...you've guessed ...the gold lamé suit with a little note assuring me that she was still alive."

"That's so funny."

"I think that was the beginning of my love of clothes. I spent nights in front of the mirror draped in gold lamé. I was beyond happy. I've never stopped wanting to dress up. I love accessories, scarves... I love scarves. You should see my collection. Funny that. I collect them but don't wear them much. I suppose I'd have liked to work in fashion, but it's far too late for that now."

"I don't believe that for a minute Deirdre."

Sally's tone was firm.

"I'm realistic. If you were telling me you'd like to be a sky-diving instructor, I might tell you to lower your expectations, but there are plenty of ways to get involved in fashion, I'm sure."

"I suppose..." Deirdre hesitated. "It must be great to have a clear sense of what you want to do from an early age. Niall always knew. He still has...sorry, 'had' his Meccano kit from when he was a child."

"What did he do?"

"He was a mechanical engineer. We had a little business. I helped in the office. It kept me busy; we'd work all hours though, machinery breaking down, cars needing hauling out of ditches. After Somhairlin was born, I couldn't have any more children, so I focused a lot of my time on her, worked in the school as a teacher's assistant for a while. Niall sold the business only last year. He'd only been retired three months. We had all these plans; buying a little house in Donegal, going back to Big Sur and San Diego, that was to have been..."

Her voice trailed off. She slumped into the chair.

"I'm sorry. I think I'm fine and then..."

"Take your time, Deirdre." Sally said quietly.

"Just give me a second please. I'll be okay in a moment."

She turned away from the screen squeezing her eyes tightly, then with a little shake of her head looked back at Sally.

"So sorry. Where was I?" she said. "Oh yes..."

"Are you sure you're feeling strong enough for this conversation Deirdre?"

"I am. I really am okay. I'm sorry. I don't know what came over me there. I think I was about to explain why I didn't worry about not having my own career?"

"Take your time."

"Thank you... So...well, it's only since Niall passed away that I've realized I've nothing to fall back on. I've been a wife and a mother. I was a good daughter too, looked after my own mother for a long time... My brother lives in Canada. He's not the best at keeping in touch, so there was only me, but nobody needs me much now."

"I can see how it must feel like that, but maybe this is the time in your life where you get to focus more on yourself and what you need, not what others need from you."

"I hadn't thought of it like that. It sounds selfish."

Sally took a sip of water.

"It's not selfishness Deirdre, it's about getting strong again so that you can find a new way to be in the world and a new way to be needed."

"Okay. I'll think about that Sally. I will. I'm already feeling guilty talking endlessly about myself in our sessions."

"There's nothing to feel guilty about Deirdre. This is your mental health. It's important."

"Yes. You're right. It was drummed into me to put other people first. It might not be an easy thing to undo."

"We can talk more about that Deirdre. It's not about who goes first, it's about respecting your own needs as well as other people's. So, let's get back to you! What was your favorite subject at school?"

"Drawing. I was always drawing. Oh! And I loved dancing as well."

"Do you still draw?"

"Not for years... I enjoyed art, but I wasn't all that good at it. Niall and I would go to galleries. We went to quite a few exhibitions in Paris and London. Dublin's become something of a center for art now too you know."

"Yes. I know. I love Dublin. I've been a few times. It's such a vibrant city. I saw an Impressionists exhibition at the National Gallery of Ireland a while ago."

"I love them too. Did you ever visit Musée d'Orsay in Paris?"

"Yes. A few times." Sally nodded. "So...are you okay if I ask you more questions?"

"Ask away, Sally. Now I'm not supposed feel guilty talking endlessly about myself, I'm really enjoying this."

Sally gave her an encouraging smile.

"I'm glad." She said, looked down at her list. "How about music. Did you play an instrument?"

"Piano for a while, but I didn't persevere. Of course, now I wish I had. I imagine it would be very therapeutic."

"What kind of music do you like?"

"Ah! Sally where would you start? I've such a broad taste for it. I suppose if you're asking about classical, my favorites are Chopin and Massenet, but I'd have you here all day with the rest, so many. You can probably guess; The Stones, Dylan, Bowie..."

"The sixties, then."

"Yes. I missed all the flower-power and hippy stuff, but I got the music. I loved dancing."

"Do you enjoy cooking?"

"Sometimes. There's not much pleasure in it anymore, but over the years I did; who wouldn't with this lovely kitchen? Do you cook?"

"I can just about make an omelet." Sally laughed. "My husband's the cook in our house. I've never really had much interest in it..."

She glanced at her notes.

"You said you enjoyed dancing?"

"Yes. Niall and I, we..."

Deirdre paused mid-sentence, recalling how Niall would have her up for every waltz at a wedding. How sometimes after a couple of glasses of wine, they would glide around the bedroom listening to Leonard Cohen and fall together onto the bed...*show me slowly what I only know the limits of...and dance me to the end of love.* Her heart was aching as the memories crowded in.

"I'm sorry if this isn't easy for you, Deirdre."

"What? Oh! Sorry, Sally. I was miles away there. What were you saying?"

"We were talking about dancing."

"Ah! Yes. Yes." She caught herself. "I did, but I think my dancing days are behind me now."

"I bet they're not." Sally smiled. " Deirdre, I'm afraid we're running out of time, but I've been making notes as we've been going along and I can email you some other questions. You don't have to answer any you don't want to; it's all designed to go at your own pace. It's important you're comfortable."

"Thank you, Sally." Deirdre said, stifling a yawn.

"Take care. Enjoy your day, Deirdre."

Sally smiled and stretched across to close out the connection.

"Thank you, Sally. You too."

Deirdre stared at the blank screen. The vivid images of dancing with Niall had left her aching for the physical comfort of him, for the intimacy they had shared, for the arms she longed to have around her. It had been interesting to reminisce about her childhood dreams and to be reminded of her younger self, but not for a split second did she wish her life had been different. Yes, she may not have had her own career, but while Niall had been with her, she had never wanted any other life. There might have been other choices, but she had made the right ones.

She closed over her laptop and began to pack away dishes. A while later, she propped a mop behind the utility room door and surveyed her immaculate kitchen.

'All those years complaining of the mess and I'd give anything to see Niall's oily overalls on the floor and muddy boots by the range,' she thought. 'I'd give the world to have the baby cot over there and the rows of dresses and tiny pajamas drying on the rack. I want it all again. I want my life back. I liked my life. I was happy. What happened? Where did it go?'

She switched on the dishwasher and dropped heavily into a chair.

"This was never the plan, was it Niall? We took it for granted we'd be together in our dotage, didn't we? We thought we'd be Derby and Joan, the folk who live on the hill. I really believed that would be us. You did too. You're not supposed to lose your soulmate, are you? It's too cruel."

Looking across the room, she had a vivid image of Niall framed in the doorway. Why had they not had one last proper kiss? Why had she not given him a hug? Why? Why? The answer was obvious; it had been an ordinary day;he would be back for his lunch. She was drying the dishes. Life had been normal. It would never be normal again.

Shuddering at the memory of the call that came a few hours later, Deirdre jumped up, snatched her coat from a chair, grabbed her phone and tore down the path. She had to shake off this mood, or the day would be lost to yet another afternoon staring at the mantelpiece. Slowing down when she reached the lane, she walked along a stretch of unmade road and up a track to the ruins of an ancient house where she knew there would be no danger of coming across a neighbor.

'Life's not meant to be easy,' she thought, taking off her coat and spreading it out over a rock. 'How hard it must have been drawing water from a well, fighting the bitter winds, and with no heat except for the fire you'd have to light yourself. Our generation has been lucky so far, Niall. We had 'the troubles,' the army on the streets, and the helicopters flying over, but we had a grand old life despite it all. Just think where we've been, what we've done, and we had our house exactly the way we wanted it. It's just a house now, Niall, not a home anymore. I loved it so much, but it may as well be like this one for all I care.

She ran her hand over the weathered stone, then climbed through the bramble, over the rubble and moss to a barbed wire fence where a flock of sheep ambled towards her with their lambs in tow. They stopped and stared directly at her. She stared back, then pulled out her phone. "Say cheese," she told them.

Back from her walk, she made a cup of tea and took it over to her desk in the corner of the kitchen. She scanned through the latest series of photographs she had taken, editing and deleting, then overlaying a few images and printing them off.

In the last twelve months, she had taken hundreds of photographs of old stone walls and crumbling buildings, portals, openings, windows, and archways, as well as a collection of tree trunks, bark, and stone that had caught her eye on the endless walks alone. She had no idea where the impulse for this had come from or why she was storing them in files, other than that they too were a journal, a record of what she was going through, some tangible expression of her pain.

Now, browsing through the printed pages, she remembered how being out in nature had brought her solace. The falling leaves had mirrored her intense loss in the early days, and the dark days of winter reminded her of the words of a song, that 'to everything, there was a season, a time to break down and a time to build up, a time to mourn and a time to dance.'

Spring had brought intense memories of happier days, when she would pick wild daffodils from the roadside and put branches of lilac from the garden into jugs all over the house. She would shake the rugs and clear out the closets. Niall would be working in the garden, turning over the soil and planting. They would marvel at the buds pushing through and the days getting longer. It had been so hard. She felt as though nature were betraying her; she wasn't ready for renewal. Flicking over an image of apple blossom, she saw the Yeats' poem that had captured the essence of that time so perfectly:

"Through wintertime we call on spring and through the spring on summer call, and when abounding hedges ring, declare that winter's best of all."

She had read it to him as if he were listening, at the graveside on their wedding anniversary in April, the last line resonating in ways it never had before: "*Nor know that what disturbs our blood is but its longing for the tomb.*"

Niall would never read poetry for himself, but he loved it when she would open her Yeats anthology and read aloud from the pages.

Deirdre didn't aspire to being a photographer. She had observed that everyone seemed to have become one, photoshopping sunrises, augmenting the night skies, abstracting images. She didn't draw comparisons. What she was producing didn't need validation, or "likes." It was deeply personal. The only person she wanted to share them with was Niall. It was ironic; if he were still alive, she would not be taking them.

Closing down her computer, she saw Sally's latest attachment of links to books and videos that might be of interest. She'd get to them later; right now, she needed a nap. Settling into the kitchen armchair, she woke up an hour later as the light was fading. The prospect of another long evening alone was depressing. Caroline might be free; she'd call. Her friend picked up right away

"Are you busy?" Deirdre asked, her tone lighter than she felt.

"Nothing that can't wait. How are you?"

"Not so bad. Do you fancy coming over this evening?"

"I do. I've been in the house all day. Have you eaten yet? There's Marks and Spencer pasta here and some salad, and I think I've a bottle of red wine somewhere."

"That sounds lovely. Bring the food. I've plenty of wine."

"Okay, be there in twenty minutes."

'What would I do without her?' Deirdre thought, clicking off the phone. Putting out two place settings, she glanced across at Niall's empty chair, then taking out two goblets from the cabinet, she opened a bottle of red wine, poured a glass, and raised it.

"Your favorite Malbec," she said. "Sláinte."

Taking a sip, she set down the glass and carried a couple of fresh logs into the living room. After several failed attempts at lighting the fire, it burst of flames. She stood back satisfied with the result and heard the door slam as Caroline let herself in the back way. She turned on the sidelights, poked at the logs, and went back to the kitchen. Caroline was already busy at the stove, humming away to herself. Deirdre took a few more sips of wine, shook salad into a bowl, and whipped up a dressing. Within minutes, they were at the table, relaxed in the familiarity of being together, having barely spoken a word.

"So, how're you getting on with Sally?" Caroline asked, after they'd eaten, kicking off her shoes and settling into an armchair.

"Really well. She's lovely. Thank you so much for connecting us."

"I thought you two would click. That's great to hear."

"It's not like the grief therapy. She's asked me a lot about school and what subjects I liked.'

"Not a lot, if I remember rightly." Caroline laughed. "Sister Philomena and you didn't exactly see eye to eye."

"True. But I'd forgotten how much I enjoyed Miss O'Malley's dancing classes.

"And the musicals. Do you remember *The Mikado*? Who was the other maid? There was you, me and yes, it was Bridie McCabe.

On an instant, Caroline leapt up and began the geisha dance, shuffling sideways across the carpet. Deirdre joined her.

"'*Three little maids from school are we, pert as a schoolgirl well can be.*' You know we hadn't a clue what we were singing did we? You'd not get away with that line nowadays." Caroline giggled. "'*One little maid is a bride Yum Yum*'". She collapsed onto the couch convulsed with laughter.

"'*Life is a joke that's just begun*'...and it was, wasn't it Dee, we had no idea, God, we were so innocent back in those days."

"We were that." Deirdre agreed.

"It's great to see you laughing."

"It feels good. We've laughed a fair bit over the years, haven't we?"

"Yes, and if God spares us, we'll laugh some more. I hear you had supper with the Larkins last Saturday."

"News travels fast." Deirdre said. "I did. They've been asking me for a while. It was strange to be there, just the three of us, but I'd better get used to it. I can't end up a recluse."

"No danger of that while I'm around. Here, is there any more of the wine left?"

"I'll open another bottle.'

"Good woman."

Caroline threw a log on the fire then curled back up, pulling a tartan throw over her lap. "I think I'll stay over tonight."

"The spare bed's made up already."

"Ah great, thanks. Here, do you remember the day Máire told us she was pregnant? She'd only turned sixteen."

"I do, just think her little girl must be forty-odd by now."

"Where does the time go?"

"Do you remember..."

The two women reminisced well into the night. Deirdre woke in the early hours as the sun rose in the distance, and her bedroom filled with golden light. Heavy clouds rolled in after a while, and she lay awake in the darkened room. As the sky lightened again, she watched a couple of kites fly between the tall trees, swooping and circling. Then, hearing her friend moving around in the bathroom, she pulled on a robe and went down to make breakfast.

"Well, that's a smell to gladden a woman's heart." Caroline declared, coming into the kitchen as Deirdre was lifting bacon rashers from a skillet.

"Here, pour yourself some tea; the toast'll be ready in a minute."

Deirdre turned the eggs and slid them onto plates.

Sitting down, she took a deep breath. Saying out loud what she had been thinking would make it real.

"Caroline. I was awake early... and I think I've made a decision."

"You have a brain to make a decision?" Caroline yawned, "My head feels like someone took a chain saw to it."

"I tried to get you to drink some water, remember?"

"I'll be okay once this kicks in." Caroline groaned, assembling two pieces of bacon between slices of toast and reaching for the sauce bottle. "So go on. You've made a decision?"

"Not definitely. I want to run it by you first."

"Okay."

"I'm thinking I should sell this house. It's too big for me and it feels like it's full of ghosts."

Caroline's shoulders collapsed.

"Aw, Dee, I can't be objective about that. What would I do without you down the street? You know how much I love this house; I pretty much grew up here too." She grabbed Deirdre's hand across the table.

"I'm sorry. That was so selfish of me. I'm sorry, this shouldn't be about me at all."

"It's okay Caroline, if it was the other way around, I'd be the same."

"Are you thinking of buying a cottage in the village? There's one for sale by Murphy's pub; I saw a sign going past the other day."

Deirdre lifted the teapot and walked over to the sink. Filling the kettle, she kept her back to Caroline, understanding that this would mean a big change for her, too.

"I'm thinking of going to England for a visit. Somhairlin was all for coming home but she's working, so it'll be easier if I go there."

"That sounds like a good idea for sure, but why would you need to sell the house? I'd look after it for you, or you could rent it out on Air B&B; I'd make sure they didn't wreck the place."

Deirdre brought the fresh pot of tea to the table.

"I need to make a clean break of it," she explained. "If I don't make a move now, I absolutely know I never will. I'll be known as 'Widow Macardle, the old woman, a bit crazed in the head, who used to be married to that Niall feller.'"

Saying it out loud had indeed made it real.

"I can see me being miserable for the rest of my life if I stay, Caroline. I need to move on. I don't know how long I'm going to live, but I can't spend my time in this house, when half of me is missing."

"But you can't stay with Somhairlin indefinitely. Goes without saying there's always a bed at my house, but you don't want to find yourself adrift."

"I'm already adrift." Deirdre sighed. "I can always rent somewhere in London."

"Let's talk about it some more. I have to be off in ten minutes. I'm taking mam to the doctors. She needs another shot for the arthritis. Promise you won't do anything drastic until we have a proper chat about it."

"Promise." Deirdre agreed, but she knew that she had made up her mind.

SAM

"**M**ahalo. Welcome to The Grand Hyatt Kauai, Miss Kingsley. Please let me know if there's anything at all we can do to make your stay more comfortable."

"Thank you. You can take this thing for starters." Alexandra said, lifting a lei from her shoulders and dropping it onto the counter. "And my assistant doesn't need one either." She added, brushing off her blouse with exaggerated flicks of her enameled nails and turning on her heel.

Sam wanted the ground to open up and swallow her.

"Sorry," she mouthed, negotiating the flowers over her head. "I think it's lovely."

"I'll have it sent to your room." The receptionist told her with a reassuring smile.

"Thank you," she mouthed, dashing after Alexandra, who had already reached the elevator at the far end of the lobby.

"Sam. Could I remind you that you're not on vacation," Alexandra snapped, stabbing the call button. "I'll meet you back here in half an hour."

"Okay. Not a problem."

"Why would there be a problem? Could you stop saying that please. I'll be sure to let you know when there is one."

Sam heaved a sigh of relief as the doors slid closed. She didn't need reminding that she was here for work. The previous weeks of preparation for the conference had been a logistical nightmare. She had been pulling all-nighters for weeks.

A girl in a neon string bikini and array of garlands reached the doors seconds too late.

"She could have held it for me," she spluttered.

"Try working for her," Sam muttered.

"Your boss?"

"Yes."

"Poor you. Want some?" She asked, proffering her wine glass."

"Not right now, thanks."

"Good luck." She waved, skipping into the elevator.

Sam strolled onto the terrace into a wall of tropical heat under the bluest sky she had ever seen. She wandered around the property, along the plumeria scented paths, past a pool of iridescent koi to a rocky lagoon by the dunes. Ahead, the ocean shimmered against an unbroken horizon. She stood in the shade of a palm tree watching the beach staff open umbrellas and set up loungers. Nearby, a woman in a cabana set down her cocktail glass, stretched out, and positioned a wide brimmed hat over her face.

'She looks so happy,' Sam thought, turning away. 'I can't remember the last time I was happy. It doesn't matter where I am or what I'm doing; this ache won't go away.'

She kicked her foot against the sandy verge, kicked it harder again, then turned back towards the building.

Crossing the lawn, a flock of tiny birds with red beaks fluttered out from a hedge. She watched them dart and hop between the flowers,then, stood back to let a bridal couple and their photographer go past.

"Congratulations!" She smiled at them.

Back in the lobby, weaving her way through the lines of delegates waiting to check in, she spotted Alexandra standing by a billboard scrutinizing her phone. Sam glanced at the banner headline above the headshot of the speaker. *The Human Factor in Human Resources.*

'I have absolutely no idea what that means,' she thought.

"Oh! You're here." Alexandra said curtly. "Let's go."

The ballroom was empty apart from a few staff removing the last of the tablecloths and flower arrangements from a wedding reception.

Are you sure we're in the right room?" Alexandra said, glancing at her watch.

"It said 'Grand Ballroom' on the wall outside, so I suppose we must be."

"You suppose."

Sam said nothing. It was only five minutes past the hour, but she felt uneasy. 'Do hotels have lots of ballrooms?' She wondered.

"You might want to fix your hair."

"Sorry?"

"Your hair. It looks like you've had your fingers in the mains."

Sam hastily smoothed it down.

"Sorry. It's the humidity," she said.

"That's what elastic bands are for." Alexandra quipped as the fire doors banged open and a woman wearing a white pantsuit stretched at the seams clicked towards them in precariously high heels.

"Ah! Hello. Lovely to finally meet you, Alexandra," she said, extending her arm. "It's been such a pleasure dealing with your bureau; you've a great team. Sandra has been so helpful."

"Thank you so much, Suzy. At AISB, we think of our speakers and agents as family," Alexandra gushed.

'One big dysfunctional one,' Sam thought, 'You haven't even introduced me.'

"Here. Take a seat," Suzy said, pulling out a gilt chair for her. Sam sat down opposite them, fighting off a familiar feeling of invisibility as she opened the conference pack.

"I was happy you settled on Jon Porter to close. I know he'll leave your audience with lots to think about," Alexandra said, gliding into a chair and carefully crossing one leg over the other.

"It was the right decision. Our chairman originally thought we'd ask him to open the symposium. I was behind that idea because he's such a draw, and it would have guaranteed all the delegates attending the first morning session. Some of them are flying in late tonight from Hong Kong. But you were right. It will keep everyone looking forward the final dinner, and we'll end on a high note."

"Could you run me through the final itinerary, Suzy?" Alexandra said, shooting a withering look at Sam. "I'm afraid I only received it a few minutes ago. Thank you, if you wouldn't mind."

Sam felt the blood rush to her temples. This was an outright lie. She'd worked late the previous nights so that Alexandra could read the full program on the plane.

32

Suzy set her laptop on the table and swiveled it around so that Alexandra could see her presentation.

"We were so disappointed Jon won't be attending the welcome dinner this evening," she said. "I was hoping that might have changed?"

Alexandra whipped out a pair of tortoise shell glasses from her purse and perused the screen.

"I'm afraid that's still the case," she said. "He's had a grueling couple of weeks on the road. He needs the down time this evening."

"Yes. That's a long flight from Vancouver. You'll still be joining us though?"

"Absolutely. Thank you for including me. They were setting out tables on the lawn as I came down. It looks fabulous."

"It really does, doesn't it. We've had a few events here these last few years. It's spectacular at night. Have you been to Kauai before?"

"No, only to the Big Island and Maui."

Sam was suffering through their small talk. How she longed to be back outside in the sunshine.

"Last year's main conference was at 'The Four Seasons' in Maui," Suzy continued. "This is a smaller venue. It's more intimate for our in-house event. It should work perfectly for the break-out sessions."

"Yes, I can see that it will."

"We had two thousand attendees in Maui. It was quite a challenge logistically."

"I heard. You had one of my clients, Fred Watts speaking there. I wasn't involved directly. As you might imagine, I can't be at all our clients' events; we have so many. But I always make sure that either myself or one of my associates gets to hear our top talents at least three times a year."

'Can we get on with whatever we need to get on with?' Sam was thinking when her phone pinged. She read the text and picked her moment to interrupt.

"I'm sorry." She said, "I've just had a text from Sophie to say Jon Porter's line check has been moved to three o'clock. That's in fifteen minutes. You're busy here Alexandra, would you like me to collect him?

"Of course." Alexandra said with a tight smile. "Thank you, Sam. Please explain that I have been delayed and will text him."

"Of course," she said, jumping up, thrilled to escape the tedium.

Running over to the front desk, she asked to be put through to Jon Porter's room.

"Who should I say is calling?"

"Alexandra Kingsley's personal assistant. From AISB Speakers' Bureau."

She was handed the phone.

"Hello Mr. Porter. I'm calling to let you know there's been a time change for your line check. I'm so sorry to give you such short notice, but it's in ten minutes in the gardens. Would you like me to meet you at reception? I'm in the lobby."

There was a pause before he replied.

"I was asleep."

"I'm sorry to disturb you."

Another pause.

"Mr. Porter are you still there?"

"Yes. Okay. Give me five minutes." He yawned. "Okay."

Firing off a text to the technician to say they were running behind, she watched the elevator for signs of

Jon. Twenty minutes later, he emerged clad in a heavy leather jacket, jeans, and biker boots.

'He's going to melt out there.' She thought, freeing up her hand from underneath her laptop. "Good to meet you, Mr. Porter."

"Oh! Shit." She cursed as a folder slipped out and papers spewed across the marble hallway. "Sorry. I mean damn."

"I think I know what you mean." He laughed, scooping them up and handing them back to her with a grin. "Jon. Pleased to meet you. So, where's Alexandra? Has she checked in yet?"

"She's trapped in a meeting, I'm afraid. She's in the ballroom with the event coordinator and sends her apologies. She said she'll be in touch the minute she's free."

"Okay. Lead on. You're her personal assistant?"

"Yes."

"So how's that going? This is the fourth gig I've done with AISB this year and you're the third PA."

"I've only been with the agency three months," she said. "I understand there's been a lot of internal restructuring."

"Very tactful." He grinned, holding open the glass door onto the terrace. "After you."

The grand lawn was bustling with staff ferrying stacks of chairs to folded tables and caterers setting up food stations. Stepping around boxes and over wires to the stage, Sam found a crew member who directed her to the sound technician. He nodded to Jon.

"Great to meet you, man. Won't keep you long. Greg here will mic you up."

Sam moved away from the stage down the central aisle to a far table, praying the earsplitting noises would stop soon and wishing she had brought her sun hat. The heat was intense and there was no shade.

'One two, one two. Testing, testing...one, two, three.'

Jon began parroting speech-testing words.

"Press the pants and sew a button on the vest... The fish twisted and turned on the bent hook. The swan-dive was far short of perfect."

His voice echoed across the gardens. Watching a string of nene geese wandering across the lawn, Sam had a sudden flash of unreality. Everything around her seemed alien. A surge of fear gripped her throat. It was as if she were seeing and hearing everything from behind a pane of glass. Her body tensed, and her heart began to race.

'Not now. Not here. Breathe...Breathe...One, two, three, four... Exhale...' she told herself.

"One two, one two," The speaker blasted. "Press the pants. Press the pants."

'In for three. Out...' she thought. 'Stay grounded. Name three things... chair, shoes, hand... chair, hand, back of chair.'

"Press the pants." Jon's voice boomed.

'You're safe. Breathe. This won't last,' she said. 'This will pass. This will pass.'

The blasting from the speakers stopped abruptly, and she saw Jon was moving across the stage. She hurried over and took a bottle of water from the crew table.

"Okay. What's next?" he asked, jumping down.

"That's it for now," she said, grateful he was unclip-ping his microphone and not looking directly at her. Her hand was shaking as she drank.

"Alexandra will text you to meet up. Would you like me to walk back with you?"

"Thank you." He laughed. "I think I can find my way. Catch you later."

"Okay."

Sam waited for him to turn the corner before taking off her shoes and cutting across the lawn towards the sand dunes. The grass felt prickly under her feet. Reaching a line of empty loungers, she threw down her bag and meandered towards the beach. Reaching the water's edge, she kicked at the shallow waves, picking up stones and tossing them into the ocean. Then, lifting her dress, she waded up to her knees and splashed along to the end of the cove. Doubling back, she ran in and out of the shoreline, turning and skipping, until catching her breath, she dropped her head to her knees and swung her arms. She looked up and scanned the dunes.

"Where am I? Where've I left my bag?"

Dashing up the side of the cliff, she orientated herself, standing with her back to the property, then raced towards the clump of palm trees by the lagoon. Spotting the lounger, she rifled through her tote and checked her phone. The lack of communication from Alexandra was both a relief and alarming.

She began texting.

'Do you need me to do anything Alexandra?'

'Delete, too broad a question.'

'I'm available if you need me.'

That was obvious, Alexandra knew how to contact her.

'The sound check went well, and Mr. Porter has gone back to his room.'

'Okay that's about right,' she thought, pressing "Send".

Picking up her shoes, she cut across to the kiosk and ordered a smoothie. As she waited, a little girl in a daisy bikini came toddling towards her. The mother dashed after her swooping her up in her arms.

'Will that ever be me?' Sam wondered, returning the woman's smile.

Collecting her drink, she set off for the room. Hopefully, she would have time for a shower and a change of clothes before she was needed again.

Sam pushed open the door to her hotel room and gasped. Dashing across the suite, she slid back large glass doors and went out onto the balcony to take in the uninterrupted view of the ocean. A flotilla of boats was sailing off in the distance and looking across the gardens through the waving palm trees, she could see the swimming pools and lagoon.

Stepping back inside, she wandered around the mirrored table and chairs, admiring a giant centerpiece of pink orchids, then across to the marbled bathroom. She did a little skip seeing the walk-in rain shower and stack of folded towels. Running into the bedroom, she bounced across the width of the sumptuous bed, then opened her case, pulled out two shift dresses and hung them onto the padded hangers in the walk-in closet. She undressed and stepped into the shower. Wrapped in a fluffy hotel robe a while later, she went back out onto the balcony.

Struck by how quickly her mood had lifted, she smiled.

'Dad would have laughed so hard.' She thought. 'I know what he'd have said: "Turns out all it takes to cheer you up, is a Hawaiian island, a five-star hotel, and an ocean-view room."'

Tears sprung up and stung the back of her eyes. How she missed his one-liners, their chats, their texts. How she ached to see him, to tell him how she was struggling, to get his advice on this job, to feel safe again, to know he was there, her rock, her anchor. The year had passed by in a fog. This job had seemed to be the right move; it had felt as though the universe were guiding her, that her dad had played some part in orchestrating her life from beyond, delivering her an opportunity that involved travel and paid well. But she wasn't so sure now. She wasn't sure what she believed in. She wasn't sure about anything at all, and the panic attacks were back.

The house phone startled her back to the moment.

"There's been a mistake in the room allocations." Alexandra greeted her.

"I'm sorry?"

"You are in my room. I need you to bring me the key."

"I'm sorry Alexandra, but I don't think you'll want my room, I've had a shower and I've used the towels and things and robe and..."

"Call housekeeping. Get them to refresh everything. Tell them I need it cleaned within half an hour."

The line went dead.

'I knew this was too good to be true.' Sam thought, pressing the button for housekeeping. "Sod it. Engaged."

She clanked down the receiver and ran into the bathroom. Grabbing her clothes from the floor, she dressed, scooped up her toiletries and threw them into her suitcase. Flying down the corridor, she remembered her dresses and raced back, yanked them from the hangers, and stuffed them into her tote.

She joined the long line at reception and was finally explaining the situation to the duty manager when Alexandra called again.

'Is the room ready?

Still trying to sort it out.

"I'm sorry. That was my boss, this really needs to be sorted quickly."

"I understand Madam and I am trying to help you, but from what you say, the two rooms allocated were as requested.'

"Yes. I requested them weeks ago, but we were handed the wrong room keys."

"I apologize for that Madam, but surely you and the other person can simply swap keys?"

Sam's was aware that her voice was going up a register every time she spoke.

"As I am explaining. I didn't know I was in the wrong room, and I took a shower."

"Then we can arrange for fresh towels to be sent up."

"That's what I was hoping, but it's too late now. The thing is..."

Her phone rang again.

"What's going on?" Alexandra snapped.

"I'm with a manager and I...

"Put him on to me.'

"My boss would like to speak to you," she said, handing over the phone.

She waited while with a flushed face, the manager searched the screen.

"Absolutely Madam. Yes, I do apologize for all the inconvenience. Let me see... I am able to offer you an upgrade to a suite on the eleventh floor. It has a panoramic view of the ocean. We would also like to offer you a complimentary amenity," he gushed.

Sam was reluctantly impressed by this result. It was comforting to know that other fully grown adults crumpled in the face of Alexandra's fury. New keys were issued, then once Alexandra was suitably ensconced in her suite, Sam made for the correct room. It was dull by contrast and faced the wall of the spa building.

'Not so much as a pineapple,' she thought, unpacking her suitcase and sorting through the chaos of clothes and toiletries. Her eyes lit up when she spotted her lei garland curled on top of the bedside table. She lifted it gently and inhaled the floral scent. Then, climbing onto the top of the bed, she closed her eyes.

Waking up with a start an hour later she scrambled around and checked the clock. Alexandra would be at the welcome dinner. Sam was wide awake now and ravenously hungry. As she sat on the bed working her way through snacks from the mini-bar, she heard the trill of ukuleles coming from the gardens. She rolled on her swimming costume, threw on a pair of shorts and tee, and followed the music.

Hula dancers were swaying under a pergola, their arms undulating the familiar movements of the luna. She watched, entranced, as they came to the end of their performance, her body moving in time with the melody. As the applause broke, she ran down to the lagoon, folded her clothes onto a rock, and dived into the water. Flipping onto her back, she floated in the shadows of the lush greenery. The sky was a blaze of stars. She watched the moon reappearing from behind an occasional cloud and the palm trees swaying in the breeze. Diving under the water, she swam under a bridge along the waterway and circled back to the rocks.

Climbing out after a few more laps, she discovered that the area had been closed up for the night and the towel cubbies were empty. She shook out her hair, peeled off her swimsuit, and struggled into her clothes. Running up the path, she hesitated at the entrance. Through the glass doors, she could see Alexandra chatting with a group of delegates.

Water puddled at her feet as she twisted her hair. Her shorts were clamped to her legs and her tee shirt was clinging like a second skin. 'This is not a good look,' she thought, 'and dripping across that marble floor is not an option.'

The automatic doors flew open and shut in front of her. Alexandra glanced up at the sudden gust of wind, looked in her direction, then turned her back.

"Aloha. Can I help you miss? You seem lost."

An employee had appeared by her side.

"Yes. Yes. Thank you," she said. "Could you tell me how to get to Room 212 without going through the lobby? I've been swimming, as you can probably see, and couldn't find a towel."

"Of course. Let me show you. I can take you through the spa."

Back in the room, Sam showered and checked her phone. The string of missed calls from Alexandra was alarming. She panicked. Was she supposed to be available twenty-four seven? Surely, she was allowed some down time of her own? She'd not been invited to the dinner; what was she supposed to do?

'What time is it in London?' she wondered, counting out eleven hours on her fingers and debating calling her friend.

'No. It's time to get a grip. I'll deal with whatever this is tomorrow. If Alexandra needed something all that important, she'd have left a message. I'm being paranoid.'

Blinking in the early morning sunshine, Sam picked up her phone from the nightstand and checked her emails. Alexandra had sent through an exceptionally long list of admin jobs for her to complete before the end of the day. 'Was she keeping her tied to the computer out of bloody-mindedness from last night?' she wondered.

Unsure of the protocol for ordering breakfast on the company, she went down to the Starbucks and joined the line of guests checking their phones. Taking her order, she reluctantly made her way back to the room, reading her itinerary between sips of coffee and bites of egg sandwich.

She was to be available by phone all day and at the outdoor venue at six p.m. to check that Jon had a comfortable chair, a side table, carafe of water, and a glass on stage. She was to collect him at six-fifteen, bring him down for another quick mic check, and show him to his assigned place at the table near the front where the chairman and VIP guests, including Alexandra, would look after him. At the signal for him to go backstage, she was to go with him. All of this seemed straightforward apart from where she was supposed to stay during the dinner. Would she get any dinner? She wondered.

Her phone buzzed.

"Hi. Can you run off another copy pf the press questions ASAP. Bring it to the mezzanine. Jon's forgotten it."

Alexandra clicked off.

Sam located the file on her laptop, raced down to the business center and printed off a copy. Leaping up the staircase, she pushed open the door and spotted Jon across the room. She handed it to him.

"Thanks, Sam. Sorry. My bad," he said.

"No problem." She smiled, smoothing back her hair, conscious that moving at speed in the humidity had done nothing for her professional image.

A girl waved to him from the corner of the room.

"Right, then. I'm going over to make up. Won't take long. How can you possibly improve on 'this'." He grinned, circling his face with his finger.

Sam watched the effect he had on the make-up artist.

"Hi there," she gushed, taking his jacket and admiring his skull bracelet.

"Ooh! Cute. I love that."

"Thank you," he said, holding out his wrist.

"Ready whenever you are Jon," a technician shouted.

Jon took his seat in front of the logo backdrop.

"We can stop anytime if you need another take."

"Good to know," he said, flicking through the notes, then handing them back to Sam.

" Finals done. Camera ready. Quiet everybody. Let's go."

There was a loud clap.

"Hello Kauai. This morning, I have the pleasure of chatting with Dr. Jon Porter. He is here to address the annual conference of The Council of Human Resource Development, which is being held at The Grand Hyatt this weekend. Mahalo, Jon," she said. "Thank you for giving us your time today. I hope you're enjoying our beautiful island."

"Mahalo Jane. It's a pleasure to be here." He smiled.

"Good. So, Jon, many people know you from the panel show *Clue Time*, but maybe they're not aware you are a psychologist and a renowned speaker. It's not an obvious combination. I wonder if you could tell us a little about how you balance it all?"

"You know, Jane," he paused for effect, "I have absolutely no idea!"

Jane laughed, and Sam saw Alexandra suppressing a smile.

"No. Seriously," he continued. "I suppose I've always had an interest in what makes people tick. I was the kid at school that drove the teachers mad. I'd question everything and argue my corner to the death. You know the 'why?' phase kids go through when they're about three? Yes?"

Jane nodded.

"Well, I'm still stuck at that stage. So, psychology and behavioral science were obvious choices of subjects for me to take at university."

Sam was quietly making her way to the door, catching snippets of the interview. 'His life sounds so easy,' she thought. 'Like he's always had a strong sense of who he is.'

Back in her room, she plonked down with her laptop and worked through Alexandra's list systematically. After taking a shower late in the afternoon, she pulled out her new dress, a simple black silk shift that she had ordered online after reading in *Elle* magazine that it would 'take you anywhere.' It was perfect with her bronze pumps, and now, she thought, 'I am 'anywhere'.'

Tying back her hair, she decided against the mascara that had melted in the humidity the day before. She also had second thoughts about lipstick, remembering Alexandra's barb about not being on vacation. Catching herself in a long mirror, she smoothed down the creases on her dress.

'They'll drop out,' she thought, packing her folder into her tote and making her way to the lift. The space that had been so chaotic a few hours before looked enchanting now, with tables draped in satin cloths set with exotic flower arrangements and sparkling tableware. Fire torches were being lit at different points along the pathways, and the sky had taken on a pinkish tinge.

"Aloha, Sam." A voice boomed.

Startled by the sound of her name resonating across the gardens, she went across to the sound engineer.

"Aloha," he said. "Almost there. Does Jon know we need another quick mic check?"

"Aloha." She smiled. "Yes. I'll bring him down soon. I just came ahead to make sure he has everything he needs up there."

"Hi, Sam,," Sophie shouted across. "Lovely to finally meet you in person."

"You too," she said, climbing the aluminum steps to the stage. "Came to check on things, but I can see you have it all in hand. I'm bringing Jon Porter down in a few minutes; will you still be here? I'd like some direction. I've not done this before."

"Yes. Don't worry. I'll be here."

"Great. Thanks."

Sam walked back towards the building and called Jon's room.

"Ready in five," he said. "Where'll I meet you?"

"I'll come to your floor. By the lift in five minutes?"

"Okay."

Sam rode up and waited by the console next to the elevator, checking herself in the ornate gilt mirror and smoothing out the stubborn creases in her dress. She straightened quickly when he turned the corner, greeting her with a grin.

"Hi Sam. How's it going?"

"Good," she said, pressing the call button. "It's all set up for you outside."

They rode down in companionable silence. He glanced in the mirror and ran his hands through his hair as they reached the ground floor.

"See you on the other side." He said, stepping back to let her lead the way. They checked in with the tech guy for a quick mic check, then she took him to his designated table near the stage.

"Alexandra should be here in a few minutes. She's at the drinks reception doing a 'meet-and-greet.'"

She hovered, unsure what to do next.

"Thank you, Sam," he said. "You can leave me here. I like to take a few minutes on my own to gear up for a talk. Enjoy the sunset. See you in a bit."

"If you're sure."

She hesitated.

"I am. Thank you."

"Okay then."

She left Jon at the table. Glancing back, she saw him flicking through his notecards. As she walked a few yards down a side path, the island came alive with color: vibrant reds, pinks, and orange streaked the sky. She stopped and watched as the sun sank into the Pacific Ocean and the long, low tone of a conch trumpet filled the air. A frisson of tiny shivers ran across her shoulders. She stood perfectly still, savoring the moment: the flaming sky, the perfumed breeze, the swaying palm trees, and the silence left in the air after the sounding of the Pū.

Hearing the chatter of delegates coming into the garden, she took a lingering look at the sea and reluctantly turned back. Alexandra, sporting a short red cocktail dress, was at the table, tossing her hair coquettishly as a man held out a chair for her. Jon didn't look up.

Sam saw Sophie signal to her from the side of the stage and went over.

"Hi," she said.

"Hi. What happens next?"

"We wait here while they have the main course, then you bring Jon over as they serve dessert."

"Okay. So how long will dinner take?"

"Not sure. Depends how long our chairman speaks for; it's supposed to be fifteen minutes," she said, pointing to the man sitting next to Alexandra. "Then they'll clear away and serve dessert. That'll take about ten minutes before the he goes back up and introduces Jon."

"Okay," Sam said, noticing that the guests were being served a starter.

As if reading her mind, Sophie lifted a tray of canapés from a stool and held it out to her.

"Stole them," she whispered. "Dig in."

"Thank you." She said, lifting a sweetcorn fritter. "These looks amazing."

As scheduled, Sam escorted Jon backstage and waited with him in the wings while the chairman ran through his resumé. She listened in awe to his academic achievements; his Masters in Behavioral Science, Ph.D. in Applied Psychology, the journal articles, and the consultancies. She caught Jon's eye.

"All true," he whispered with a grin.

She suppressed a giggle.

"...and of course, no introduction would be complete without a mention of his regular appearances on *Clue Time*, the show that has been nominated for an Emmy Award.

This prompted a round of applause.

"Tonight's presentation promises to be both entertaining and informative, and I am delighted to introduce Dr. Jon Porter."

Jon strode out from the wings.

"Thank you, Peter," he said, shaking hands with the chairman and waiting for the applause to die down.

It suddenly dawned on Sam that she had no choice but to listen to this speech. It was all she needed right now, to be trapped in the wings for the next hour while Jon addressed three hundred business executives on a subject of absolutely no interest to her. Her throat tightened. She wiped a bead of sweat from her forehead and took a couple of deep breaths. Jon's voice seemed a long way off. She forced herself back to the moment.

"Hello everyone. Isn't this the most spectacular evening. How're you all doing?" He began. "Let me ask you a question. Please do not feel that you have to share your answer, or you might have a bit of explaining to do later."

He waited for the chatter coming from the far tables to stop.

'Okay. Take a minute and ask yourself ,'Do I love my job?"

Sam knew her answer.

"I'll come back to this later." He continued. "But for now, I'm going to assume that you do, and that you are not just here for the Mai Tais. I'm going to be talking about what we really mean by 'human resources.' Your resources are your people, human beings who hopefully are also doing a job they love to do. How do you recruit the right people, keep them motivated, keep them working as a team when they are all such different personalities? How do you put the 'human' aspect front and center in 'Human Resources?'"

'We're not a team at the bureau.' She thought. 'They're all in competition with each other. I'm not convinced Alexandra is human either.'

"A while back when I was doing my Ph.D.," Jon went on. "I came across an article in 'Evolutionary Psychology Magazine.' By the way, that'll tell you the kind of social life I was having at the time..." he quipped.

Sam laughed along with the audience. "Jon now had her undivided attention. He took off his jacket, put it on the stool, and took a drink of water.

"The article was about a study of human behavior from, as you may have guessed, an evolutionary perspective. As a psychologist, I'm fascinated by the structures that we put in place so that we humans can function together." He continued. "Too often, we put efficiency at the forefront; we design linear systems based on industrial models, a hierarchy designed to separate people rather than bring them together. Systems need to keep pace with the changes in society and adapt rapidly to the developments in technology we are experiencing in our lifetime.

'That's another reason I don't fit in at AISB,' she thought. 'I'm invisible. I'm never involved in the decision-making process. I just get told what to do, like I don't have a brain myself.'

Jon was warming to his theme.

"In the next hour, I want to talk about talent, about the range of talents that may be hidden in the most unlikely places and how you might develop them in yourself and your workforce. I want you to challenge yourself to think differently, to take risks within your company, to see it as an organic structure that needs to be flexible and innovative. I want to talk about the need to be creative and how to discover and nurture the untapped potential that is undoubtedly in your team."

'He's so right. There's no space to be creative at all. I don't know what I was thinking taking this job. It's a dead-end. I've been coming at everything from the wrong angle.'

Jon continued building to the crescendo of his talk.

"We are all much more than the label we are given with our job title. Remember the question I asked you to ask yourself earlier on? 'Do you love your job?' I want you to think hard about this, because if you are not doing something that you love to do, it will be hard to encourage and inspire other people in your work place, and more importantly, it will be a waste of your own human resources. Do yourself a favor. Love your work and you will come home to yourself, then, like Confucius said, 'You will never have to work a day in your life.' Thank you very much."

The delegates burst into spontaneous applause and Sam clapped furiously. The hour had gone by in a flash. She stayed rooted to the spot, it was as if a light had been switched on, as if he had spoken directly to her. The chairman was on stage again, shaking Jon's hand and as the final applause of the evening trickled out, he escorted him off the far side of the stage and down the steps where Alexandra and a couple of the VIPs from their table greeted him.

Snatches of the talk were whirling around in Sam's head. She needed to walk to process them. She crossed the lawn. The moon was almost full and seemed larger and closer than she had ever seen it before. The breeze was gentle on her arms. From somewhere close by came the lilt of ukuleles and laughter. She ambled beyond the restaurants and lines of cabanas then sat on a rock by the lagoon listening to the waves lapping the shore. 'There's more to life than running around after Alexandra,' she thought. 'I used to have bigger dreams. What happened to them? This job isn't leading anywhere. I don't have a plan for my life at all.'

Standing up, she wandered towards the cliffs, then turned around when the path became dark, and she felt too far away from the hotel. Coming back up the narrow path from the lagoon, she saw Jon studying his phone in front of her. He looked up.

"Hi," he said "Not joining the drinks party?"

No. I'm not exactly sure where I should be. Are you taking a break?" she asked. Then, glancing around, "Is Alexandra here?"

"Alexandra...Alexandra..." He shouted into the night air. "Doesn't look like she is." He laughed.

"Oh!" Sam said, jolting back into work mode. I'm so sorry. Someone from the agency should be looking after you. I feel bad if it's supposed to be me, I assumed it was Alexandra's job. Sorry. I didn't mean to make it sound like you need looking after...or that you're a 'job.'" 'Stop speaking,' she told herself.

Jon went to answer, but she didn't pause for breath.

"I'll text her, maybe she got caught up with some delegates."

She rooted around in her bag. "I should have stayed longer after your talk. Do you need anything? Are you okay?"

"Relax. I don't need anything. Here. Sit down a minute."

He gestured to a lounger. "Alexandra will be networking like crazy. I made good my escape. 'Early start' is always a great exit line, I find."

Sam hesitated. Then, dropping her phone back in the tote, she perched on the end of the recliner. Jon leaned back on the one next to it, folding his arms behind his head.

"I'm off the clock, and so are you presumably. You said you haven't worked for AISB all that long?"

"This is my first event." She said, sitting back a little. "It's why I'm a bit jittery. Sorry."

"Don't worry, Alexandra makes everyone jittery. What were you doing before?"

"I was PA to the director of a not-for-profit, 'Irish Heritage,' she said. "It was a lot different. I enjoyed your talk, by the way." 'Understatement of the year,' she thought.

"Thank you," he said. "It seemed to go down well."

They looked up at the night sky for a few moments. Jon broke the silence.

"That really is something. No light pollution, all those stars."

"It's magical, isn't it. You know, when I learned that some stars are dead planets, I found it really depressing, worse than knowing there's no such thing as Santa."

"What? You don't believe in Santa?" he said, with an expression of mock horror.

"No more than I believe in a white man in a robe in the sky."

"So what do you believe?"

"Oh!" She paused. "I'm not sure."

"Me neither. It's why I think it's important to make the most of the time we have here. Did you know that the chances of being born at all are something like one in four hundred trillion?"

"I didn't." Sam said.

"It's to do with the probability of our parents meeting and then the probability of fertilization and birth. I often bring it into my talks. Turns out the odds are against us. To be born at all is a miracle. Fascinating stuff."

Sam could listen to him for hours. She gazed back up at the sky.

"I also found it hard to understand how the world can be spinning but it doesn't feel like it. They explained gravity to us at school, but I still struggle with it."

"It's because everything else, the oceans and the atmosphere are spinning too, like when you're high up on a plane and you don't feel it moving."

"That makes sense. It's such a bizarre thought though, isn't it?"

"It is."

"Do you want to walk?" he asked, sitting up. "Talking of planes, I'm on the 'red eye' tomorrow night. Vegas. I tell you, if you're looking for somewhere to make you question the meaning of life, that would be it."

"I've never been, but it does sound unreal." Sam laughed, standing up.

Jon pointed towards the end of the property, where a grass verge led down to the sea. "Let's explore some more of your magical island."

They climbed down the dunes, kicked off their shoes, and walked across the beach. As they reached the shoreline, Sam stopped and gasped, pressing her foot down and lifting it again she watched the sand light up with sparks of blue light.

"Look," she said. "What's happening? Look. Ahead there, the sand's glowing."

"I'm not in a rush to tell you. You might want to believe in Hawaiian fairies." John smiled, trailing his foot in the sand and watching the flickers.

"What is it? What?" she asked. "Whatever it is, it's beautiful."

"It's plankton."

Sam rested one foot after the other and watched the light flare. Then, circling her leg, she created a luminescent sphere.

"It's still magical though, isn't it?"

"Absolutely." He grinned.

Alexandra was already waiting outside the lobby when Sam came to check out the next morning.

"Finally," she greeted her.

"I don't think I'm late. Didn't you say to be here at ten?" Sam countered.

Alexandra's eyes flashed. She climbed into the car, clamped on earpieces and stared fixedly at her phone. Sam supervised the loading of bags and then slid into the seat next to her. As the car turned onto the winding roads to the airport, she felt almost overwhelmingly sad to be leaving. She had seen so little of the island, and there was so much to explore: the Wai Poo Falls, the canyons, the gardens, and the Na Pali coastline. The pictures in the hotel brochure had been so enticing.

She relived moments from the previous night. There had been something surreal about being in moonlight at the edge of the luminous ocean. For the first time in her life, she had experienced a visceral sense of the size of the cosmos. Looking out into the seemingly endless sea, she had been reminded of infinity, and when Jon began to talk about the theory of singularity, she had stopped him. "Please leave me to my imagination," she'd said. "I could get my head around the reality of it all, but I prefer my version of the universe, the one with no black holes."

He had laughed, telling her he preferred hers too, and that as long as she didn't tell him she believed the world was flat, he was okay with it. He'd shared something of his "life in the fast lane" as he called it. He'd seemed pensive, told her he didn't want to be traveling so much.

"Sometimes you end up doing something because the opportunity seems too good to turn down. Serendipity. You have to be careful not to get derailed."

She'd felt a pang of envy. Why hadn't serendipity come her way? What had he meant about getting derailed? You'd have to have a sense of direction to get derailed from it. He'd talked about finding your talents.

'How do I find mine?' She wondered. 'Some people are just lucky. It was all well and good him inspiring an audience to take control of their lives, but how were you supposed to do that?'

She leaned back and closed her eyes.

A while later, after negotiating passport control and guiding Alexandra to the Premier Lounge, she wandered around the airport gift shops in search of souvenirs. Her mother collected snow globes and would be thrilled with this musical one with two barefoot girls in hula skirts dancing to "Aloha 'Oe".

'Does it ever snow in Hawaii?' She wondered, taking it over to the check-out.

The flight to L.A. went quickly. Curled into the seat with her blow-up pillow under her neck and her legs across the folding table, she slept for most of the way. After the drag of waiting in line to get through customs, she finally met up with Alexandra at the baggage claim.

"Infuriating." Alexandra muttered as Sam lifted her own case from the carousel.

"What's the point of priority labelling when you have to wait for all the other bags?"

'Here's yours." Sam said, spotting the logos on Alexandra's case and yanking it from the conveyor belt. Heaving them onto a trolley, she steered unsteadily towards Customs.

"I had a text from the driver. He's here." She panted, pushing up the incline to the arrivals hall.

Once in the car, Sam had a rush of adrenalin as the Lincoln swung along the freeway onto an overpass and the city sprawled out below them in a matrix of street corridors.

Alexandra looked across at her.

"Before we get to the hotel, I need a word." She lowered her voice.

"I don't want to see a repeat performance of your drowned rat impersonation. That event was with one of our top clients and there are codes of conduct when you're working for me. While we're traveling, you are representing the bureau at all times. I called you several times the other night and you didn't pick up. You are here to assist me. I expect to be assisted. Is that clear?"

"Y'all comfortable back there?" The driver boomed before Sam had a moment to respond. "I'm Benjamin. You can call me Benjie. How are you folks doing today? There's water and mints. Let me know if the AC is okay."

"Thank you, Benjamin. We're fine." Alexandra shot back. "We will let you know if there is anything we need."

"I love your accent." He said, grinning through the rearview mirror. "I want to go to London; weather's not so great there, but I'm from Detroit, so reckon I can probably hack it. Want some music?"

"No thank you."

"I can sing for you ladies if you'd like."

"Benjamin, we have had a long flight. Please stop talking."

"Gotcha." He said, revving up the engine and swerving across three lanes in one parallel move.

Sam stared out of the window and grabbed hold of the seat in front as the car braked sharply.

Alexandra continued. "This is a relatively small event tomorrow. I expect you to be professional. Is that clear?"

"It is," she said quietly.

The car was at a standstill. She read the graffiti on the walls of the freeway as they edged forward in the lines of traffic. Taking a bottle of water from the side pocket, she drank in silence, pulled out her phone and searched for a Wi-Fi connection, anything to distract from the flight instinct that was making her palms sweat.

After what seemed an interminable stretch of time, they swung through the wide approach to the hotel in Santa Monica. Two young valet guys in shorts and tees descended on the car doors.

"Welcome to The Fairmont Hotel. Have you stayed with us before?" One of them asked, lifting out her case.

"I haven't," she said, pulling down her sunglasses from the top of her head. "But it's wonderful to be here." 'You have no idea,' she thought.

Alexandra disappeared to her room within minutes of checking in. Sam had her own bag sent up and went back outdoors. She'd glimpsed the ocean on the way in and wanted to see it properly, stretch her legs, and shake off her mood. She was in Los Angeles; she was at least going to see some of it. She wandered along Ocean Boulevard taking in the scene, the Ferris wheel on the Santa Monica Pier, the pizza parlors, the crowded beach, and the skaters on the crowded board-walk flying in every direction against a cloudless blue sky. Beginning to feel the late afternoon sun burn the top of her head, she turned back to the hotel.

Sam's room overlooked the gardens. It would have been good to have an ocean view, but at least it wasn't facing another building. She was about to take a shower when her phone buzzed.

"Hey, you jet-setter you! Are you in L.A.?"

"Hi Bets. I think so." Sam laughed. Where did her friend get her relentlessly high energy from? "It feels unreal, like I'm on the set of *La La Land*."

"You have to have at least one 'sighting.' As long as it's not Jake Gyllenhaal, I'll still speak to you." Betsy laughed. "Tell me all."

"Nothing new. Alexandra's still being a pain. It's really hard to deal with. I had a lovely walk with Jon Porter after his talk the other night and was feeling all positive, but then as we were in the car on the way to the airport, Alexandra..."

"Woa... You skipped over that too quickly. You went for a walk with Jon Porter?"

"There's nothing to tell, I just bumped into him by the pool, and we wandered around the beach for a while..."

"And?"

"And nothing. I'm working, Bets, and anyway, why would someone like him be interested in me?"

"Excuse me! Don't be ridiculous. You're gorgeous and smart, and why wouldn't he be?'

"He's brilliant. I'm not in his league."

"Sorry? Now I'm getting really pissed with you."

Sam caught herself quickly. Betsy had recently been watching a lot of Mel Robbins videos and using positive self-talk.

"Well, forget I said that. Anyway, we had a walk and that was all, but I had my phone switched off, and it was like the second time Alexandra tried to reach me at night. She read me the riot act on the way here. It was probably my fault. I forgot to turn it back on after the talk."

"Stop beating yourself up. Shit happens."

"I suppose. How about you? What've you been up to?" she asked, pulling out her wash bag and placing bottles on the shelf next to her toothbrush.

"Still a desert here, met up with the girls from work for drinks at Soho House Saturday night. Wrote off Sunday. Nothing new. I need to detox. Back on the wagon tomorrow. How many days are you in Tinsel Town?"

We leave tomorrow evening. I can't wait to get home. L.A.'s wasted on me right now. I loved Kauai though. I really didn't want to leave."

"It looked amazing. Oh! Sam, sorry I want to hear all but I've gotta go, I'm supposed to be meeting Helen ten minutes ago. Call me tomorrow. Don't put up with any more of that woman's crap. Remember to use those affirmations I sent and try the meditation. Did you look at the link?"

"Not yet. I will."

"Promise?"

"Promise."

"Okay. Talk soon. Love you. Bye."

Betsy's latest obsession, in addition to running, was yoga and with the zeal of the newly converted, she'd been nagging Sam endlessly to try meditation, promising it would help with her anxiety.

Sam felt flat. She was angry with herself for talking about her insecurities. Trying to be more upbeat than she felt had exhausted her. She hadn't intended to mention the walk with Jon. Sure she was attracted to him, but he had such a brilliant mind, why would he be interested in her? She was even boring herself these days. She'd searched online for everything she could find out about him and there was a lot of it. He seemed to be two different people. It intrigued her. On the one hand, he was this established academic, and then on *Clue Time*, he had a completely different persona. The evening had been special, but not in the way Betsy imagined. Something of it would be lost if she tried to put it into words. She felt more alone than ever. There was only one person in the world she wanted to talk to right now, and she would never hear his voice again.

She ordered a pizza from room service, took a shower, and wrapped herself in a robe. Flopping onto the bed, she turned on the television and surfed the channels. *Pretty Woman* might be the perfect distraction needed; how curious to think Rodeo Drive was just up the street. Frustrated by the adverts cutting in at frequent intervals, she switched off the TV, finished her supper, and searched her phone for the app Betsy had suggested.

Stretching out, she closed her eyes and listened.

" Take a deep breath, one, two, three and gently out...one...two...three."

She inhaled deeply.

"Relax your eyes, your jaw, your shoulders...feel the tension slip away, relax your arms, your hands, your chest....your toes, your legs...your hips...

Now, acutely aware of her limbs, Sam struggled to switch off the voice inside her head. She felt even more tense than when she'd started.

"Let go of your thoughts. If your mind wanders bring yourself back to your center."

'"Where's my center?" Feck this,' she muttered, yanking out her earpieces. Plonking her phone on the bedside table, she climbed under the duvet, bashed the pillow with her fist, closed her eyes, and eventually drifted into a fitful sleep.

DEIRDRE

Deirdre clicked out of the TED talk she'd been watching. Sally had sent it earlier in the week. A younger woman, who had been widowed a few years previously, was explaining how "we don't move on from grief, we move forward with it." It was timely. Maybe it was okay to be planning changes and trying something new. It didn't mean that she was somehow "over" her grief, it meant she was working "with" it. One phrase particularly resonated: "In the wake of loss, we get to assemble something new with whatever is left behind." She would print that out and put it on her notice board as a reminder.

She checked the time and propped the computer on top of some books to make it the right height for the Zoom, then dialed in.

"Hello Sally." She waved. "Hope you can see me okay; I'm in the front parlor, and there's not a lot of light. I could move if you like."

"It's okay. I can see you just fine. That's a gorgeous red couch. I love your cushions."

"Thank you. It's cozy in here for sure."

"Thank you for sending back the questionnaire, Deirdre."

"Sorry it took me a day or so to get around to it. I've had so many forms to fill in this year, it's been a nightmare putting everything into my own name, the bank, the gas, electricity, phone...it was endless, and I hate forms at the best of times."

"Oh! I'm sorry..."

"It's okay. As you can see, I left a lot of it blank. I thought it'd be easier to talk.

"That's fine, Deirdre. They're just prompts to get you thinking, and of course you can share as little or as much as you want with me."

Putting on a pair of retro-framed glasses, Sally read out the first question. 'What do you want to experience in your life moving forward?'"

"'Moving *forward*, not moving *on*,' Deirdre thought.

"Before Niall died, it would have been a completely different answer," she said. "Now, as you can see, I've narrowed it down, but it's still pretty broad. I would like to have new experiences and to go to new places."

"That is such a positive answer. We can work with that."

Deirdre was pleased. She had agonized over the question, never having asked herself anything like it before.

"I have absolutely no idea where those places are, Sally. I just know I don't want to go back to anywhere Niall and I went together yet. I don't think I'm running away. It's a big world, so why put myself through the agony?"

"That makes perfect sense. Who knows how you might feel in the future."

"It took me a while to come up with answers, Sally. It was a great exercise. I can't share what I'm about to say with anyone else but you."

She ran a hand through her hair.

"The thing is...I'm stuck! My days are so long, and there's no real comfort in them. I want some kind of adventure. I look at the people around me, and I don't want this sort of life anymore. It didn't feel predictable with Niall, but now... I'm over-familiar with everything and everyone here. There are no surprises anymore. Maybe it's just another of the stages you go through when you're widowed..."

Sally looked at her over the top of her glasses and took a moment to reply.

"It may be a grief stage Deirdre, but whether it is or it isn't, it's a valid feeling, and I believe you should acknowledge and respect it. Boredom is a powerful tool. It can be a positive driver."

"That's so interesting, Sally. I've never had the luxury of boredom before."

"Well Deirdre." Sally said with a mischievous smile. "If you'd care to move onto the next question, it may well be short-lived."

" Which one was that?" Deirdre asked. "Sorry. I don't have them in front of me."

"It's 'What new skills would you like to develop?'"

"Ah! That one. Yes. There are a few skills I'd like to learn. I've taken a ton of photographs on my phone when I'm out walking. It's become something of a compulsion actually. I really like editing and chopping them around. I spend hours on it, and the time flies by."

"That's a sign you're in flow.'' Sally agreed. "When we get immersed in an activity and lose track of time it means that we're totally living in the present moment.

It's a sign that we're doing something we really love to do.'

"Yes. You're so right about the time thing. I started editing the other afternoon, and the next time I looked up, it was dark. The thing is, I don't know what the value in it is, Sally. I'm not in a rush to sign up for a photography course. I still have brain fog, and the time I tried to learn how to use a digital camera I was useless. What I love about the phone is you just point it and press. I don't want to jinx it. I think if I formalize it, I'll lose it."

"To be sure I'm clear: you're saying that this is something where you'd like to master a new skill but you want to be careful how you go about it? Am I understanding that correctly?"

"Yes. That's it. That's exactly right!"

"Let me think about it." Sally nodded. "I do know someone who runs art therapy classes. She's a photographer, too. You said you loved art at school. Maybe there's a way to combine the two. I'm out of my depth here, but let me do some research. I'll talk to her. She's based in Ibiza."

"Ah! That'd be great Sally. I don't see me becoming the next Ansel Adams but I really enjoy it and I would like to learn some new techniques."

"I'll call her tomorrow."

"Thank you."

'I think we're making good progress, Deirdre. Do you?"

"I do. I'm making progress in another direction as well."

"Go on."

"I've decided to sell the house. They tell you not to make big decisions in the first year, but I'm a year out now, and I think it's the right thing to do. I'm haunted by memories here and anyway, it's too big for me... I'm sorry. Give me a second, I wasn't expecting...."

Deirdre's face had crumpled. She pulled a tissue from her sleeve and blew her nose.

"Sorry Sally. I'm not sure what happened there. You think you're doing well, and then from nowhere it all floods over you."

"Take your time." Sally murmured. "Do you want to take a break?"

"No. I'll be fine. I'm fine. I don't know where that came from... I was telling you about the house."

"You were. How long have you lived there?"

"Most of my life...It's been in the family for four generations... Niall and I...Sorry. Excuse me, Sally. Give me another moment, please."

Deirdre went into the kitchen and poured a glass of cold water. She drank it quickly, then, checking her reflection in the hall mirror, she wiped her eyes and ran a hand through her hair.

"Okay. I'm back." She said, resting the glass on the coffee table. I just caught sight of myself, Sally. I look a complete wreck. I'm sorry. I think I'm more emotional about the house sale than I thought."

"Deirdre. Do you want to stop? We can if you like. I could find time tomorrow."

"Thank you, but I'm okay now. I need to pull myself together. I'm not sure what came over me. It's been the family home for four generations. That's why it's such a big decision."

"It looks lovely from what I can see. Is it on the market yet?"

"I've an agent coming this afternoon."

"What time?"

"Oh! Not for another forty minutes."

"Well, let me know if you have to jump off."

"I'm fine, the place is straight, and he'll be late anyway. It's Ireland."

"Do you have plans to buy a smaller one?"

"I haven't thought it all through. I don't want to buy another one yet. It'll be a while before it's sold, and I'm hoping in that in that time, things will have become clearer. I plan on staying with my daughter in London for a while."

"We've not known each other long, Deirdre, and it's not my place to advise you on this, but I can be a sounding board if you like."

"Thank you." Deirdre smiled. "It's great to have someone who can be objective about it. I don't know anyone else who can."

"Good. You can talk to me about anything at all in complete confidence."

"Thank you."

"So would you like to share a little more about your photography?"

Deirdre instantly came alive talking about the process of editing and was pleased that the call ended on a positive note. She'd felt self-conscious about breaking down again.

'It's okay. She isn't judging me,' she told herself, shutting her computer. "Why do I feel the need to appear stronger than I am?"

She made herself a cup of tea, becoming increasingly nervous waiting for the agent. This was a huge decision to be making on her own. What if she regretted it? Should she be hanging onto to it to leave to Somhairlin one day? Would Niall approve? Would her grandmother be turning in her grave?

Her grandparents had lived in the house way back when it had been a smallholding with a few outbuildings, a pig pen, a hen house, and a couple of fields. It had been passed on to her parents and then to herself when her father had died not long after she and Niall were married. Deirdre's mother had moved out to live with her sister, and the house had become theirs. Over the years, the house had settled well into its new incarnation.

Niall had been in his element drawing up plans with the architect to extend and renovate it. He'd spent his weekends plumbing and wiring the kitchen. The place was almost ready to move into when Deirdre discovered she was two months pregnant with Somhairlin. Together, they'd prepared a little nursery, and Niall had grassed part of the field for a children's play space. Deirdre had enjoyed picking out furnishings and creating a kitchen garden.

Hearing a car pull into the driveway, she went to open the door.

"Sorry I'm late Deirdre, the Ardoyle Road was closed from the flooding." He greeted her, stamping wet boots on the step. "That was an awful downpour."

"It was indeed. Come on in, Dermot," she said, as he shook off his raincoat. "Give me that here."

She hung it onto a peg.

"How are you? Been a while since I saw you."

"Not so bad. Can't complain. Awful business you losing Niall like that. Ah! He was one of the best, me and the lads really miss him at the quiz nights."

"Yes. He'll be missed at them alright. Would you like a cup of tea? Kettle's just boiled."

"That'd be grand."

He followed her into the kitchen.

"You have it lovely here., he said, casting his eyes around the room.

Deirdre could see that he was checking out the appliances, not admiring her decor.

"Ah! Thanks," he said, taking a cup from her.

"Would you like a piece of currant bread?"

"Och, you know I wouldn't mind. Go on then."

Deirdre went over to the work island, cut a slice of bread, and buttered it thickly while Dermot hovered, unsure whether to sit down and make himself at home. When the invitation didn't come. he took the plate and balanced it on the side of the kitchen table.

"So you're up for selling the old place?" he said, through a gulp of tea.

"Yes. I am. At least I think I am. The mortgage is paid off, so I suppose it depends on what I can get for it."

Taking a last bite of bread, Dermot drained the cup and set it down. "Okay, well, can I take a look around? Shall we start upstairs? You told me you've the two bathrooms now?"

"We do. I mean 'I' do." She corrected herself. "One of them's connected. I think you'd call it an 'en suite'."

Going up the winding staircase ahead of him, she waved him into her bedroom. She hovered outside, embarrassed for him to be seeing the intimate space she had shared with Niall.

"That's a fine view you have there." he said, pulling the curtain to one side.

"Indeed," she said." The bathroom's through there."

'Why was he taking so long to check out one room?' she thought.

"Good size, nice and modern," he yelled. "The young ones go mad for these rain shower yokes."

"That was Somhairlin's idea," she said. "The other bedroom's just here."

She closed the door behind them, directing him across the landing to the guest room, then opening the door next to it.

"And this is Somhairlin's room," she said.

"How's she doing? I heard she's in London these days."

"She is, although she travels with her job, so she couldn't get back for the Anniversary Mass, which..."

"Good size too," he interjected. "Plenty of storage space."

Deirdre, who had never judged a room by its square footage, was feeling increasingly disappointed with Dermot's disregard for how lovely it was all looking.

"The other bathroom and shower are over there." she nodded.

In her mind's eye, as she stood in the doorway, she could see the rocking chair where she had cradled Somhairlin as a baby, the cot with its swinging mobile, and the frieze of Peter Rabbit across the walls. She swallowed hard.

Going downstairs to the parlor, she had a flash image of Niall reading on the couch, his newspaper littering the floor, empty plates on the coffee table and magazines on the rug in front of the fire. The room seemed foreign now, so orderly with its cushions plumped into perfect squares and the velvety throws neatly folded on the arm of the couch.

"The dining room's through there," she said following him through.

"Hmm. It's quite small; might make a good office."

"The table's too big for the space," she volunteered. "We should have bought an extending one, but this belonged to Niall's mother."

She lingered as Dermot went to the kitchen to take some measurements.

For a split second, the room was alive with the memory of what was to be their last Christmas; wood-scented candles flickering along the mantelpiece, holly and crackers on the tablecloth, Niall clinking a glass to make a toast, the uproarious laughter, the sense of being home and being content. Deirdre's throat constricted. Coming back to the reality of the moment, she shut her eyes, until the intense wave of grief passed, and then she joined Dermot in the garden.

The rain had eased. They walked down as far as the shed, which had been turned into another of Niall's workshops. Deirdre had nagged him endlessly to keep all the tools at work and leave her space for the plant potting.

"Och Dee! You complain of me having the stuff here, but where would you be if I couldn't sharpen the shears or sort out the auld lawnmower?"

"We could buy new things, you know. They are for sale. Not everything has to be mended."

He would rub his head and laugh.

"Ah! now, give over, you know you'd be lost without me," he'd say.

And she was.

SAM

The California sunlight streamed through Sam's hotel window. She had tossed and turned through the night and woken up with a sense of dread. Bleary-eyed, she stumbled to the bathroom. After a long shower and seeing that she had an hour before the breakfast opened, she determined to shake off her mood with a walk. Leaving the hotel, she crossed the street, surprised to see the amount of early heavy traffic on the Pacific Coast Highway. The scale of the beach amazed her. There was no way she would be able to get across to the water's edge and back to the hotel in good time.

Objectively, it was beautiful and uncannily familiar from so many movies, but it felt alien; the streets were wide and the gardens along Ocean Boulevard were overly manicured. It reminded her of Promenade de la Croisette in Cannes, but she felt it lacked the charm of the pavement cafés and the splendor of the architecture. There was something artificial about it all; even the sky seemed too blue to be real. The contrast between this coastline and Kauai was marked. There had been something intimate about that beach, a natural quality that had spoken to her soul. This panorama could take your breath away, but it didn't draw her in. Sam was aching to be back in Kauai and to have that evening under the stars all over again. She shook off the image of Jon firing pebbles at the water and how easy their conversation had been.

She strolled for a while, then turned back to the hotel, where a breakfast buffet had been laid out in stations. She loaded a plate with pancakes, fresh strawberries, and bacon and took it over to a long oak table. She perched on a stool, relieved that Alexandra was nowhere in sight. This would be a short trip. The itinerary was straightforward; the speaker would be done by lunchtime, and their car to the airport was booked for three o'clock to catch the evening flight.

She had decided not to leave anything to chance. At exactly nine she would text Alexandra, ask what was needed throughout the day, and stick to the letter of her instructions. Avoiding another run-in was a top priority. Within forty-eight hours they would be back in London. She could do this.

By ten o'clock, Alexandra had not replied. Sam tried her again. When she still didn't pick up, she went across to the conference venue.

"Hi. Hello. I'm looking for Alexandra Kingsley from AISB," she told a woman with a name badge and clip board who looked like she might know. "Have you seen her anywhere?"

"I've been trying to get in touch with her myself," she said. "I'm not sure what she looks like."

"She's about your height, long blonde hair, slim and probably wearing a beige leather jacket," she offered, resisting the urge to describe Alexandra in unflattering terms.

"That just about describes every woman in L.A." She laughed. "Except me, of course... Okay honey, if you find her first, tell her Suzanne is waiting in the ball room to take her to meet our chairman. Here, take my number."

She gave her a card.

"Thank you."

"You're welcome."

Sam tried Alexandra's phone again. When there was still no response, she asked reception to call the room and was told that the line wasn't connecting, maybe it was off the hook. She decided to risk going up to the room and knocking. It was the only option left. Tapping the door tentatively at first, then increasingly harder, she called her name and waited. It remained firmly shut.

'She's probably at the event by now and I'll be choked off for not being there,' she thought turning back toward the lift.

An hour and a half later, with the speeches finished and lunch almost over, there was still no sign of Alexandra. At this rate, they were going to miss their flight. She spotted the duty manager across the lobby and explained the situation.

"I've told security," he told her. "They'll be here in a minute."

Moments later, two heavily armed men in uniforms crossed the lobby.

"What seems to be the problem, Ma'am?"

Sam had not been expecting this level of help.

"Oh! I'm sorry, I don't think it's quite an emergency... well it might be, but I don't think it is quite as... I thought maybe the manager could just open the room, you see my boss hasn't turned up today, and she's not answering her phone, but she might have just slept in...and....I mean is this necessary, can't I have a spare key maybe?

"Ma'am we can't permit that. Accessing a guest room is against hotel policy."

"Well, yes, I can see that, but I mean you'll use a key, you won't just break down the door or anything? If she's fallen asleep, she'd not thank me for having you wake her up. I mean, you have guns and that can be frightening...I mean for English people."

"Even Americans try not to use them," he assured her, finally relaxing into a smile. "Let us handle this, okay Ma'am?"

Sam followed them into the elevator feeling decidedly uncomfortable. The tension in the air was making it hard for her to breath.

"Wait here, Ma'am," one of them told her as the doors opened.

"Stand back." He barked at a hotel guest who was turning the corner.

What was happening? This was straight out of a movie. Waiting while they knocked on the door her mind was racing. Had Alexandra been murdered? Given her personality it was entirely possible.

A few moments later the door had been levered open. One of the officers stepped inside cautiously while the other scanned the corridor before following him into the room. He swiftly reappeared, yelling into a two-way radio.

"We need an EMT now... Fairmont Hotel, yes thirteenth floor. Room 589."

He gestured for Sam to join him. Her legs could hardly support her. Had Alexandra been attacked?"

"Is she okay? What's happened?" she asked.

"She's going to be okay. She's fallen. I've called for the paramedics. You can go in and stay with her while we're waiting, but don't try to help her. That's their job."

Entering the suite, she found Alexandra slumped on the tiled floor clutching the side of the bath, her leg was at a curious angle to her body.

"About fucking time," she greeted her, trying to lever herself up from the side of the bath and collapsing back onto the tiles. Sam said nothing, rooted to the spot. The more Alexandra yelled at her, the more detached she became. She heaved a huge sigh of relief when the paramedics arrived and began unpacking equipment, checking her vitals, asking a string of questions, then strapping her onto a gurney.

"Are you okay, Ma'am?" a medic said kindly. "You can come in the ambulance to UCLA with us. Your friend's going to be okay; her oxygen levels are good and her heartbeat is regular."

'Nothing about this woman is regular, much less her heart,' Sam thought.

A small crowd had gathered outside the front entrance of the hotel, watching Alexandra being lifted into an ambulance. Sam noticed a woman taking a selfie in front of it and was horrified. Suzanne walked over to her.

"What's going on? Is she okay?"

Sam nodded. "I think so."

"What happened?"

"She slipped on the marble on the bathroom floor," Sam told her. "She couldn't reach the phone to call for help, so by the time we found her she'd been stuck there for a few hours."

"Holy shit! That's awful. I had a feeling something was wrong when she didn't show up. Thank God you found her. Did she bang her head? Why are they taking her to the hospital?"

"I think it's just her leg. That's all I know, except they said her vitals are normal, and unless there's some internal bleeding, she'll be okay."

"Are you alright, honey? I have a diazepam here." Suzanne shook open her handbag.

"Er. No. Thank you," Sam said. "I'm okay. They're ready now. I have to go with them. Would you book me a room for tonight? We've missed our flight now. Do you think they'll keep her in overnight? Should we book two rooms, do you think?"

"Unless she's dying, I'd imagine they'll release her later tonight. Call me when you know what's going on. There'll be plenty of rooms here once most of the delegates go home this afternoon. I'm not leaving until tomorrow. I'll see if they can reserve two rooms for you guys."

Sam was relieved. The travel arrangements would need to be changed, but someone at the bureau could handle that. She would call them from the hospital. Now she knew Alexandra was not concussed or likely to die on her watch, she was beginning to feel resentful. All she'd had so far from her was abuse. 'You would think I'd oiled the floor, the mouthful of obscenities she came out with.'

The wait at the hospital was interminable. Once Alexandra had given her insurance details and been whisked away, Sam sat on the awkward plastic chairs trying to tune out the constant blare coming from several television screens. The vending machine was out of order, and the air conditioning was brutal. Eventually, some doors flapped open and a nurse came across to her.

"Miss Kingsley is out of the operating room." she said. "It went well. All good, but it'll be a while before she's able to walk. We'll keep her in overnight. The MRI was clear, but it's as well to monitor a knock on the head. She was lucky. It's an isolated fracture of the tibia, the fibula was still intact, the bones have been realigned..."

Sam had stopped listening, she felt queasy. This was far more information than she needed.

"She's in the recovery room. Do you want to wait and see her or come back in the morning?"

"I'll come back in the morning." Sam said, not missing a beat. "Thank you. Do you know where I can get a taxi? I mean cab.'"

All the way back to the hotel, Sam berated herself over every aspect of the day.

'I should have asked them to open Alexandra's room sooner. What if it had been more than her leg? If she'd bled to death? If I'd not waited until after the speech...I should have known it was serious. I should have...'

It took her a moment to register that her phone was ringing. It was Suzanne.

"Any news?"

"She's okay. She's broken her leg, but they've reset it; they said she'll be fine. It'll just take time. They're keeping her in overnight."

"Oh, okay! That's obviously not great news, but it's a relief to hear she's going to be okay. I'll cancel her room reservation then. When do you think you'll be back? We're at the patio bar, come and meet us when you get here."

"Absolutely," Sam said. "Thank you. I'll see you soon."

Arriving back at the hotel, she went directly to the bar and ordered a large glass of white wine.

"That was fast!"

Suzanne had appeared at her side as she was lifting the glass to her lips.

"You've had a long day, next one's on me," she said. "We're over there. Come join us."

"Great. Thanks." Sam said following her outside, where they joined a group of delegates sitting around a large table under heat lamps.

"Everyone, this is Sam. The 'shero' of the day!"

A guy stood up and pulled over a chair for her.

"Hi. I'm Bob. I was today's main speaker. We all heard what happened. Well done! Suzanne said, you were something else, organizing everyone, calm as a cucumber."

"Thank you." Sam mumbled, stunned that she had come across like that. "I really haven't done anything remarkable."

"Not what I heard." He said, shunting his chair to the side of hers. "I love your accent. Where are you from?"

"Ireland," she said.

"Always meaning to go. My family's Irish, the O'Rourkes, County Wexford, I think. I've heard it rains a lot, but it's beautiful."

"Wexford is beautiful. Where do you live?"

"Vancouver. Not so far, but I like to stay overnight when the gig's in L.A. Love it here."

Once the focus had shifted away from her, Sam finally relaxed. Bob turned out to be easy company, and she let him regale her with his family history and life in Canada.

Back in her room, a knock on the door signaled the arrival of her room service order.

"Good evening. How are you today? How's your stay going? Are you with us for long?"

Without waiting for answers, the waiter set down a tray. "Is there anything else I can get you?"

"No thank you."

He hovered.

"Oh! Ah! Yes of course." She rifled in her purse for a tip.

"Enjoy," he said, folding the note into his pocket.

"I will," she said. "You have no idea how hungry I am."

Sam's head was racing as she tore into the sandwich. She glanced at the time, deciding to wait until midnight to call Sandra, when it would be morning in London. The agents were technically available twenty-four hours for emergencies, but there was no need to wake anyone. It would be another eight hours before Sam would know when Alexandra would be able to fly.

Sam realized that she knew absolutely nothing about Alexandra's private life. Did she have family that should be called, or even maybe a partner who would fly out to make sure everything went okay?

What would have happened if she, Sam had been the one who'd had an accident? No way would Alexandra have gone to the hospital or looked after her if things had been reversed. Did they both have insurance? Had the bureau looked after her too? Again, she doubted it. The other evening when Jon had asked why she had become a personal assistant, she hadn't hesitated. She liked being needed and valued. Working for Alexandra had turned that on its head. It was soul-destroying.

"Please hold. Can I have your name again?"

Sam was on the phone to UCLA Medical Center the next morning. She had given her name three times already and was trying to keep the irritation out of her voice.

"Sam Macardle." She said, drawing out the consonant.

"Please hold."

After a full ten minutes of a recording of the hospital facilities, someone picked up the other end and told her that Alexandra was being prepared to leave, that she was fit enough to fly, but would need to use a wheelchair. As this was something the hospital could not provide, she was advised to contact the airline to inform them of Alexandra's condition and arrange for another wheelchair to meet them at the airport.

Hiring a wheelchair turned out to be far more complicated than expected. By the time Sam had located one and arranged delivery to the hotel, Alexandra had been discharged for three hours. She'd texted and called Sam at regular intervals, her voice becoming increasingly shrill.

'This is not going well,' Sam thought, helpless to do anything other than wait. 'If I have to carry her onto the plane myself, I'm getting her on to it,' she thought, relieved when it was finally delivered. Her phone rang as the valet was negotiating it into a yellow cab.

"Hey, Sam. Sandra here. How's it going? Is Alexandra with you?"

"I'm on my way to get her now," she said, watching the driver give the cases a final shove into the trunk. Hang on; I'll be able to talk in a minute."

"UCLA Medical Centre please," she told him, climbing in.

"Okay, I can talk now," she said, clicking her seat belt.

"Did you get all the travel documents?"

"Yes. They were there when I woke up this morning. Thank you."

"Good. Sam, I don't know if you saw the email I sent an hour ago?"

"No. I haven't checked recently. I just clocked the time of the flight, so we don't miss it, but I've not had a chance to do pre-check, and I still have to sort out a wheelchair this end. It shouldn't be a problem though; apparently, they meet people with them even if you've not booked."

"Great. The thing is, we can't get you on the same flight, there was some kind of over-selling on tickets, and there isn't a seat in coach anymore. You didn't get back to me, so I called Alexandra, and she said to book you tomorrow or whenever there's availability. I checked and there are seats on the red eye tomorrow night or a late afternoon one on Thursday."

Sam was aghast. 'I'll be stuck here, rather than have the bureau cough up a business fare for me?!' she thought. 'I'm rushing around here like a blue-arsed fly and they couldn't give a toss when I get home?'

"I think we're just coming up to the hospital. Can I get back to you?" she managed.

"Sure. Let me know. I think Alexandra would prefer you to fly tomorrow night as we won't get the same the hotel rate as we did for the conference. Sorry."

"Right. Okay. I've got to go now," Sam said, knowing they were still a good ten minutes away, but wanting to moderate her response. "I'll call when I've checked her in."

She flopped back in the seat. 'Great,' she thought. 'So much for the bureau "family" Alexandra's always going on about. I am so low down the pecking order here. They'd have bought another ticket if one of their speakers was stranded. Oh! And nice touch, 'we're not paying the full rate for the hotel for you either.'

She stared out of the window, outraged.

Pulling into the hospital entrance, the driver extended the wheelchair and piled the suitcases on top. "I'm really grateful," she told him.

"You're welcome, Ma'am," he said, wiping beads of sweat from his forehead.

"Keep the change," she told him, handing over a fifty-dollar bill. "That tip is on my boss."

"Have a wonderful day." He beamed.

Flying through the hospital doors, Sam followed the signs to reach the discharge area where Alexandra was strapped into a wheelchair flanked by an orderly.

"Hi Ma'am," he said, unlocking the brake with his foot. "Where's your car?"

"Oh!" Sam mouthed. "I should have had the taxi wait for us. I didn't know how long I'd be. I'll order an Uber now. Sorry," she said, then remembering, "Oh!

My Uber account doesn't work in America. Do you have a number for a taxi?".

"No, but you can ask at reception."

"Can you come with us then? Maybe stay and help me get her into the cab? I don't think I can do it by myself." 'And god knows how I'll get her out the other end,' she thought. 'Perhaps I'll just tip her onto the sidewalk.'

"I'm still here," Alexandra snapped. "I've a broken leg, not a broken brain. How long am I expected to wait for a taxi to arrive now? This is imbecilic."

Sam exchanged looks with the orderly, who bore all the hallmarks of someone who had been in Alexandra's company way too long.

"You push that one and I'll push her," he said, ignoring Alexandra and steering her rapidly towards the corridor. "Don't worry miss. We'll help you."

To Sam's immense relief, Alexandra fell asleep within minutes of being in the cab.

The traffic to the airport was more congested than when they came in from Kauai. 'Has it only been two days?' she thought. It seemed like a lifetime, and now she would have to go back to the hotel on her own, and she hadn't a room booked.

'It's okay,' she told herself. If I have to find somewhere else to stay tonight, then I will. I've a Visa card. There are plenty of hotels. Nothing bad is going to happen. Breathe...one...two.'

She looked across at Alexandra, who was slumped awkwardly to one side, her head back, mouth gaping, the hospital identity bracelet still on her wrist. She saw a thin, vulnerable woman. She also saw someone who put themselves first, who was mean to people she didn't consider to be important, and who was unpleasant to work with.

The thought of going back to the bureau and working for AISB after this was unthinkable. She was leaving her here in L.A. to save the money on one extra air fare? Was that how much she was valued? It was untenable. It would be a risk to be without a job, but it was a risk she would take. She would get Alexandra on board, call her mother, then change her flight for one to Dublin. She was going home.

DEIRDRE

After the agent left, Deirdre had wandered around every room in the house again. Could she make new memories here? Impossible. Dinner parties without Niall to greet their friends and serve the drinks, sitting on her own after the guests had left? It was unthinkable. At the thought of another Christmas, her stomach lurched. It was the right decision. She had called Dermot, who told her he would pop round with the paperwork the next morning.

The time had flown by in a whirl of activity preparing for the photographer. The lawn had been mowed, windows cleaned, fires lit, and on Dermot's suggestion, a table was set out in the garden replete with Royal Albert china for afternoon tea. Apparently, there was a rush on from Dublin buyers. Young couples were snapping up weekend houses in the countryside.

'Tea in the garden? This is Ireland, not the Costa Brava,' she thought, but didn't say.

Scrolling through the details. she struggled to recognize the place. The garden looked to be the size of a bowling green and the pristine sweep of countertops made the kitchen look surgical. Dermot had told her the market was hot right now and she could prepare for it to go quickly. He advised her not to accept the first offer or even consider lowering the price. Her mouth had dropped open when he told her what the house was worth. Six hundred thousand euros? It was an amount she found impossible to grasp. How she longed to share the news with Niall. He never would have believed it.

She sank back in the couch, resigned to another night in front of the television, when her mood soon lifted as her phone rang and she saw Somhairlin's number.

"Hello sweetheart," she said.

"Hello Mum. How are you?"

"Ah! Somhairlin, it's lovely to hear your voice, the texting's fine, but it's not the same. Are you still in Hawaii, or is it California? I can't keep up with you. Are you having a wonderful time?"

"Great to hear you too. Mum. I'm in Los Angeles. I'm thinking I might come home for a few days."

Deirdre sensed something off in Sam's tone. She sounded strained.

"Well of course. Of course," she said. "Is everything okay?"

"No bother, Mum. I'm grand."

"Okay, just making sure. So, when might you be coming?"

"This weekend."

Deirdre lit up.

"Really? Really? This weekend. What a lovely surprise. That'll be just wonderful."

"I might be able to go into Belfast or Dublin, not sure yet, but I'll probably get in on Saturday afternoon. I was making sure you'd be home."

"Where else would I be?" Deirdre laughed. "Let me know the flight details and I'll come and meet you."

"Thanks Mum. I'll email you the times and see you very soon. Can't stop now."

"Okay darling."

Deirdre's moment of exhilaration passed moments later, remembering that Somhairlin didn't know that the house was about to go on the market.

'That'll be another anchor gone and she might not take the news well.' She sighed. 'Why is life always so complicated? Ah! Well. As Scarlett O' Hara said, "Tomorrow is another day."

Climbing the stairs with a fresh energy, she changed the bedding, pulled out towels from the hot press, and laid out Sam's dressing gown and pajamas at the end of the bed. Searching for the hot water bottle, she was reminded of their first Christmas after Niall died, and how she had prepared the room for Somhairlin with such a heavy heart. That holiday had been so hard for them both. Locked into raw grief and aware of the other's pain, they had steered the conversations and navigated the new terrain cautiously, neither wanting to trigger the other's emotions. A few days before she was due to leave, Somhairlin had suggested she might stay in Ireland to help her. Much as she would have loved that, she knew it would be a mistake.

"You've your own life to live," she'd told her, "You've a job and a nice flat; why would you come back here? You're only across the water. I'll be just fine."

There'd been talk of a boyfriend, but that seemed to have fizzled out. How she wished she'd been able to give her a sibling, but Somhairlin did have Betsy, a true friend who had dropped everything to fly over with Sam for the funeral.

Settling down in front of the fire a while later, Deirdre switched on *Flight of the Swans*, the David Attenborough documentary she had been storing up for this kind of evening when she had no energy left, but it was still too early to go to bed. Before Niall died, she had not been particularly drawn to natural history programs, but there was comfort in them now. They were a reminder that she was part of something bigger and that maybe there was some divine order to the world. Life and death were a circle in harmony with each other.

Swans mated for life. She had never thought of that before. They had something in common. This was fascinating. As the program continued, a wedge took flight in a spectacular display of strength and synchronicity. Left behind, a solitary swan drifted far across the lake. In that moment Deirdre saw it as a metaphor for her life. She was the "swan" left behind.

'Is there no bloody escaping this?' she cursed, turning off the TV and flinging the remote at the couch. 'I'm going to watch nothing but comedy from now on.' Then, remembering the call with Somhairlin, she brightened for a moment, before her shoulders drooped.

'How am I going to tell her I'm selling up? She's going to want to know where I'm going. Where am I going? Where? I can't just run away like Shirley Valentine and hope someone turns up to rescue me. Nobody's coming. Caroline's right. I have to make a proper plan.'

SAM

S am was surprised at the ease with which they passed through LAX. Alexandra was pushed at high speed through the lines of tourists to the check-in desk, where Sam was told that she would not be allowed further. She left her with the escort and stood watching as Alexandra was wheeled away. She was somebody else's problem now. Going across the concourse to the ticket desk, she booked herself onto the night flight to Dublin, delighted she wouldn't have to spend another night in L.A.

After security, she wandered around the shops until her flight boarded. Then, settling into her seat, she closed her eyes and heaved a sigh of relief. Once the seat belt signs had been turned off and drinks served, the passenger next to her raised her glass.

"Sláinte," she said.

"Sláinte." Sam smiled.

"Going home?"

"I am."

Not wanting to be drawn into a long conversation Sam smiled and pulled out the book she'd not opened since leaving London. The words danced in front of her as she struggled to remember the plot. She snapped it closed as the meal trolley arrived. Twisting the top from the miniature wine bottle, she picked at her salad, reliving the last twenty-four hours, and beginning to feel anxious. She was out of a job, and it was highly unlikely Alexandra would give her a reference for another one.

'"When one door closes, another one opens." That's what dad always used to say,' she thought, remembering the time she had woken up sick the morning of a gymnastics display that she had been practicing for all year. She had been inconsolable.

"How?" She'd blubbered. "You don't understand."

But he understood her disappointment and opened another door,' by booking them seats at 'The World Gymnastics Championships' in Liverpool for later that month. She still had the tee shirt and the vivid memory of it. Next day, they'd taken the 'Magical Mystery Tour" in an open topped bus around the city, singing along to "Yellow Submarine" and "All You need is Love." They'd had dinner in Chinatown and fallen helpless with laughter trying to eat noodles with chopsticks. Sam smiled at the memory and sighed. He had been the most wonderful dad. Why could she not have had him for longer? She handed her tray to the attendant and scrolled through a few of the movie channels until the lights were dimmed and she was overwhelmed with tiredness. Pulling the blanket around her, she closed her eyes, amazed to wake up to the pilot's announcement. She had slept the entire journey. Hearing his accent cheered her.

"We'll be touching down in Dublin in forty minutes. I hope you had an enjoyable flight. For those of you visiting, Fáilte go hÉirinn, Welcome to Ireland and to those of you coming home, Fáilte abhaile."

"Yes." She thought, 'I'm coming home.'

Shaking a cramp out of her arm, she saw the outline of the island and a patchwork of green fields become visible through the clouds. As the plane circled across the sea and began making its descent, she felt a sense of relief coupled with an aching sadness that her dad would not be there with her mother to meet her.

"That was a good flight," her neighbor remarked as the plane taxied along the runway. "Hardly any turbulence."

"Yes." Sam replied. "Did you get any sleep?"

"Not as much as you did." She laughed.

"I'm sorry, was I snoring?"

"No, but I climbed over you a few times to go to the loo and you were out for the count."

"Oh! Thank you for not disturbing me."

She opened the overhead locker and pulled down her bag. "All the best now," she said.

Joining the line of weary passengers at immigration, she waited impatiently until finally, through customs, she dashed into the arrivals hall and spotted her mother waving from behind the barrier.

"Come here 'til I hug the life out of you." Deirdre beamed, throwing both arms around her. "I have missed you so much."

Taking a step back she looked her up and down. "Were they not feeding you in London at all?"

Sam smiled. Within seconds, her mother had managed to make herself conscious about her weight. She also knew that it was completely unintentional.

"I'm sure you'll have me fattened up in no time, Mum. You look well. I've missed you so much."

"Is that all you have with you?" Deirdre asked, eyeing her carry-on case.

"It is," she said. "And it's full of summer clothes, so I'm going to freeze."

Deirdre gave her a conspiratorial smile as she steered her towards the car park. "They've a sale on in Dunnes."

Once in the car, Deirdre switched off the radio and turned up the heaters.

"So how was the flight? I was surprised you didn't come by Aer Lingus."

"It was all very last minute, and it was fine."

"Did you manage to sleep? When we went to San Diego, I had an awful time with the jet lag and your dad said it was because I stayed awake the whole way back. How you're supposed to sleep upright in those sardine tins I've no idea. But you know how he could sleep for Ireland."

"I do." Sam said stiffly.

Aware of a moment's awkwardness after the mention of Niall, Deirdre spoke rapidly.

"What was the weather like in L.A.? I heard something about wildfires; that had me worried for a minute there."

"They weren't near where we stayed. I'm not sure I like L.A., although I didn't see much of it. I'll tell you all over a cup of tea. I've not had one in days."

"I can't wait to hear all about Hawaii, or Kauai, I think it was," Deirdre said, swinging the car onto the motorway and looking across at her. "I always dreamed of going ever since I saw Elvis in *Blue Hawaii*. 'Night and you and blue Hawaii ee eee'," she crooned.

"It was magical, Mum." Sam softened. "I took lots of pictures. I can't wait to show you. The ocean is so clear and at nighttime, the moon and the stars are awesome."

"Well, it's been a beautiful day here today, too." Deirdre said. "And all the more special for having you home."

Sam looked out as the familiar shape of the mountains came into view and the car sped down the narrow lanes, swooshing through puddles to avoid the potholes. As they turned onto the street, the sky had turned leaden. Inhaling the damp country air, she knew she was home. It felt so good. It had been the right decision to come back. She was safe. There would always be this place in the world with a welcome, and even though her dad wasn't here, for as long as her mother was alive, it would always be home. As the car cruised up the driveway she leaned forward with excitement, then stiffened.

"What the...Mum? MUM!!!!!! What's THAT?"

Deirdre's jaw dropped with shock. A 'For Sale' sign had appeared at the end of the garden. Sam leapt out as she was stopping the car.

"What're you thinking? You're selling up? Where are you going? Did you not think to tell me? This is my HOME. You can't do this! Is this how you're telling me you're moving? Did you not think how I'd react just seeing it like that?!"

Sam's cheeks were burning. She hardly paused for breath, turning in circles then pacing in front of the door.

"I was going to tell you this evening. I can explain..."

"Explain what? Did you not stop to think this might affect me at all?! This is my home!" she yelled.

Deirdre stood helplessly in front of her daughter waiting for her rage to pass. When all the fight was out of her and she dissolved into tears, Deirdre went to put her arm around her. Sam knocked it away.

"Somhairlin, I was waiting for the right moment." Deirdre said quietly. "I only made up my mind a week or so ago. You've been abroad and the sign's been put up while I was on my way to meet you. Do you honestly think I'd have wanted you to find out like this?"

Sam's lip was trembling. "I suppose not," she mumbled, "but you might have thought to talk to me about it before you just went ahead and did it."

"Let's get into the house," Deirdre said quietly. "That was a shock for me too."

Sam dropped her case in the hall, went into the kitchen, and swept her eyes across the room. There was none of the usual clutter; no boots by the door, or stack of newspapers piled high in the basket, no fishing rods, no red plaid jacket on the back of the chair. She stood motionless, overcome with a yearning that was so intense it frightened her.

"I'll light the fire," her mother said from behind her. "Why don't you go up and have a shower or maybe a nice bath? I've a casserole to heat up. It'll be ready in about an hour. I'll bring you up a cup of tea. Go on now. It'll make you feel better."

Sam couldn't speak. She gave a weak smile, nodded and left the room.

Deirdre went into the sitting room, scrunched up papers, stacked the kindling, and had the fire going within minutes.

'Keep the home fires burning,' she thought, standing back to admire the flames. 'How ironic. I couldn't have done a worse job of that today if I'd tried.'

She sighed, knowing that now there would be no going back. That sign was a punctuation mark. It made it real. She turned on the side lights and drew across the curtains. In the flickering firelight, the room felt cozy and welcoming. Back in the kitchen, she laid out the table with candles and a pottery jug filled with the cow parsley and daisies she had picked on the mountain. Lifting the casserole dish out of the stove, she felt a rush of tenderness. Somhairlin was home. She would cherish this. They would never get this time together here, like this again. It was precious.

The evening passed affably enough, both side-stepping the larger conversation. Sam showed her mother some pictures from Kauai but didn't tell her about Alexandra or quitting her job. Deirdre was delighted with the snow globe and told her that indeed she'd heard that sometimes it did snow in Hawaii. She tried to keep things upbeat, sharing something of the conversations she'd been having with Sally and the possibility of taking a course. They said goodnight early with unspoken apologies still lingering in the air.

Sam lay awake until the early hours of the morning. She snuggled into her bed. It felt like a cocoon as she hugged the hot water bottle. This had always been the place she felt most safe, her childhood room, with all its memories and she was going to lose this too? Where would home be now? Where could she run once this had gone?

Mulling over the afternoon's events she felt bad about her outburst. It had been selfish. What did she imagine her mother was going to do, sit around covered in cobwebs like some Miss Havisham? Of course not. No. It made perfect sense that she would need to make some changes, but this was a bit extreme, surely, and what was all this talk about 'connecting with her inner child?' Who was this coach and that other woman in Ibiza? Was her mother being brainwashed? She sounded like she was building up to some crazy 'Eat, Pray, Love' expedition. 'I should have come home more often,' she thought, 'But at least I'm here now.'

DIERDRE

The call from Dermot came early the next morning.

"There's a couple live in Drogheda. They'd like to come over and take a look at the house this afternoon. I know it's short notice, but it's going to be dry today, and they're cash buyers," he told her, his voice barely masking his excitement.

Deirdre hesitated. Sam was still in bed, and they hadn't had the conversation she needed with her yet.

"I'm not sure Dermot. Somhairlin's home unexpectedly. What time were you thinking? Maybe later on, after three maybe? I could leave the key under the mat for you."

"I'll ask. I'm sure that'll be fine. I'll call you right back."

Sam had appeared in the doorway.

"Who was on the phone, Mum? Are you sure you should be leaving the key under the mat these days?"

Side-stepping the question, Deirdre gave her a big smile. "Good morning. Kettle's just boiled. Did you sleep well?"

"Eventually. That bed has to be the best ever." Sam yawned, "Took me a while to get off, but then I passed out."

"I was thinking. Do you fancy a run into town?" Deirdre asked her, setting out two mugs and arranging slices of bread into the toaster. "We could get you the bits and pieces you need and maybe stop off and have our tea out.

Before Sam could answer, her phone rang again.

"Hello Dermot," she said, catching herself before could stop.

Sam scowled.

"Yes. Okay. Yes for sure. Yes, fine. Okay."

"So that was Dermot Flanagan, the very same Flanagan of Flanagans Estate Agents on the 'For Sale' sign in our driveway," she snarked.

"Somhairlin, I know this has come as a shock, and believe me, I wish it hadn't, but now you know, and we need to have an adult conversation about it. I know you're upset, but in the name of God, what's going on with you that you're so angry? Is everything okay in London? Is there a reason you decided to come here straight from America? I know you too well. Something's going on."

Sam slumped into the kitchen chair.

"You're right. It isn't all about the house. I'm not doing great, Mum."

Deirdre sat down next to her and put her arm around her shoulder.

"Here."she said, pulling a mug of tea towards her."You're exhausted. Why don't you go back to bed for an hour or two and let's go for a walk this afternoon. We can go into town another day."

"Let's walk this afternoon, but I need to go to the graveyard this morning before I do anything else."

"Do you want to go on your own?"

"Yes, if that's okay."

"Of course it is. I was just making sure."

"Thanks for understanding mum."

"Of course sweetheart." Deirdre said standing up again. "What would you like to eat before you go?"

A few hours later, Deirdre drove up the winding roads through the mountains, and pulled into a lay-by overlooking the estuary. They walked to the vantage point of an old stone wall and gazed out over the expanse of dark water set against the backdrop of pine covered hills and woodland. Deirdre flung her arms out wide and filled her lungs with air.

"I'd almost forgotten how beautiful this spot is." Sam said, pulling her phone from her pocket and snapping a picture of the heart-shaped lake.

"This has kept me sane this last year, Sam. When you see the mist here in the mornings, it's hard not to believe there's a god. Just look at the sun streaming through the clouds there, isn't it just like some kind of apparition?"

"It really is."

"I'm forever walking the feet off myself these days. I come here or up Slieve Mullion. It lifts my spirits no matter how rough a day I'm having."

"I understand that. I've been running away from my feelings all year, trying to block them out, dashing around the city, taking the new job, but by the sea in Kauai, I reconnected somehow. There was a moment, a sunset, when I felt like I was in the right place, that I understood something I couldn't find words for."

Deirdre turned to look at her.

"Was it a feeling of peace?"

"Sort of. It was like I knew that it was all happening like it should be, like I don't have to worry. But then of course I got back to the hotel and started worrying."

"I've had a few of those moments too. They're hard to hang onto, I know, but you don't forget them. Why don't we go to Clough beach tomorrow?"

"I'd love that."

"Me too. Shall we walk on?"

"Yes."

"This way." Deirdre said, pulling back a bramble and climbing over a stile onto an unmade track. "Ireland will always be home Sam. I know it's hard with the house going, and it'll be strange for a while, but you'll find your way, I know you will."

"You sound all wise and accepting Mum. What's going on with you?"

Sam jumped down after her and brushed off her jacket.

"Ah! You know Somhairlin, sometimes knowing what you 'don't' want is the way to find out what you 'do.'"

"That sounds incredibly Irish." Sam laughed.

"Well, there'd be a reason for that alright." Deirdre smiled. "You young people think that we older ones have it all sorted out. The truth is, we don't. I'm feeling more lost and confused than I ever did, but I do have a bit of wisdom to fall back on, much as that might surprise you."

"Ha! It does! No, seriously; I know you're not going to do anything mad, but I'm having to adjust to this new version of you Mum. The next thing, you'll be off with some gigolo and living in Italy."

Sam drew back suddenly.

"You've not met someone, have you?"

Deirdre giggled.

"Now where do you think I'd meet anyone in these parts, Somhairlin Macardle? Don't worry, there aren't any more shocks to come, and I can tell you here and now, it would have to be a gigolo with a fortune. I'm not up for anyone else's rejects or some widower needing looking after in his old age."

"That's a relief. I'm not ready for that, but Mum, you do know that I'd want you to be happy if you did meet someone."

"Well, that's good to hear sweetheart, but it's not the plan. Your dad would be a very hard act to follow."

At the mention of her father, Sam's eyes welled with tears.

"Mum. I'm really lost right now. I wasn't going to bother you with it, now you've so much on, but I quit my job."

Deirdre glanced across at Sam before going ahead of her up the narrow path.

"It was only a job, Somhairlin. There'll be plenty more." She looked back over her shoulder. "Is that why you're home?"

"I was planning on coming soon anyway, it's not the only reason." Sam said, batting off a swarm of midges.

"Were you not enjoying it at all? I thought you were."

"My boss was a narcissist. Mum, can you slow down a bit?"

"Sorry. Of course." Deirdre dropped back.

"But the job. You were enjoying parts of it weren't you? All the gadding about?"

"Not really. I heard one of our speakers recently. He was talking about how we only have one life and we should be doing something we really love with it."

"I couldn't agree more."

"Well, I wasn't."

"Sorry to interrupt you, Somhairlin, but don't miss it. Look."

Deirdre put her hand on Sam's arm. "There's the grey heron at the edge of the water. Do you see him?"

"I do."

"Hang on while I take a picture."

As Deirdre pulled her phone from her pocket, Sam walked on a little and looked back at her mother. She freeze-framed the moment in her head, then taking out her own phone, took a picture.

'One day she will be gone too, and this will be another memory,' she thought. 'I need to look after her while she's still here.'

"Got a few," Deirdre said, coming over to show her. "I just love you can do that without having to set a camera."

"That's great mum. It really is, you've captured the reeds so well."

"Ah! Thanks. I'm going to stop doing this the moment it stops being such a joy. Sally is putting me in touch with a teacher and I'll talk to her, but it's precious. I don't want anyone to start getting analyzing or criticizing it like they did in school."

"I get that. The only thing I ever felt good at was dancing, and we didn't get any of that at school."

"I've always found it really frustrating how much you doubt yourself. You're so talented at so many different things."

"Like what?"

"I wouldn't know where to start, sweetheart. You're a great cook. You're a brilliant organizer, you write really well, you've great style, and you're kind and really good with people. Somhairlin, don't underestimate the importance of that. You're a force for good in the world."

"Ah mum, thank you. It's not how I see myself at all."

"Well, you should. Just a thought: Sally's sent me quite a few websites and books. You can take a look at them if you like. They might give you some ideas, get you thinking like they did for me."

"I'll take any help I can get at this point," Sam said. "Send them to me."

As the path became steeper and narrower, Sam dropped behind her mother and they continued climbing in single-file until they reached a clearing, where they rested for a while on the felled logs before turning back.

"Are you getting hungry yet?" Deirdre asked on the stroll back to the car.

"Always."

"Okay. What do you fancy? We can go into town or pick up some fish and chips and take them home. You choose."

"Let's do chips. I can smell the vinegar already." Sam smiled. "Mushy peas and pickled onions too. I could slaughter it."

"And I'll make us a nice pot of tea."

DIERDRE

The next morning, Deirdre carefully blew out her hair. 'Still my crowning glory,' she thought, curling the sides with tongs and letting it fall across her face. She pulled out a pink blouse, applied a matching shade of lipstick, then added one of her many floral scarves. Seeing herself on Zoom last week had been a wake-up call. "Table top dressing," it was called. She'd read about that; you put the focus on the part of you people will see most.

The overwhelming grief waves that had begun to ease were back with a vengeance. She was glad of the timing of this call. Lately, she had been feeling less resourceful and increasingly apprehensive about her future. The brain fog had descended again just when she needed to deal with the paperwork and inspections the house sale involved. The strain of masking her emotions was also telling on her and she was still finding it hard to sleep in that vast empty bed.

'Today is a new day,' she thought.

She waited. Sally was running late.

"Ah! Good morning. How are you?" she said when Sally eventually appeared on the screen.

"Hi Deirdre. So sorry to keep you waiting, I've been dealing with something of a crisis this morning."

"Nothing too serious, I hope."

"Just trying to work around two kids and a husband with a 'man cold'." She laughed. "Right now, you are what's important. How is the house sale going? Is it on the market yet?"

"Ah! Sally, it's been quite a week. My daughter's home from London, via Los Angeles."

"How lovely."

"It has been, although it hasn't been exactly what she was expecting; I didn't get a chance to tell her about selling the house, so it was strained at first, but she's on side now."

"Well, that's good to hear."

"Yes, and the other thing that I wasn't expecting at all is that I've had two offers. Can you believe it? Two offers in the space of a few days, and one of them wants to move quickly."

"Oh! Sorry Deirdre," Sally said. "Could you repeat that?"

"Of course. I was saying that I have a buyer, actually two buyers."

"How are you feeling about it?"

"I'm a bit thrown in truth, thought I'd have longer to adjust to it, but there's no going back now. Somhairlin's going to stay on and help me. We haven't really got much further than that."

"It must be good to have her there."

"It is, and I've a call booked with your colleague in Ibiza tomorrow. I'm not sure if it's good or bad timing. I mean, I'll not be able to do a course remotely if I'm packing everything up, but I also saw that she has some residential courses coming up, so that might be something worth thinking about."

"Good idea," Sally said, then hesitated. "Deirdre, would you mind awfully if we reschedule this call? I don't want to waste your time, but a text from my daughter's school just popped up on my screen and I need to deal with something."

"Of course. Of course." Deirdre shook her head. "Go right ahead Sally. No bother at all."

"Thank you for understanding. I'll text you some new times if that's okay?"

"Absolutely, and you know now I'm thinking, it might be better to talk after I've had the other call with Isabelle. You can help me decide if you think it's the right thing for me to be doing. I'll let you go. Take care of yourself, Sally."

"Okay. We'll talk soon. Thanks, Deirdre."

The screen went black. Deirdre closed over her computer.

'It's a reminder,' she thought. 'I'm so tied up with my grief, I forget other people have their own crap to deal with.'

Although she understood, she felt flat. She'd been looking forward to focusing on herself for the hour. Having Somhairlin home was wonderful in so many ways, but it had thrown her off track. Knowing her daughter was struggling had put her back into her maternal mode, and with that had come the stark reminder that she didn't have Niall to lean on anymore. For the first time, she understood something of the difficulties of being a single parent. In fact, it seemed unimaginable, superhuman to raise children alone.

'Where does the time go?' she mused, thinking back to when Somhairlin had been at primary school, to the concerts, the swimming, dancing, and the sports days, all over in the blink of an eye. Deirdre's life had become even fuller with Somhairlin at secondary school with the gymnastic competitions and trips up and down to Dublin for ballet classes when she outgrew the dance academy in town.

Those years were the happiest she could remember, driving to the city on Saturday mornings, singing along to the radio, hearing the craic about school. She could still picture Somhairlin climbing out of the car, her hair pulled tight in a bun, blue serge jacket fastened over her pink leotard. Deirdre would spend a few hours wandering around the art galleries or window shopping in Grafton Street. Niall often caught the train down to meet them, and they would go for pizza. Inevitably, as Sam grew older, all she wanted was to hang out with her friends at the weekends, and she lost interest in the dancing classes. Deirdre had felt horribly redundant.

Now, after their recent conversation, Deirdre was wondering whether she should have pushed her more at school. The report cards were always peppered with references to her lack of concentration. She had no interest in going to university even if she'd had the grades, which she didn't. She was adamant she wanted to go to the local tech. Deirdre knew she was being swayed by the boyfriend at the time.

At college, Somhairlin had changed courses so many times that Deirdre lost track. Would she have a profession by now if she'd gone to university? She had been bright enough. Would she be happier?' That was the thing about parenting, no matter how hard you tried, you got a lot of it wrong.

'Ah! Feck it,' she thought. 'I'll go for a walk to clear my head, have a chat with Niall. I haven't done that in a while.' Catching herself in the kitchen mirror, she froze in front of her reflection. Who was this old woman? She put her face closer to the mirror, tracing her finger along the lines that grief had etched into her face, noticing the hollow circles around her eyes and the deep crevices in the corners of her mouth. In all the years she had been with Niall, she had never examined her face in this way. Why would she? Niall had found her beautiful and never tired of telling her that she was, and always would be, the girl that he had married. It struck her now that no-one would ever see "the girl in her" in that way, ever again. It was a stab to the heart. She took off the scarf and rubbed at her lipstick with the back of her hand. What was the point of all that effort?

SAM

Sam came downstairs after she heard her mother leave the house, happy to have the place to herself for a while. She made a pot of coffee, cut a large slices of currant bread, loaded it with butter, and went into the sitting room. It was good to be home in so many ways, but she was finding it hard to keep up an appearance of feeling okay. Everywhere was a stark reminder of her dad. Now she understood better why her mother needed to make a new start.

Looking out at the garden, she could see her father so clearly in her mind's eye, shirt sleeves rolled up, taking sly puffs on his pipe at the back of the shed. As a child, she was his conspirator, but of course her mother would have smelled the tobacco smoke from the kitchen.

The shed still held some of her childhood toys; her bicycle and crash helmet. Maybe he was keeping them for his grandchild one day? There were tangles of old rope still twined round the branch on the apple tree where he'd built her a makeshift swing. She could "see" him sitting on the garden bench, working on some broken part of machinery, or mending a scooter or some other contraption a neighbor had brought over for him to fix. At night, coming home from seeing a friend in the village, she half-expected to see his shadow hovering behind a curtain, anxiously waiting for her to come back from a dance. He would have gone upstairs before she turned the key in the latch, knowing she was safe and saving her the embarrassment of trying to appear sober. He was her rock, and she had missed him intensely all year, but now it was impossible to escape the sadness.

Taking the last bite of bread, she put the plate on the coffee table, curled up on the couch, and scrolled through her emails. There was no reply from Alexandra. Sam had emailed to explain that she had been called to Ireland urgently and would not be coming back. She'd spoken to Sandra, who told her Alexandra had only taken two days out of the office and was more bad-tempered than ever, limping around on crutches and demanding everyone stop the second she needed anything. Hearing this, Sam knew that she had made the right decision.

She put down her coffee cup and went upstairs to shower. Remembering she needed to call Betsy, she was searching for her phone when it rang.

"Hi Bets. I was literally about to call you."

"I would hope," Betsy quipped. "What's going on? I left you to get over the jet lag but this is taking the piss."

"Sorry. Honestly, I was about to call the minute my coffee kicked in and I could form sentences. Are you still in Sussex?"

"You are forgiven. Yep. Still here. I'll be back in town at the weekend, can't wait, my sister's driving me insane. I have absolutely no idea how we're related. How was the trip?"

Sam clipped on a pair of earrings.

It's a bit of a story. I was waiting until I had time for a long catch up. I've quit my job.

"Oh! Really? Good. It was making you stressed."

Sam had expected more questions from Betsy, but reminded herself it was hardly a surprise, she'd been moaning on about work endlessly.

"I'm not back at the flat by the way. I'm in Ireland at Mum's," she said.

"Oh! How come? Is she okay?"

"She's fine. I just took a notion to come home for a while. I knew you were away anyway. Can I call you this evening? I can hear Mum back. We're going out for our lunch. She's selling the house and it looks like there's a buyer, so I'll probably be staying on for a while to help her move. I've been here almost two weeks and I've absolutely no idea where the time's gone."

"Oh!" Betsy's voice dropped. "How long do you think you'll be away?"

"I'm not sure; a few more weeks, maybe longer. Why don't you come over?"

Betsy's voice brightened. "Really? I love your house. If it's not going to be there for much longer, I'd like to come one last time. I could help with the packing, and we can go to that pub with the session and that seriously cool bartender. Is he still there?"

"At Malones? I'll check for you." Sam laughed. "I've not been back myself yet. It won't be a deal-breaker, will it?"

"Erm...well..."

"Ha! I'm sure he won't have gone far. Okay, Mum's shouting me. Let me know when you're coming, and I'll pick you up. I'll call you later."

"Okay. I'll look at flights. Talk later, I'm off to find my wooly socks and wellies. Love you. Love to your mum. See you soon."

Sam stopped in the doorway before taking the stairs. It was true that she was staying on in order to help her mother, but also true that she was in no rush to go back to London. The idea of job hunting, putting herself out there again, was too depressing. It wasn't like she could see any future back in Ireland, but she would stay for as long as it took her to make a plan. She had drifted long enough.

"Sam are you coming? Can we go? Caroline will have the lunch ready for us."

"Almost, give me a minute," she yelled, pulling on her padded jacket. "Sorry. Coming."

She caught up with her mother on the path.

"Sorry Mum. I was on the phone to Bets. Would it be okay if she came over? She could help with the packing."

Deirdre smiled.

"Of course. That'd be great."

"She sends her love."

"What's she up to these days? Does she have a boy-friend, girlfriend, or significant other yet?"

"Mother you are so 'Woke.'" Sam laughed. "She's with no-one right now, and stop fishing, I'm not with anyone either."

"Sean Campbell is still unattached."

"Well, good for Sean Campbell, Mum, I'll be sure to let you know when I get that desperate."

Unlatching the gate at Caroline's cottage, Sam leapt back as her border collie charged towards them. "Sandy! Here Sandy!" Caroline yelled, running down the path and waving a dishcloth at him. "Get down. Get down!"

"Sorry. He gets over excited," she said, yanking him back by the collar. "What a welcome, Somhairlin. How are you? You're looking well. Come on in. I've the lunch almost ready."

They followed her into a tiny hallway, squeezing past a jumble of coats and boots. The smell of peat fire and yeasty bread gave Deirdre a jolt. The year of living alone and all the house clearing had left her own house soulless by comparison.

'This is how home should be,' she thought, surveying the parlor with fresh eyes.

Caroline's clutter felt cozy; the oak dresser crammed with jugs and bric-a-brac, the prints and water colors lining every inch of wall, the scrubbed pine table set out with mismatched plates and the wild daisies in homespun pottery bowls. Deirdre wanted to curl up next to the cat in the basket by the fire and never wake up again.

"How are you, Aunty Caroline?" Sam asked her, loosening her coat and struggling to get into the room past the dog.

Caroline's eyes crinkled with warmth. With no children of her own, Sam knew that she had always thought of Somhairlin as the daughter she never had.

"Not so bad, Somhairlin. Not so bad. And yourself? I hear your boss wasn't treating you so well. I want to hear all about it. What was L.A. like? Did you spot anyone famous? Sit down, sit down. Give me a minute while I get the pie out of the oven before I forget all about it. Here, Deirdre, lift that pot for me, will you?"

Sam settled into the well-worn sofa and shifted across to let the dog jump up next to her.

DIERDRE

Deirdre had yet to sign contracts on the sale of the house but had made a start on clearing out the cupboards.

'Why did we hang onto all this crap?' she thought, opening a dresser with rows of unused Waterford crystal. 'Wedding presents still in their boxes forty- odd years later. What were we thinking, saving things for best? We should have been having our dinner off the fine bone china. What was the point of having it? What had they been saving it for? Poverty mentality, that's what it was. It had to stop right now.'

Several hours later, surveying the bags designated for the charity shop and the box of clothes for Caroline to take for her car boot sale, she remembered an article she'd come across about the benefits of clearing out. It was something about Feng Shui and how clutter can be a metaphor for our internal landscapes. Clearing was supposed to make a person feel lighter, but it was having the entirely opposite effect. She felt so heavy. Every single object held a story. There wasn't so much as a handbag, or a thimble, a vase or a pair of gloves that hadn't sparked a memory. The woman who had pulled on those gloves had been deeply happy, secure, and certain. It was as if she were a completely different being. Even though Deirdre had learned to smile again and had moments of optimism, that person, the one who trusted her world and her place in it, was gone. She knew beyond a shadow of doubt, that losing Niall had changed her utterly.

Sapped of energy, she considered taking a nap before remembering that she had the Zoom call with the artist in Ibiza. Checking the clock, it crossed her mind to cancel, but decided that it would be unprofessional and anyway, what else was she going to do with the afternoon? She ran upstairs, splashed her face with cold water, put on some lipstick, and pulled a brush through her hair. Racing back down to her kitchen desk, she dialed in to the call.

This was always a strange moment for her, waiting for someone to magically appear. The technology was all so new. A face appeared. Inevitably, it was the face of a younger woman. Everyone was younger these days. Recently, Deirdre had become overly conscious of her age. With Niall there had been the illusion of youth; the look in his eye that made her feel sexy and attractive. Now she had only the mirror, and her reflection was not nearly so kind.

"Lovely to meet you, Deirdre." Isabelle smiled warmly

"And you too."

"Sally told me you might be interested in the possibility of taking a course or class."

"I am."

Isabelle spoke softly. "Before we talk about that, I want to say that she also told me your husband passed away last year. I am so sorry. I am sure it must be very difficult coming to terms with a loss like that after so many years."

There was genuine warmth in her words, and Deirdre appreciated her sympathy and the way it had been expressed. New people were often awkward around her, uncertain what to say.

"Thank you," she said. "It's not been easy. Sally's been helping me to try to find a way to express my grief through some form of creativity. She had an instinct that you might be able to help. I had a look at your website, and it all looks so impressive. I'm not a photographer at all. I don't know how to use a digital camera even, all I have is the latest Iphone."

"That's what I mostly use these days, too," Isabelle replied.

"What? Really? Surely not."

"Yes. The quality's the same up to a certain point as long as you know how to use it properly, and the rest is playing around on the computer on different apps. I warn you, you can get lost for days."

"I do know what you mean. I spend hours on the Snapseed App. It really does surprise me that you use your phone too. Your work is incredible."

Deirdre had done her research; Isabella's website was professional and her credentials impeccable. She held a Master's in Psychology and the Expressive Arts, and had held exhibitions in major galleries. Her specialism was collage.

"I have to confess; I nearly cancelled our call. I found it all a bit intimidating, I'm not at any level really, a complete beginner, and honestly, my brain is still fuddled a lot of the time, so I'm not ready for anything technical."

"That's perfectly fine. We can take it slowly. The process of photographic collage is a metaphor in many ways. You deconstruct in order to reconstruct."

"My life is turning into one big metaphor." Deirdre thought.

"It's fun. It's play." Isabelle continued. "You get lost in the moment and create something from nothing. You aren't evaluated, you're simply being creative, and I promise, some magic always appears.

"It does sound really interesting."

"Good. So how about I send you a schedule of the time I have available and my costs? I'll also give you a sense of how the private class might work and a list of art supplies you'll need. Take a look and email me if you want to move forward. Online and Zoom would be the place to start, and if at some point you'd like to take a course in my studio, here in Ibiza, we can look at making that happen."

"That sounds perfect. Thank you. I've never been to Ibiza. I hear it's beautiful."

"It really is. I've been here ten years, and I only came for a month."

"Ah! Now I'm sure there's a story there."

"There is... Is there anything else you need to know? Do you have any questions for me?"

Deirdre did have a few questions, and by the time the call ended, was genuinely interested to learn more about the process. Sam was shouting from the hall as she clicked off.

"I'm going into town now, Mum... See you later."

"Enjoy yourself," she shouted back.

'Enjoy yourself...'That was what Niall always told her, wasn't it?

"It's your treat," he'd say when she'd hesitate over taking a dessert in a restaurant. "You've earned it," if she dithered whether to have another glass of wine. "Enjoy yourself. Buy something lovely," when she was going shopping in town. She would come back and model her new dress for him, show him her latest bargains. She'd heard some women hid their shopping from their husbands. How bizarre a thought. She couldn't get home fast enough to show him and see his eyes twinkle with delight as she twirled around the kitchen.

Oh! How he had loved her, spoiled her, made her laugh, such a kind and generous man. They'd been incredibly lucky to have found each other. She knew that. People recently told her that she should be grateful for having had such a love in her life. And she was, she really was, but what they may not appreciate, was how hard it was to lose it when it had been your whole life.

'Enough,' she thought, getting up from the chair quickly. 'What's next on the "To Do" list?'

After storing the donation bags littering the floor, she sat back at the table and looked through links she might share with Somhairlin. They all seemed more pertinent to her own situation and interests: art courses, photography exhibitions, a grief forum for widows, and a TED talk about the power of gratitude. As she scrolled through, Deirdre became increasingly conscious that she had been so besieged by her own grief, so preoccupied and resourceless, that she had left Somhairlin to pretty much cope on her own. She would step up now and do the research, find books and links on coping with the loss of a parent, and maybe help her to find her own "Sally," a coach or a therapist. She would suggest that, offer to pay for it and guide her as best she could.

SAM

S am raced down the path and onto the lane as the bus was coming towards her.

"Ah! Thanks Michael," she said, panting up the steps. "I'm not used to the royal treatment. Bus drivers in London don't stop for anyone."

"Awful place, London. Why would you ever leave here? How's your mam?"

Sam swiped her card.

"She's doing okay."

"Heard she's selling the auld place."

"Yes." She nodded, grabbing onto a pole as the bus lurched forward.

"Tell her I was asking after her."

"Will do."

She took an empty seat by the window as the bus drew to another halt at the crossroads. A teenage girl climbed on, barely glancing up from her phone. She plonked down next to Sam and began texting.

'How long is it since I was wearing that exact school uniform?' Sam wondered. 'Twenty years? Twenty? Surely not? How did that happen?'

As the bus trundled up the hill, Sam had flashbacks to her own teenage years and shuddered. 'Who'd be a teenager again?' she thought. 'All that angst.'

Gazing out of the window, she recalled how she had opted out of the culture. Terrified of drugs and not interested in playing around, she had fallen insanely in love with a boy from school. They'd been like an old married couple, playing Monopoly on Saturday nights while their classmates were out doing all the things teenagers were supposed to be doing. Looking back, Sam thought of it as one of the happiest times of her life, despite the agony of breaking up with him while they were at college.

Betsy was of the opinion that Sam was in a pattern of serial monogamy that wasn't healthy.

"Why not live a little?" she'd suggested, after Sam's next long-term relationship ended.

Betsy's idea of 'living a little' in no way appealed. Sam had heard far too many stories of black-out drinking and humiliating morning-afters. She was not going to sleep or drink her way out of the grief or the depression, that much she knew.

Sam hadn't been in the town since her father died. On recent visits, she'd had no interest in going out or shopping. A few school friends had come to the house and brought her up to speed with the gossip. She'd heard tales of the few who, like herself, had moved to England and the ones who had gone to different parts of the country as far away as Aaron Island. Most of them were married. She heard rumors of affairs, of break-ups, coming-outs, and the accidental overdose of a classmate. It seemed that all life was here, a microcosm of everything that was happening in the cities.

As they drew up next to the canal, Sam had an image of her dad waiting to meet her off the bus, and her heart sank knowing he would never be there again. She jumped off, pushing the memory away.

Walking along the walled path, lost in thought, she turned onto the main street and heard someone calling her name.

"Well, if it isn't Somhairlin McCardle."

"Madame."

Sam's eyes lit up at the sight of her old dance teacher, who apart from appearing to have shrunk six inches, was exactly as she remembered, dressed entirely in black with her silver hair tied in a topknot.

"Somhairlin, you've not changed at all. I'd have known you anywhere. How are you? I heard you moved to London a few years back. What brings you home?"

"Lovely to see you too." Sam beamed. "You're looking great. How are you?"

"Not so bad, there's life in the old dog yet. I was so sad to hear about your father. He was a lovely gentleman. I remember him so well at the performances, he would be bursting with pride for you."

"Thank you. Yes, we miss him terribly."

"How's your mother doing?"

"She's trying her best. It's still early days, but I think she's stronger than I knew."

"It must be so hard...so hard. So where are you off to now? I can't stop for long, but I can't let you get away that easily. Fancy a quick cup of tea in Delaney's?"

Sam was delighted. Though "Madame" probably didn't know, she was the only teacher who had made a positive impact on her life.

"I'd love to," she said. "I've plenty of time."

"Okay, grand. Here, let's cross."

Taking Sam's arm, she hurried her across the road. "London must be marvelous. Haven't managed to get over there in an age. I want to hear all about it. Did you see the Royal Ballet's *Romeo and Juliet* recently? I was mad I couldn't get away. Steven McRae's incredible. He's a brilliant tap dancer too, like a young Fred Astaire. Sadlers Wells has been doing brilliant work recently, did you see their *Rite of Spring*? I'd give anything to live in London. You must be in seventh heaven."

The question was rhetorical.

Now was not the time to tell "Madame" that in the years she had lived there, she had not once been to the ballet, all that culture was on her doorstep, and she had not even been to the theatre. Not once. How had she let that happen?

The atmosphere in Delaney's took her right back. There wasn't the slightest nod to sophistication. Tea was served from giant brown teapots and the stained cups had seen better days. There was something reassuring about its unpretentiousness. Maybe she had style fatigue after years of living in London?

"You'll take a wee scone?'" The waitress asked, coming back with a sugar bowl and a couple of spoons.

"Yes please. They chimed in together and laughed.

"So do you still have the Academy Madame?" Sam asked her, pouring the milk.

"Oh! Sam, you're an adult, enough with the 'Madame.' Call me Bridget."

Sam was thrown. She might have managed "Mrs. O' Leary," but it would take a while to make this transition.

"Yes, the Academy's going from strength to strength."

"Are you still teaching?"

"I keep my hand in for sure. A few years back I had a grant from the Arts Council and brought in more staff, but here come on, tell me what you're up to."

Sam sighed.

"It's not as wildly exciting as you might imagine." She began. "I've had a few jobs, mostly as a personal assistant, but I left my last one recently, so I'm in a kind of no-man's-land right now."

"Really?" Bridget looked thoughtful. "You know, Somhairlin, I've had a lot of students, but I never forgot you. I always felt that you have something special to share with the world."

Sam smiled. "That's so kind of you, but I haven't really found what I'm supposed to be doing."

"How old are you now?"

"Thirty- two."

"Well, that's no age at all." Bridget smiled. "People think they should have everything worked out by the time they leave school, but life's not like that. It doesn't go in a straight line. Well, not for most of us. Life's messier than that."

"Well, mine certainly is." Sam agreed.

"You've the rest of it in front of you. How exciting."

Sam stirred the milk in her cup slowly.

"Do you remember the class song?" Bridget continued.

"How could I forget." Sam laughed. *This little light of mine, I'm gonna let it shine...*"

"There you go. You have to let your light shine or what's the point of anything? My God, this scone is good." She added, wiping the crumbs from her lips.

"But if you don't know what your light is, how do you let it shine?" Sam asked.

Mrs. O'Leary took a sip of tea and set down the cup.

"You have to think hard about what you love to do. I struggled at school, I'm dyslexic, I was incredibly shy, but the moment I found dancing, I felt a happiness I couldn't put into words."

Sam felt privileged that 'Madame' was confiding in this way.

"I understand what you're saying," Sam said. "But if you can't make a career out of dancing, how do you find something else you love to do?"

"But it doesn't have to be a career. You don't have to stop dancing altogether. Some of us need to move to think. We can't sit still. Nowadays, they call it a condition, and maybe it is, but in my experience, you shouldn't suppress your need to move, and maybe you'd find your true north if you danced or swam or bounced your way towards it. You should get a rebounder. I use mine every morning."

Sam pushed away the startling image of Madame on a rebounder

Bridget glanced at her watch. "I have a meeting in half an hour," she said, gesturing for the bill. "How long will you be home?"

"I'm here for another few weeks."

"Grand. Then why don't you call the office and fix a time to come to the Academy?"

"I'd love to."

"Good show. I'll tell Teresa to expect your call. Have a look at our website too. We're all bells and whistles these days. This has been lovely, Sam," she said, taking the receipt from the waitress and getting to her feet. "I'm looking forward to showing you around."

"I can't wait." Sam replied, opening the door for them.

After another "goodbye" on the street, Sam wandered by the canal for a while, amused that "Madame" had suggested she should literally bounce her way through life. Picking up a brisk pace, she walked in the direction of the town, humming as she went.

'This little light of mine, I'm gonna let it shine. Let it shine. Let it shine. let it shine.'

DEIRDRE

Deirdre had closed over her computer and was about to take a nap when she looked across the room and saw Caroline passing the window.

"I was on my way back from seeing my mam and thought I'd drop in. Here. Sausage rolls," she said, closing the door behind her and handing Deirdre a paper bag.

"Lovely. Thanks," Deirdre said, taking them over to the fridge. "Cup of tea?"

"I'm swimming in the stuff, but go on," Caroline said, surveying the boxes piled high next to the kitchen dresser and lifting a picture from the shelf. "Love this, Dee. Didn't ever see it before. Where'd you buy it?"

"I didn't. It's one of my own photographs. I took it a few weeks back. I've been enlarging some of them," she said over her shoulder as she filled the kettle.

Caroline studied the image of a large flock of sheep staring directly at her. She swung her head to the left a little and then to the right.

"They look at you wherever you're standing. Every single one of them, even those wee lambs and look at that one at the back peaking over. It'd put you off having your Sunday roast for sure."

"I know. It was quite a moment. I took another before they came across the field towards me. I mean to enlarge it, too - It'd be like the before-and-after pictures of kids graduating. Do you know the ones I mean?"

"I think so. Show me."

Deirdre went over to her desk and ran off a copy. Caroline took it and laid it out next to the other. She stood back.

"That's hilarious," she said, "'before-and-after' pictures of sheep."

"I mounted the first one on stock card. It makes a difference."

"It's like a painting. Dee, you're so talented."

"Ach! I'm not so sure about that, but I am rather proud of it, for sure."

Deirdre was aware of a slight flutter in her stomach. This was the first time anyone had seen her recent pictures and she hadn't expected this response.

"I love the grey heron, too," Caroline said, lifting another photograph that was propped up by a jug on the windowsill. Could I have a copy? You know you could be selling these Dee. I'd buy them for sure."

"Give over, Caroline. Who'd spend good money on my pictures when they can go down the lane and take as many snaps of the sheep or the heron as they like?"

"Really, Deirdre. I mean it. People would buy them. I could stand there all day with my camera and not get anything like that. Would you just look at the arch of the branch. It's like a Chinese watercolor."

"Well, I do have to say I'm rather proud of it."

"As well you should be. I expect a copy of both of these, and I know the very place I'm going to hang them."

"Ah thank you. I do think I'm going to carry on with it. I had a call with an artist in Ibiza earlier on. Did I tell you Sally recommended her?" Deirdre said, lifting the pot of tea and putting the savories onto a tray. "Shall we take it into the sitting room? I'll light the fire. You're in no rush, are you?"

"No rush at all. Yes, you did say something about maybe taking a course."

"I'd have to sort out everything here first, but I could start online over Zoom, so I'm thinking about it."

"It's a brilliant idea, Dee. Have you given any more thought to what you'll do when you sell the house? I can't believe it sold so fast! I mean, it's gorgeous and all, but that was very quick. I've not had time to get used to the idea. Your head must be reeling. Here, let me carry something."

Deirdre busied herself at the fire while Caroline set out the cups and poured their tea.

"That'll be get going in a few minutes," Deirdre said, standing back from the grate and wiping her hands on a rag.

She sat down next to her.

"Yes. You're right, my head is reeling, alright."

"When do you expect to exchange contracts?"

"Not sure, but quickly, I think. The survey's all done."

"So what are you thinking?" Caroline asked, biting into a chocolate eclair.

"I'm not sure, but I'm wondering about renting a flat in the town for a few months, putting everything in storage and hoping a plan emerges. Somhairlin isn't in a rush to go back to London, and I'm loving having her around. I've been looking, and there's that new development down by the canal."

Caroline looked wistful.

"This is really happening." She sighed. "But I'm pleased you're starting to have some kind of a plan and you won't be too far away at all."

"I'll be just down the road. You know, I kind of like the idea of being near the town for a while. I get awful lonely some nights here by myself, and if I hear a noise, I think someone's downstairs and I can't get back to sleep. Don't tell anyone, but I'm also terrified of falling down the stairs and nobody finding me for days."

"Ah! Sure there's no danger of that Dee; "Mickey the Post" would be sure to notice you weren't there with his cup of tea in the morning."

Deirdre laughed. She was relieved that the plan seemed to make sense to someone else. She hadn't been at all sure. Lately, thoughts occurred to her in the early hours of the morning that seemed insane in daylight.

'Baby steps,' she kept telling herself. 'Keep doing what's in front of you. It's all you can do.'

"So, can I help with anything?" Caroline asked, gently putting her hand on Deirdre's arm.

"You know what I'm dreading, don't you, Caroline? Niall's clothes are still in the wardrobe, just as he left them."

"I know... If you like, you can leave it all to me, go out for the day, and when you come back, it'll all have gone to a good place."

"No, Caroline. Thank you, but we'll do it together. I need to face it. Maybe it'll finally sink in that's he's really gone. I'm still half-waiting to see him come around the corner."

"I know."

Deirdre looked at her friend. "Caroline, some days I don't want to go on. How can losing someone make you feel like this? The world is suddenly a terrifying lonely place. I'm making these plans, but I have no enthusiasm for them at all. I visualize myself in a flat, and then it comes in on me that I won't know why I'd be there. Does that make any sense?"

"It does..."

"It's this persistent thought I have that I don't know why I'm here anymore, like, what's the point of me?"

"Well, Somhairlin needs you. That's a start. And I do, too."

Deirdre smiled, her eyes overbrimming with tears.

"Yes...yes...that's true, but surely there has to be something more? Something I do with my time? I'm sick of thinking about myself and what I'm going to do."

"You're allowed Dee. You have to put your own mask on first and give yourself time before you even think of what you'd be doing for anyone else."

"I'm going so fast, too fast, but I'm scared to stop. All this packing is making me wonder what's the point of it all? I never thought that way before in my life. It scares me. I just want to be with him. I need him, Dee. I need him."

She let out a sudden yelp and doubled over. Her face contorted as she rocked back and forth, her shoulders heaving.

Caroline put her arm around her friend's shoulder and waited.

As Deirdre became calmer, Caroline went across to the sink, pulled off some kitchen roll, and handed it to her. Deirdre blew her nose noisily, wiped her eyes, and sank back into the couch.

"I'm sorry. I don't know what happened."

"I do." Caroline said gently. "You're still grieving. It's as simple as that. You'll have your bad days and your good ones, and I promise it will get easier. It will."

"I hope you're right." Deirdre murmured. "I can't live the rest of my life like this."

"You won't have to." Her friend reassured her. "Wait here, and I'll put the kettle on again, and I'm thinking a snifter of whisky wouldn't do you any harm."

SAM

Sam was approaching the village on her way back from town when she saw a message from Sandra. She shot a text back then hopped off the bus. The house was dark. Going through the side of the garden, she let herself in the back door.

"Mum! I'm home."

Her voice echoed.

"Mum?"

Turning on the kitchen light, she pulled off her shoes and coat, threw her shopping bags onto the table, and called Sandra back.

"Hey. How's it going?"

"Good. How are you?"

"Unemployed."

"What? What? Sorry?"

"I resigned."

"Oh! Really?" Sam said, attempting to fill the kettle with one hand.

"It's been coming for a while. I've had enough. Just wanted to let you know.

"Jon Porter's not on the books anymore, by the way."

"Really? How so?" Sam felt an unexpected jolt at the mention of his name.

"No clue. He was in Alexandra's office for ages. She pulled down the blind, always a bad sign as you know. Anyway, they were in there for about fifteen minutes, and Jon came out and marched off without speaking to any of us, which was unusual. He always hangs around and has a bit of a laugh. She appeared a few minutes later, told me to take his name off the books, that we weren't representing him anymore."

"Oh! I wonder what that was about."

"No clue. But anyway, I'm just letting you know I've left. I'm going to take a week off to do nothing and then start looking for another job."

"I'm sure you'll find something much better. Keep in touch, won't you?"

"Of course. What've you been up to since you left?"

"Not a lot, I'm helping my mother pack up our house and trying to figure out what to do with the rest of my life."

"Aren't we all...okay...well, hope it goes well, you have my number. Let's grab a drink when you're back."

"Will do. Bye."

"Bye."

Sam clicked off as the mantel clock chimed the hour. 'Where's my mother got to?' she wondered, going up to her room to change. 'And Jon Porter's left the bureau too.' Struggling with an emotion she found hard to place, she pulled on her sweatpants, then hearing a key turn in the latch, ran downstairs.

"Hey Mum. Where've you been? I was starting to worry."

Deirdre walked unsteadily towards the hall stand and peeled off her coat.

"Caroline'n'd I went for a walk..." She slurred.

"Mum, you've been drinking."

"I have!" Deirdre responded as Caroline appeared in the doorway.

"Hello Somhairlin." She grinned, opening her arms wide and swaying towards her. "Come here and give your Aunty Caroline a big hug."

"Come on in, Aunty Caroline." Sam said, stepping neatly to one side.

Her mother was already in the kitchen. "Where's that bottle of Bushmills?" She shouted. "The vintage 1982 or whatever, the one your dad's been saving for reasons best known to himself?"

"Hang on. I'll get it. Don't even think of climbing on a chair."

Sam went after her, reached up, and lifted down a brown box with a gold label.

"This one?"

"Yes, thank you very much, take it into the sitting room please, and would you ever be a good girl and light the fire? It'll have gone out by now. We met Mary O'Rourke up the street, her and Peter are on their way round for a drink. I told them to ask Pat and Dan Murphy over too if they're not doing anything."

Sam took Caroline's coat and put it over her arm.

"Okay." She said, "I can see we're in for a bit of a night of it.

"I'll take a nice glass of red wine," Caroline announced, rattling around a drawer in search of a corkscrew.

She pulled a bottle of Merlot from the rack. "Will you be having one yourself?" she asked Sam.

"Yes, please."

"Me too and use those fecking Waterford glasses." Deirdre said, pointing to the display of crystal in the glass fronted cupboard.

Sam laughed. It was rare she saw her mother with a few drinks in her, and certainly not since her dad had died.

'Who'd begrudge her this?' she thought, dragging the log basket and taking it into the sitting room. She fired up the embers, went back to the kitchen where she made a stack of cheese and pickle sandwiches, and shook out bags of crisps into bowls. Sooner or later, people would come looking for food. Setting out the table with plates and silverware, her mood lifted at the idea of having company.

A few hours in, the room had come alive with banter, stories exchanged, and jokes being told to screams of laughter. There had been much refilling of glasses.

"Come on now, Pat. Give us a song," Caroline cajoled "We've waited long enough."

Pat, who had been chatting to Mary by the mantelpiece, turned around, needing nothing further by way of encouragement. He cleared his throat a few times and the room fell respectfully silent.

"I'll take you home again Kathleen....to where your heart will feel no pain...and when the fields are fresh and green, I will take you to your home again."

Everyone sat in rapt attention.

"Aris. Artis,' Caroline yelled, breaking the tangible moment of sadness as the song ended.

"Come on Pat, give us Mick McGuire."

Pat tapped his foot and began singing in time to the beat.

"Johnny get up from the fire get up and give your man a seat, don't you know it's Mick McGuire and he's courting your sister Kate..."

There was much jigging and clapping. Caroline took to her feet and danced the Sevens crisscrossing the room, her arms straight by her side.

Sam sipped her wine, savoring the laughter. These friends of her parents had been a part of her life since the day she was born. She loved each and every one of them. Until last year, she had never considered there would come a time when one of them would not be there. Now she could see that time had not been especially kind to them. Lines were etched into Pat's face, but as he sang, his eyes crinkled with warmth. He was such a kind man, just like her father had been. Sam was suddenly struck by the fact that they must also be missing him very much.

Mary was called upon next and after a few moments' consideration, decided on 'Scarlet Ribbons.'

'Jesus, tonight please stop.' Sam thought, glancing across at her mother who had a faraway look. 'Why are all these old songs so miserable? This one's an absolute killer.'

Mary's voice quavered as she reached the top notes.

"If I live to be one hundred, I will never know from where, came those ribbons, scarlet ribbons, scarlet ribbons for her hair."

There was a trickle of applause and much 'Well done, Mary,' then, sensing the evening might be taking a downturn, Dan jumped in with "It's a Long Way to Tipperary."

Pat twirled a couple of spoons, clicking them up and down on his hip as Mary marked the beat, drumming the coffee table. The others sang at the top of their voices, swinging in unison from side to side on the couch, waving Waterford glasses. Sam took one long look at the scene, froze the moment in her mind's eye, then slipped out of the room and climbed the stairs to bed.

SAM

The approach to the dance school was every bit as miserable as Sam remembered. A new generation of kids in garish hoodies and tracksuits were hanging around smoking outside the chip shop, swearing and kicking the ground aimlessly. Walking past the McDonalds onto a wide stretch of wasteland, she turned off the street and crossed underneath a bridge, stopping to buy a copy of *The Big Issue* from a girl whom she guessed was about the same age as herself.

'...and there but for the grace of God go I...' she thought, rolling it into her bag as she turned the corner to the academy.

The exterior of the Victorian building was unchanged, unlike the open-plan reception area, which now had vibrant red walls and posters of musicals and events. It was so different from the drab entranceway she remembered. Doors flapped open and shut as students spilled out from classes, dashing past her as she walked across to the reception area.

"Can I help you?"

A young woman with purple hair and several nose rings looked up from her computer.

"Thank you. I'm Sam Macardle; I've an appoint-ment with 'Madame O'Leary," she said.

"Ah! Of course. Hello. She told me to bring you straight to her office. This way."

She said, guiding her down a corridor where Brid-get's door was open.

"Thank you, Marie," she said. "Hello, Sam. So glad you could make it. The children are very excited to have a guest today. We've half an hour before the class. Let me show you around. You can leave your coat in the staffroom."

After introducing Sam to a couple of teachers, she led the way to the main hall, where a few older students were warming up at the barres in front of long mirrors.

"I remember this so well," Sam said. "It even smells the same."

"Is that a good thing?" Bridget laughed. "We had a new sprung floor installed about five years ago and gave it all a lick of paint, but let's face it, space is the most important thing of all isn't it? You can have all the high-tech sound systems you want, and we do now, but at the end of the day, that piano serves us very well.

Sam looked across at the upright piano and beat-en-up stool.

"Does Mrs. Winters still play during class?" she asked.

"Ah! No. Kathleen died a few years ago, lord rest her soul. We have a lovely young girl now who's also a dancer, Jenny Rafferty. You'll meet her in a minute."

"I'm sorry to hear that. I liked her. I sometimes wondered how she had the patience to play the same sequence over and over when we practiced. I remem-ber how she'd play those wonderful pieces of Chopin when we were filing out at the end. It must have been such a relief after an hour on repeat."

"Do you know, that thought never occurred to me," Brigitte said as some studio doors swung open and a group of children in pink leotards came chattering and skipping towards the changing rooms.

"Walk, everyone. Please," she shouted.

The children slowed down immediately.

"So, no change there." Sam laughed. "Everyone is still terrified of you... In a nice way, of course," she added.

"Of course," Bridget said with a knowing smile. "Discipline is underrated nowadays. Let's go this way. Did you get a chance to look at our website? What do you think?"

"It's incredible. How you've taken this from the little school with our tap and ballet classes, to this is almost unbelievable."

"You'll have seen that we have Adult classes now too; tap, ballroom, Latin, waltz, cha cha, jive...we even Argentine tango." She said proudly. "That's what I was telling you. There's absolutely no need to stop dancing. If you're going to be here for a few weeks, why not sign up. You'd love it."

Sam didn't hesitate.

"I will," she said.

"I was hoping you'd say that. Okay, we'd better get to the studio."

Bridget walked ahead of her down another corridor, past the storage areas and the rails crammed with costumes and shoes spilling from boxes, through the changing rooms, past make-up stations, rigging systems, and lighting blocks, to the stage. She stood in the wings looking out through the drapes, remembering how it had felt as a dancer in those waiting moments counting out the beats in preparation to go on stage. She thought back to standing in the wings waiting with Jon in Kauai and how he had caught her eye and made her giggle. Why could she not get him out of her head?

"I'll be retiring next year," Bridget told her. "I've a great team now. It's time. I'll join the board and focus on the community outreach program. We have an inclusive dance course and we also take groups to perform in the hospital and care homes. It's such a joy to see the little ones with the older residents.

"That's wonderful," Sam said.

"Let's go back into the hall. This way."

Bridget directed her through the theatre.

"This class is grade two." She told her opening the door. "A few of the children are older, but they're mostly about eight. You met Bronagh earlier. She trained in Dublin. We're so lucky to have her.

"Good morning Jenny." she nodded to the pianist who was busy sorting through sheet music. "I'll introduce you at the end of the class," she said, indicating for Sam to sit down.

The children, girls except for one boy, were already there when they arrived, lining up to face the barre when Bronagh walked to the front of the room.

"Good morning, everyone."

"Good morning, Miss Sullivan," they chanted.

"We are very fortunate to have Madame join us today.

"Good morning, Madame," they chorused.

"And this is Miss Macardle. When she was your age, she came here for ballet classes, and she's here today as our special guest, so let's do our very best work."

"Hello everyone." Sam smiled.

As the lesson began with the routine she knew so well; the pliés, battement tendu, battement glissé and ronde de jambe, Sam found it hard to stay in her seat. Her body knew exactly what to do and her limbs ached to be doing it. Dance had given her another language, a way to express herself; why had she let it go?" She wondered.

At the end of the hour, as the children performed a series of curtseys, she was reminded how much she loved the ceremony of ballet, the quiet elegance of it and the respect always shown to the teacher.

Thanking Bridget profusely, she had a few words with Bronagh before booking a few ballet and tap classes. On the way home, she stopped by the café and ordered a coffee and slice of apple pie. She was feeling a little ambivalent now about signing up for the barre class. What had she been thinking? She was way out of shape; she'd never be able to keep up. Tap would be fun though, and she knew exactly where she'd stored her tap shoes.

Her phone pinged as she sat down. She checked her messages.

Heard you resigned.

Hope you're okay.

Want to chat sometime?

It took a second for to register that it was from Jon Porter. She read it again, slowly this time, unsure why she wasn't simply firing back a quick reply. She began texting.

Am in Ireland. Yes, I resigned. Love to chat. Delete.

Yes, I resigned. Am in Ireland. Happy to chat.

Settling on the second version, she pressed 'send.'

"Thank you," she said, as the waitress served her, and her phone dinged again.

Great...I'm in London. Time for a call?

Am in a café, could chat in about an hour.

The reply came back.

I'll call you at 7 then.

Okay.

She waited a moment before clicking off. There was no denying the flip her stomach had made when she'd seen that text. She pushed away the plate, checked the time, and asked for the bill.

"Don't worry about the change," she said, leaping up and grabbing her bag. She pulled on her coat, flew down the street, and caught the bus as it was turning the corner. Settling into the seat, she tried to push any expectations about the call out of her mind. He was probably getting in touch for some practical reason to do with the bureau, why else would Jon Porter have got in touch with her? What was she hoping for? Looking up, she saw she'd missed her stop and ran to the front of the bus.

"If you could pull up before the crossroads that'd be great." She told the driver. "I just went past my house!"

"You're alright," he said, slowing down and opening the doors. "Safe home now."

Racing down the road and up the path, she stuck her head around the kitchen door. Her mother was at the kitchen table surrounded by packing cases, tissue paper, and pots of paints and glue.

"Hi Mum. I've a call in half an hour," she said. "What time's dinner?"

Deirdre looked at her blankly for a moment.

"Sorry Somhairlin, sorry what did you say? I was miles away."

"I don't want to disturb you, just wondered what time we're eating."

"Goodness, look at the time... I haven't even started cooking."

"No problem. Let's get a takeaway."

"Good idea," Deirdre answered, switching off the printer. Indian?"

"Yes please, and extra popadoms; let's go wild."

"Okay. I'll call them in half an hour."

Sam was lying on top of the bed with her phone in her hand when it rang. She waited a few seconds before answering.

"Hello," she said. "This is Sam."

"Hello, this is Jon." He echoed her, laughing. "How are you?"

"I'm good...how are you?"

"I'm good too."

"That's good." 'Too many "goods"' she thought.

"Alexandra told me you'd suddenly quit for no reason, but I find that hard to believe."

"Well, yes. I did have a few reasons."

"I can imagine." He laughed.

'Why has my brain frozen?' she thought.

"I'm back in London," he said, breaking the moment's silence. "Would you like to meet up for dinner, celebrate our emancipation from AISB? They're not representing me anymore."

Sam swung her legs off the bed, stood up and began pacing the room. 'Am I hearing correctly?" she thought.

"That'd be lovely," she said. "Sandra told me you'd left."

"It wasn't the friendliest of exits. Alex didn't exactly throw me a leaving 'do'. But it's been coming for a while. So, what about you? Why did you leave?"

"It's a bit of a long story." She hesitated.

"Are you okay?"

"I am," she said. "It was the best decision I've made in ages."

"Good. I look forward to hearing all about it over dinner. What part of London are you in?"

"Clapham," she said," But I'm in Ireland at the moment."

"Ah! Okay. When're you back?"

"I'm not exactly sure, about a week or so, I think."

"Why don't you shoot me a text when you know?"

"Okay," she said, "I will. Okay. Bye." She clicked off.

'Why did I cut the conversation short like that?' she wondered. 'That was so rude of me. He must think I'm really odd.'

Hearing her mother call, she ran downstairs.

"Smells amazing. Did you order naan?" She asked.

"Yes. The one with coconut you like, peshwari and that cucumber thing, should be in there too."

"Ah! Yes, raita, it's here," she said, lifting out the foil trays.

"Great. There's some lager in the bottom of the fridge."

Sam ferried their plates to the table, prised the lids off their drinks, and pulled out a chair.

"This looks so good. I'm starving."

They passed the dishes back and forth, relishing the food.

148

"So how did you get on at The Academy? How was 'Madame'?" Deirdre asked, breaking the silence after a while.

"You mean 'Bridget.'" Sam laughed. "I get to be on first-name terms these days. She's great, still got incredible energy, although she plans on retiring, or at least stepping down soon. It was so lovely to be there, brought back so many memories."

"I'm sure it must have done."

"You know, I was thinking, I can't remember the last time I felt passionate about anything in the way I used to when I was dancing. I miss it. I love that world."

"You did love it. You were obsessed from any age. I still have your collection of ballet books upstairs somewhere. I'll dig them out for you, and I know your dad kept all your old CDs with the soundtracks on."

"I'd love to look through them again. So why did I stop? I don't really remember anything except getting self-conscious. In Dublin, the girls were all so thin and willowy and I thought I was fat."

Deirdre looked up from her plate.

"You never told me that. I wish you had. I'd have talked some sense into you. Look at you, you've never put on an ounce. You certainly don't take after the Macardles in that department."

"Well, that's teenagers for you, I suppose. Pass me the rice please."

"Here you go," Deirdre said, lifting a bowl. "I rest my point. You've hollow legs Somhairlin."

"Well anyway, I'm going to take some classes while I'm here."

"That's a great idea."

149

Deirdre pushed her plate away and sat back in the chair.

"I'm full to the rafters,"she said. "I can hardly move."

"Me too. Go on ahead to the sitting room. It'll only take me a minute to clear away."

Deirdre stood up.

"Okay." She yawned.

Sam straightened up the table and joined her mother by the fire. They sat watching the flames lick the logs.

"Do you remember when I was little, we would make stories about inside the fire?"

"I do indeed. I still do it sometimes. You can imagine a whole world in there once you get your eye in."

"Yes. Look. I can see a bridge and a dragon face."

"I can see a bridge too.

"I have such happy memories of growing up, Mum," Sam said with a deep sigh.

"I'm so glad. I have too," Deirdre said softly. "So many.

"I miss him so much."

"I know you do darling. I do too. It's so terribly hard, isn't it."

She took Sam's hand.

"Do you want to talk about it?"

'I'm a bit talked out today, if it's okay. Could we watch some telly?"

"Of course. Let's find something to take us out of ourselves." She said, "Have you watched *Clue Time* at all? Caroline and I are addicted. She's a lot faster than me with the answers, though."

Sam sat up.

"Mum, do you remember me telling you about the speaker I heard in Kauai?"

"I do."

"Well, that's him. The speaker."

"Who's 'him'? You mean the bald guy who asks the questions? What's his name? Peter Walker, that one?"

"No. The other one, not the one with the beard. The younger one, Jon Porter."

"Oh! I love him. He's great with the one-liners, and he's so clever."

"I know. He really is. I was talking to him on the phone, just now before the dinner arrived."

Deirdre's mouth dropped open.

"You know him?"

"Kind of. I told you. He was the speaker in Kauai, the one who made me think about leaving the job."

"I feel really bad not knowing what you did in your job. I know you were PR-ing."

"PA, mum. Personal assistant."

"Sorry, I knew that, sorry. Yes, I knew you were assisting someone, but I didn't really know why you were in Kauai. I feel terrible, Somhairlin, I've not been paying proper attention at all. As long as you were doing okay, that was all I needed to know. But why were you talking to him now you've resigned? Were you PA -ing for him?"

"No. My boss owns the bureau."

"I'm beginning to feel really stupid."

"Mum, don't be daft. I never explained it to you, how would you know. The Speakers Bureau is like a manager, an agent. They take on speakers and find them events to speak at. I was there with Alexandra, the woman who owns the bureau, the one who was impossible to work for. Jon Porter was the guest speaker, so I had to show him around, make sure he had everything he needed, and be there to help Alexandra, too."

"Okay. So, was that the kind of thing you were doing at 'Irish Heritage' too?

"Kind of. It was different in some ways. It was more interesting. I got to meet people, show visitors around London, that kind of thing. The boss there gave me a lot of different things to do."

"Like what?"

"Oh, you know, working on the website and a lot of the social media stuff. She would give me a project and then let me get on with it. We did events. You remember I sent you the photographs when the Taoiseach was over in London."

"Ah! Yes. I remember that, and wasn't there some girl from the Eurovision song contest at something too?"

Sam laughed.

"Yes, she was, but it wasn't quite the same kind of event. That was a fundraiser."

"Well, what would I know?" Deirdre laughed. "You know I'd be more into the singing than the politics. So here, you were telling me about Jon whatshisname."

"Yes. After his talk, which was brilliant, we bumped into each other and went for a walk along the beach. He's so easy to talk to."

"He comes across that way."

"He's quick. It's like there are two of them. In real life, he's actually quite serious. I mean he's funny, but he's intense."

"I can't wait to get telling Caroline. She'll never believe it. Shall we watch one?

Why don't you get it set up while I make us a cup of tea."

Deirdre looked up as Sam came into the kitchen the next morning.

"How did you sleep?" she asked. "The kettle's just boiled."

"Not too badly." Sam yawned. "What time did you get up?"

"Too early." Deirdre said.

Sam made herself a cup of tea and joined her mother at the kitchen table. She lifted one of the photographs from the pile Deirdre was sorting through.

"I remember that day so well," she said. "Look at dad there. What an eegit."

Deirdre glanced across at the picture of Niall and Sam with ice cream moustaches and cones in their hands.

"That was in Donegal, the day we made the sand turtles."

"Here." Deirdre handed her a few more photographs of sand sculptures with Sam and her dad standing proudly next to them.

"Do you remember the wave that came in about ten minutes later?"

"Yes, and how the car got stuck in the sand"

"What was he thinking, driving onto it?"

"I can't remember. I think we were on it before he realized it was the sand."

"And this one."

"Yes. I remember him building you that house with all those boxes. I can't remember what came in them. He said you got as much pleasure from the empty boxes as you did from the toys inside them."

"I did.'

"And this, continuing the theme..." Deirdre laughed, handing her another.

Sam gazed at the childhood picture of herself skiing down the hill at the back of the house. She swallowed hard, remembering the Christmas morning when thick snow had fallen overnight, and her dad had stayed up making her a sledge from flattened boxes wrapped in shower curtain."

"It took you a moment to see the funny side, I seem to remember, Mum." Sam grinned.

"It did." Deirdre smiled. "I didn't know what he'd used until I was standing stark naked in the shower and there was water spraying all over the bathroom."

"He was so inventive."

"...and kind. I couldn't stay cross with him for long, you had so much fun with it."

They smiled at the memory before the silence between them landed. Sam drank her tea and her mother looked away, covering her mouth with her hand.

"Okay Mum. What's today?" Sam said, jumping up after a few minutes and going over to the fridge. She pulled out a carton of orange juice and poured a glass. "What do you need me to do?"

"Nothing at all. I think we should go out for our lunch. Betsy will be here soon, and we might not get another chance to be just the two of us. I want to hear what's going on with you. I was mortified last night when I didn't know what your work was about."

"It's okay. I told you. How were you to know?" she said,

"I was thinking after I went to bed that, on top of whatever's been going on with you and that awful woman, I've pulled the rug out from under you, quite literally. Let's make up for lost time, catch up properly."

Sam poured milk into a bowl of cereal and brought it back to the table.

"I'd like that, Mum." she said. "I've missed you. I haven't wanted to worry you. I know how hard it's been, but I'm a bit lost right now."

"Okay. Let's go to Kinloch and walk along the strand.

Later that morning, deep in thought, Sam looked out across at the mountains and sea that was turning dark under the ominous clouds gathering overhead. Deirdre pulled into a parking spot next to the medieval castle and turned to her.

"Are you still up for this? It'll certainly blow the cobwebs away."

"I am." Sam said, yanking up the hood on her cagoule. "Are we women or mice?"

"Squeak." Deirdre laughed.

The storm blew in as they made their way across the street. Sam turned her head to the sky and let the rain lash her face as Deirdre tightened her coat and put up her hood. They walked around the peninsular, occasionally nodding a "Hello" to other walkers, side-stepping the puddles, and making their way until the path ended. As the rain eased, they stood looking out across the bay. A flash of light behind a cloud signaled the sun's appearance. Deirdre crossed the shingle to a shallow inlet and Sam followed her.

"Would you take a look at that." Deirdre said, as the beginnings of a rainbow appeared above the mountain.

"So beautiful." Sam agreed, watching the colors deepen and form a near perfect arch. They stood together in wonder.

"They're a sign of new beginnings, Mum. Did you know that?"

Sam took her mother's hand.

"If I knew, I've forgotten." Deirdre said.

They stood a while longer, then as the sky brightened, they turned back towards the road.

"Tell me what's going on with you, love. It's not just the grief, is it?" Deirdre said, shaking the rain off her hood and stuffing it in her pocket.

Sam hesitated. "No, it's not just the grief, but it's somehow connected. I'm sorry I didn't hang around with you for longer last year. I just couldn't."

"What are you talking about? You did offer. Have you forgotten that? I was the one told you to go back to London and get on with your life."

"Honestly, I don't remember. It's all a bit of a fog. I tried to make a new start. I thought this job would be perfect with the traveling, but it was so stressful. I need to do something more than run around after some egomaniac."

"You do."

"Have you any suggestions?"

"I don't think I'm very well equipped to help you there.' Deirdre sighed. "I didn't even know there were jobs like the one you had. There's a lot of opportunity that wasn't there in my day or if there was, I didn't see it. Maybe you could do a few sessions with Sally. She was brilliant at getting me started on the right track."

Sam hesitated.

"I'm not sure about that. Sally's your coach. I might need to find some kind of support, but Sally is there for you."

"Fair enough, but if you think it'd be useful to have someone in your corner, I'm happy to pay for them."

"Maybe. Thanks, Mum."

Shall we have lunch at the hotel? If it stays dry, we can sit outside."

"Sounds good."

Linking arms as they walked across to the SeaView Hotel, they found a table near the bay window overlooking the lough. Glancing around Sam saw that little had changed since the last time she had been there many years before. The dark wood interior and mid-century furniture felt oddly reassuring. She scanned the menu which gave little indication of having changed much either.

"They still have Coquille St Jaques!" She laughed. "I haven't seen that on a menu in years. I'm going to have it for old time's sake."

"I'll join you." Deirdre said. "Your dad loved the mussels here. We came a lot when we were courting."

Sam closed her menu over.

"Mum, did you know when you first met Dad that he was special? I mean did you have a feeling, even before you got to know him properly?"

"I hadn't met all that many men before, but yes. Yes, from the first time we met I knew he was different for sure."

"And you had a feeling he was right for you?"

"I did." Deirdre's eyes softened with the memory. "We didn't need many words. We both just knew. We never talked about it or analyzed it. Why do you ask?"

"Oh! Nothing," Sam said. "Nothing. I was just wondering."

DEIRDRE

Deirdre kept an eye on the clock as she finished seasoning a chicken casserole and piling carrots into the slow cooker. Straightening up the countertop, she went back to the kitchen table and dialed in for the call with Sally.

"Hello Deirdre," Sally greeted her. "How are you? I'm sorry I had to cut short our last session."

"Ah! No bother at all, Sally. Things happen." She said, "Excuse the state of me. I've been cooking. I can see myself there. I look like the wreck of the Hesperus. I hope you were able to sort out your problem."

"Yes. Thank you. So how are you? Are you still finding space to take your photographs in between the move? Fill me in."

"Yes. I'm still snapping away. Caroline's taken a couple of them to frame. She was saying I could sell them, but I'm not so sure about that."

"Why ever not!?"

"I'm a real amateur, but I was rather flattered. I've been looking forward to telling you about the session with Isabelle."

"Great. I want to hear."

"It went really well."

"I'm so pleased."

"I can't get enough of it. It's incredible. She's shown me a way to make collages from my pictures. You enlarge and print off a photograph then just tear the shit out of it, pardon my French. Then you glue it and rearrange everything and eventually you end up with... it's hard to explain, you take another photograph... and...well here...let me show you."

Deirdre lifted a collage from the table and held it up to the screen."

"Wow! Deirdre, that is beautiful, the colors, the shapes. It's lovely."

"Ah! Thank you, Sally. This started out as a photograph of a flock of sheep. I call it 'Sheep Wreck.' Weak pun I know, but it amused me. Isabelle said to name each piece when it feels finished. There are about six layers on this. It's just cardboard and Pritt stick, but for a beginner, I'm rather chuffed with myself."

"As so you should be," Sally said. "You're so animated. You're really in your element with this aren't you?"

"I am. It's helping clear my mind; sometimes I destroy the paper I cry so much, but it's therapeutic and I'm so grateful for the introduction. She's so encouraging."

"She's special, isn't she?"

"Yes, so calm."

"I couldn't be more thrilled that you've found a way to express yourself creatively. That's wonderful."

"I've also been trying to answer more of the questions you sent over, asking myself who I am now."

"Go on."

"I'm trying to work out who I might have been if I'd not met Niall. What would I have done? I came across a book about Hillary Clinton, how her life might have been if she'd never met Bill. It got me thinking. I'm pretty sure I wouldn't have changed the course of history, but you know, it would all have been very different. Those questions you asked me, the ones about what I loved as a child...what I stopped doing when I got older?"

"Yes..."

"The answer is somewhere in there, I'm sure. I think I lost part of myself along the way."

"It makes perfect sense." Sally nodded. "No matter how hard we aim for balance, we all have to compromise to make marriages work, and when we have children, well, as you know, you put yourself last."

"That's so true." Deirdre said. "It's hard to put how I feel into words exactly, but I want a bigger life than I've had, not a smaller one. I know what I don't want, it's finding out what I do, that's the issue."

"There's no rush, Deirdre. You're making incredible strides. I'm sure the answer will reveal itself. Be patient if you can."

"I know I can't rush things." Deirdre said slowly. "But with the house going, I have to make some kind of plan sooner rather than later. I'm terrified of making a mistake. It's that George Harrison song; '*If you don't know where you're going, any road will take you there...*' I still have no clear sense of direction."

"You will have. This is just another stage on the journey. You're in liminal space right now. It's scary I know, but you are doing everything you should be doing. It's okay to feel lost for a while, but you're moving forward even though it may not feel like it."

"I've never made big decisions on my own before, you know. I think that's what makes it so frightening. I get scared. Niall and I would talk about everything together and looking back we never had to make any decisions as big as the ones I'm making on my own right now. Maybe we did, but it didn't feel that way when we had each other."

"I know. It must be so hard."

"It really is. I wonder sometimes how Niall would have dealt with things If I'd gone first. I think he'd have carried on pottering around his shed. I don't think he'd be trying to work out who he was. He had a better sense of himself than I do. I spent so much of my life looking after him, working with him. There was always someone dropping by needing some old tractor fixed, people around the house and in the yard. I think his life would have continued much as it was; he'd have missed me of course, I mean I know that, but I think it might have been easier for him."

"I can see why you'd ask yourself those questions, but the truth is, Deirdre, you have no way of knowing. I am sure he would have struggled in his own way. It's hard to lose someone when your lives have been so intertwined. You've lost your best friend, but also your work. You're on the path now to finding new work, new purpose; try not to dwell on the 'what ifs.' Focus on the art as much as possible, and you'll keep getting stronger."

"Sorry. I don't know where that came from, I was just trying to explain why it's so hard."

"There's no need to be sorry. I'm here as a sounding board for whatever comes into your head, but I'm also here to try to help you stay on track. Allow yourself these thoughts but try not to let them overwhelm you. It's perfectly understandable you're going to have them but keep doing everything you're doing and try to take each day as it comes."

"Yes. 'One day at a time. 'I needed that reminder. Thank you Sally."

"Deirdre, did you get a chance to look at the other video I sent, the one about integrating grief and moving forward 'with' it rather than 'through' it? I'm not trained as a grief counsellor as you know, so I hope it sits okay with you when I send those kinds of links."

"I did indeed Sally. Thank you"

"Ah! That's good. I hope all goes well for you this week and remember, if you need to check in at any time before our next session just shoot me a text."

After the call, Deirdre stayed at the computer looking through some of the photographs she'd taken one day at the derelict cottage. She printed off a series of images and began tearing them into long strips, sticking them onto card, and overlaying the deconstructed images of archways, layer upon layer until the sheet was covered. Ripping again and pasting some more, she loaded a brush with watercolor paint and let it run in rivulets between the crevices. She gazed at the abstraction, marveling at the beauty of the pools of color. The metaphor Isabelle had used was not lost on her. She was deconstructing her life in order to reconstruct it differently, just as she had done with the photograph. Even in the depths of terrible pain, she was able to create something beautiful.

Hearing a car pull into the driveway, she looked up at the clock. How could it possibly be two hours since Somhairlin had left for the airport? She leapt up, rinsed her hands and ran to open the front door.

"Hello, Betsy. Come in, come in. You're very welcome. Don't mind the state of the place. You have to step round everything to get where you're going," she said, shifting a box out of the way with her foot.

"Lovely to see you, Mrs. Macardle." Betsy said, heaving her suitcase over the step and catching her breath. "I see it's still raining in Ireland."

"Hasn't stopped since you left." Deirdre laughed. "Give me your coat and close over that door. It would freeze the life out of you. Where's Sam?"

"She's on the phone in the car, sorting out some dance class for tomorrow; said she'll come in the back way."

"Ah! Okay. So how are you, Betsy? Give me that here," she said, taking her coat. Where did you get this from? It's absolutely gorgeous."

"Ah! You know me, a charity shop. Thirty quid."

"Get away! Just look at that beautiful lining and the quality of the velvet. You shouldn't be wearing it in the rain though; you'll ruin it."

"I won't. Don't worry."

'Would you like a cup of tea or something stronger maybe. You're on your holidays. A glass of wine?"

"I'd love a glass of wine. Thank you."

"Would you be having the red or the white? I have both."

"White would be lovely."

"Now where did I pack the glasses?" Deirdre muttered, searching through the top of a crate. "My head's not on straight. What was I thinking, putting them away? Like we won't need a drink in the next week. Ha!"

"They're in there mum." Sam said, closing the door behind her. "The wooden box in the corner. I'll get them."

"Okay sweetheart," she said going over to the fridge. "I'll join you. I've the fire lit. Why don't you girls take the bags upstairs, get into your pajamas, and I'll bring the drinks in for us."

"Okay, Mum. Bets, follow me. You're in the same room as last time."

In the sitting room, Deirdre gave the fire a poke. It sprung into life, crackling and creating a golden glow. She opened the bottle and poured a glass of wine, taking a few sips before flopping down in the couch. 'I'm going to miss this,' she thought.

She stared at the bare walls, at the dusty outlines where the pictures had hung, at the empty mantel piece, the upended chairs, and the cushions piled high in the corner on top of box after box of books. A lifetime had been dismantled, packed away to be stored. 'Deconstructed.' She thought, drifting off into a sea of memories until the girls reappeared.

"Mrs. Macardle, I've brought you a little present," Betsy said, handing her a flat rectangular box.

"Ah! That's so kind of you. You didn't need to be doing that... I love this paper," she said, carefully untying the ribbon. "I'll use it again."

Betsy lifted her wine glass and sat down next to her.

Deirdre gasped as she pulled out a square silk scarf with delicate swirls of blue and green edged with the softest pink.

"It's absolutely beautiful," she said, holding it up and showing Sam. "Isn't this exquisite? Thank you so much."

She leaned across and hugged Betsy, then examined it closely.

"You're not going to believe this," she said, "Don't move."

A few seconds later, she was back holding a piece of card, a 'detail' from one of the abstract collages she had made.

"Look. Look..." She said holding it on top of the silk. "How is this even possible?"

Both girls stared in amazement. It was as if the card were a swatch from the scarf. The intensity of the blues and greens in the marbled pattern were identical. It had the same pink edging. It was a perfect match.

"Where did you get that?" Betsy asked.

"I made it."

"You made it? It's awesome, beautiful. Did you paint it?"

"Kind of..." Deirdre said, it's a process. I'll show you. Come into the kitchen."

She weaved her way through the boxes to her desk and the girls followed her.

"I have it here, somewhere," she said, rifling through a box of photographs. "Ah! Here it is. This one. The grey heron. I took this photograph the day we went for our walk, not long after you got home, Sam."

"I remember." Sam nodded.

"So this is the original photograph," she told them. "I enlarge it on watercolor paper, like this one here you can see on the printer, then I just tear it and glue it over and over and basically go a bit mad until I feel like painting over the layers, then I take another photograph of the new version, this one here...and do it all over again. Then sooner or later, I'm done, finished with it. It's hard to explain, but I can see when something beautiful has appeared. It's like magic."

"Mum's so into it," Sam said proudly. "She disappears for hours on end. Here, look Bets, this one with all the sheep, and this other one I love, especially."

She picked out a sepia-toned collage with an intricate twisting pattern of branches and cords.

"You're so talented, Mrs. Macardle. You should be selling these."

"Get away with you Betsy... I've only just started. I've no clue what I'm about."

"You could sell those on Etsy no problem," she told her.

"Well, that's very kind of you to say. My friend Caroline said the same thing, so I suppose I should be gracious; it's lovely to get the appreciation. That's all that matters to me right now. I'm still reeling from the scarf being the same. Where did you get it?"

"From the same shop I found my coat. It's vintage Dior."

"Well, my goodness!" Deirdre exclaimed. "Dior! Thank you...gosh, Dior!"

Sam interjected. "Sorry to be so plebeian, while you two are talking Dior... but that chicken casserole is speaking to me. Are we eating soon?"

"Smells awesome." Betsy said.

"Okay girls. Go on back and sit by the fire. Give me ten minutes. I'll take it out of the oven and let it cool down.

SAM

"It's great to see you," Sam said, lolling back at the end of the couch opposite Betsy after her mother had gone to bed.

"You too. Your mum looks much better than last time I saw her. She seems to be doing well."

"She's been busy packing up the house, and I've helped her find a flat to rent for a while. She gets tired easily. She has a faraway look a lot of the time, but she's like a new person with the photography thing. She's even talking about going to Ibiza for an art course."

"Ibiza? Isn't that party central?"

"The studio's in the north of the island. She says it's quiet, away from all the clubs."

"Seeing your mum tonight after a few glasses of wine, I wouldn't put money on her staying in the quiet part," Betsy laughed. "So, how're you doing?"

"I'm okay... I've missed dad a lot since I've been here. It's still hard, but I've been taking loads of dance classes. Getting back into ballet was a killer."

"If it's anything like barre method, I hear you." Betsy nodded. "You look good on it, though."

"Yeh. I feel better for it. You're coming with me tomorrow, yes?"

"Of course. I'm up for anything."

"Great. We'll take the bus in. So, what've you been up to?"

"Not much. Just work and thinking about changing jobs, then not doing anything about it...you know me... same old, same old."

Sam plumped up the cushion behind her head.

"You're so funny," she said. "You're all about me having fun jobs, but then you stay in that crappy one."

"I know, but it's easy, gives me time for my classes and messing around on Etsy." She shrugged. "I'm alright. I'm not as interested in work as you are. It's just a job." Sam glanced up at the clock.

"Shall I leave you to wake up in the morning, or do you want a shout? We need to leave at ten."

Betsy swung her legs around.

"I'll set my alarm. I'll need to. I remember that bed was so comfortable, can't wait to get into it. We're like a pair of old ladies, aren't we?" She yawned and levered herself from the couch.

"Go on ahead. I'll turn out the lights," Sam said, propping up the fireguard.

"Okay. See you in the morning. Sleep well."

Sam climbed into bed and stared at the ceiling lost in thought. Betsy was a breath of fresh air. It was great to have her here, but she'd hesitated to tell her about the call with Jon. Anyway, there was nothing to tell her, was there? It had been nothing more than a catch-up about AISB hadn't it? And the dinner invitation? There was nothing in that either was there? Or was there?

She switched off the bedside light, rolled over and pulled the covers high over her shoulders. It was a while before she stopped replaying the conversation with Jon in her head.

DIERDRE

The next morning, Deirdre dressed in a daze, still somewhere between sleep and waking, reluctant to lose the images that had come during the night when she had dreamed of twirling in blue and grey silk under a glistening waterfall. It had left her with a sense of peace. She sat for a while at the dressing table. Maybe this was the beginning of acceptance? It was almost as though she were on the edge of happiness.

There had been so many moments recently where she had felt guided. Things were falling into place in ways she could never have imagined. The thought of an apartment had been daunting in the abstract, but the one they'd found had left her with goosebumps and a sense of *déjà vu* from the moment she walked in. There were two bedrooms, each with their own bathroom, a compact kitchen, and a large sitting room running the entire width of the apartment. The view was spectacular. Stepping through the wide sliding glass doors onto a small verandah, she could see the cathedral spire and rows of houses nestled on the hillside against the backdrop of distant mountains. The waterway was jostling with walkers and joggers going back and forth on the towpath.

It was only four miles away, but a completely different world. It would literally give her a new perspective. She welcomed the idea, laughing with Isabelle recently that she now 'spoke Metaphor.' She could joke about it, but metaphors were indeed another language, and they resonated. Looking at the world from an entirely different vantage point was what she needed. Already, she could see the town with fresh eyes. It didn't stop the ache or the urge to share it all with Niall, or the lurch in her stomach when she saw two chairs at the bistro table on the verandah, but she was learning to live with these moments and to push past them.

She thought back to the previous evening and the scarf. Had she imagined the similarity with the collage? Did she dare allow herself to think she had produced something even vaguely like a Dior print? She'd had a few glasses of wine; it must have been her imagination. She jumped up and raced down to the kitchen. Lifting the scarf from the desk, she rested it on top of the collage, marveling again at the similarity. Then, flicking through some of her other work, she felt a flutter in her stomach.

'This would make a beautiful one,' she thought, pulling out a sepia toned abstract. '...and this could work wonderfully as a large silk square that you'd maybe wear over a jacket.' Turning over one after the other, she had a rush of adrenalin at the possibilities, how she could crop sections, and expand others, the textures she might use, the fabrics, the details she could add with fringing or even pom moms, why not?

Then, without warning, her stomach tightened, and her mood crashed.

'This is madness,' she thought. 'I haven't the faintest clue how to go about getting a pattern onto a piece of silk or make it into a scarf, let alone sell it on Etsy or anywhere else.'

She put down the painting and stared out at the mist covering the mountain. Hearing the girls moving about upstairs, she made tea and took it into the sitting room. Setting it down on the coffee table, she sat despondently on the couch, thinking how for a few giddy minutes, she had been high on possibilities and now, all she wanted was go back to bed. It was madness to think she could create a business from a silly coincidence. It was wishful thinking, absolute fantasy.

She drank her tea and tried to recapture the sense of contentment she'd felt on waking, annoyed that her fleeting moments of happiness had been so quickly sabotaged by grief. Would she always be at the mercy of it? Would her confidence ever come back?

'Confidence...' she thought, setting down the cup, suddenly hit by a startling truth.

'That wasn't grief.' She thought. 'It had nothing at all to do with grief. That was a voice in my head telling me I couldn't do something, that I'm not good enough, that I'm too old, that it's not worth trying. I'm using grief as an excuse.'

With this insight, Deirdre had a flashback to a moment in the art room at school, to a piece of work she had proudly shown her teacher, only to be told it lacked perspective. It had been graded "C" and handed back without a word of encouragement. Deirdre felt her disappointment all over again, amazed that this one negative experience could have had such a profoundly lasting effect, that all these years later she was still holding onto the feeling of shame. How could one teacher have knocked her confidence so badly? The memories of those classes came flooding back. That same art teacher had told them that the Impressionists, whom she loved, were too 'chocolate box.' Surely, she had that the wrong way around? Was it Renoir's fault that his paintings were being used by Cadbury's?

This had been her art teacher. So much for creative expression. She felt outraged. The adult Deirdre was going to have none of this. At the very least, she would show Isabelle her collage this morning and try not to anticipate her reaction.

"We're off now, Mum," Sam said, poking her neck around the door.

"Have a lovely time," Deirdre replied. "Bye, Betsy. See you later," she shouted.

The door slammed, and Deirdre went back into the kitchen, grateful to have it all to herself to prepare for the video call. Isabelle dialed in exactly on time. Deirdre was immediately struck by the contrast in their clothes. Here she was, with the central heating on full blast and a cardigan over her sweater and Isabelle in a bright pink sleeveless top.

"I'm so envious of your weather." She told her.

"It's one of the reasons I moved here. I couldn't face another winter in England."

"This is the first year I've really felt that too, in Ireland," she said, thinking back to how the dark nights had felt endless. It was one of the hardest parts of being alone. She had ached for the companionship of a game of Scrabble with Niall or to curl up with him and watch a movie in front of the fire.

"Did you get on well this week?" Isabelle asked. "Any work to show me?"

"I did," Deirdre said, more calmly than she felt.

She held the scarf up to the screen.

"Can you see the pattern?"

"Not exactly. Could you bring it a little closer? "Okay yes. That's better. It looks like one of your last collages, part of the heron. Is that right?"

"It does, doesn't it... but it's not."

She held up the print of the collage.

"This is my heron collage."

"I'm sorry, this is so frustrating on Zoom. They both look the same to me."

"It's not the Zoom." Deirdre said with delight. "They ARE the same."

"Okay. Good. So, what do you want to show me? It's exasperating isn't it, not being in the same room."

"But you can see that they look the same?"

"Yes. Absolutely."

"Okay. Well, one of these, this one, is my collage and this one...is a silk scarf."

"So did you transpose the image onto the silk?"

"Isabelle," Deirdre roared with laughter, "I'm quite a fast learner, but no, in the last week I have not learned how to silk screen or whatever the process might be. I wouldn't have the foggiest idea where to start."

"I have to say I was a little surprised," Isabelle smiled, "but nothing truly amazes me. When we're being creative, we make magic, and the universe conspires with us to create miracles. We are supported in so many ways when we go deeper into the creative process."

She lowered her voice to a deep bass. "Be warned Deirdre, this is a rabbit hole."

"I can sense that already." Deirdre laughed. "As long as I don't meet the Mad Hatter...although, saying that, I'm on a roll...maybe I could make him a scarf to match his hat. I think I might be cracking up."

Isabelle giggled. "It's marvelous to see you so animated," she said. "I'm happy this work is inspiring you."

"It's incredible. I had no idea I could enjoy anything so much."

"That's wonderful to hear, Deirdre."

"I need to learn how to do it. How do I transfer a painting onto silk? I've no idea where to start. Would you be able to help me?"

Isabelle nodded.

"Absolutely. Yes. It's not my specialism, but I'm sure I can point you in the right direction for a course. Let me give it some thought."

"Thank you."

"So, when are you thinking of coming here?"

"I'm moving into an apartment next week. It'll not take long to get set up, it's part furnished. I could make a plan to come quite soon."

"Let me look at the schedule. I think there'll be space towards the end of next month. How does that sound? The days will be getting longer, and we should be over the rainy season by then." She laughed. "We do have a rainy season."

Registering that she was rushing ahead of herself, Deirdre was relieved Isabelle was pushing back the time frame a little. Realistically, she would need several weeks to organize everything at the apartment and to prepare for the trip properly.

"I'll confirm some dates and send you details for accommodation," Isabelle said. "You'll need to hire a car, but there's nothing that can't be sorted out."

"Perfect. Thank you,," Deirdre said.

"Have you been working on anything else?"

"I have. I've been taking shots of archways and portals, like you suggested. I loved the 're-framing' metaphor you used last time."

She searched through the mound of photographs on the desk and found the new ones she wanted to show her. "These are through an archway of tall trees, and these here are a few I took a while ago through the windows of a derelict cottage."

"How beautiful. We have so many ruins of houses here, too. I love how windows frame the picture, don't you?"

"I'm looking at a lot of things in a different way now. I used the Snapseed App to get this double-exposure effect."

She lifted another photograph.

"Abstracting is so much fun isn't it. Email them across when you get a minute and I'll tell you what comes to mind when I look at them properly. Have you named them?"

"No."

"You might like to give them a title...just a suggestion."

The hour was over too soon. Deirdre wandered into the garden and looked around her flower beds for a while, pulling out a few clumps of weed and running her hands through the rosemary to smell the intense perfume. Sighing at the prospect of dealing with the mounting paperwork on her desk, she went back inside. The creative projects were an escape, but the outside world kept intruding with its bombardment of officialdom that Niall had handled for all their married life.

SAM

Betsy was attracting looks on the bus. She and Sam exchanged glances and giggled. Startlingly incongruous in her diamanté earrings and Doc Marten boots, her lime-green hair was clashing wildly against the shocking pink of her furry coat.

They hopped off at the canal.

"Mum's flat is just up there," Sam said, pointing to a modern apartment block.

"Cool. Bit different, hey?"

"Yes. It's only until she decides where to buy. The Academy's this way, "she said, leading her under the bridge and stopping as usual to give a few coins to the girl selling *The Big Issue*.

"Thanks," she said, handing her a worn copy.

"Keep it," Sam said. "You can sell it again."

A couple of kids yelled obscenities as they passed the chip shop.

"Not the friendliest end of town, I grant you, but wait 'til you see the studio," Sam said, shouldering the heavy door to the Academy.

"Hi Teresa."

"Morning, Sam."

"Here Bets," she said, going through swing doors into the recreation area.

"The class will be over in an hour, and then I'll show you around. There's a coffee machine over there."

"Okay. Great. I've plenty to keep me busy," Betsy said, pulling out her phone.

Sam changed and joined the class. Madame had been onto something. Dancing was giving her a feeling of connection with herself that she had forgotten. She could express her intense emotions stretching her legs at the barre until they trembled with the effort, and work through her anger in the repetitive floor work. Sometimes she would stay behind and practice her pirouettes until the spinning and spotting sparked pure joy. She worked on them until her toes were on fire and she had nothing left to give.

After the class, she found Betsy at a table drinking coffee and darning ballet shoes with Bronagh.

"Thought I'd make myself useful," she said, looking up as Sam approached. "Bronagh here was telling me all about Dublin. It sounds awesome."

"Ah. Great," Sam said. "Hi Bronagh. Can I steal her away?"

"Of course." Bronagh smiled up at her. "Thanks Betsy. Hope to see you again."

"She seems really nice," Betsy said, going down the corridor. "You Irish are all so friendly."

"I don't know her all that well, but she does seem lovely. She's a good teacher. This way," Sam said, taking her down a wide ramp and pressing a button. The doors opened into a large hall.

"Let's go up the far end. I'll pull a few chairs over. This used to be the main space before they built the extension."

A few minutes later, the door flew open and a woman with short blonde hair set off with scarlet lipstick whizzed across the room and spun her wheelchair around to face them.

"Hi Sam." She smiled.

"Hi Eileen. This is my friend Betsy. She's over from London."

"Hello Betsy. Glad to have you with us."

"Eileen and I were at primary school together." She told her.

"And then she got the eleven plus and went to "Our Lady's.""

"Our Ladies?"

"The grammar school," Sam explained. "Eileen went to 'The Brit School' in London. I wish I'd gone."

"How come?"

"It's a Performing Arts School," Sam explained. "I hated 'Our Lady's'."

"Sorry. I'd better get started, running late as ever," Eileen said, turning to the group that had assembled while they'd been chatting.

"Good morning, everyone. Let's make a nice straight line, shall we? Peter, are you with us today?"

"Sorry Eileen." A teen blushed, steering his wheelchair from the far end of the room to the end of the line.

"We'll start with the Adagio in C minor, Mary. Thank you," Eileen said, nodding to a girl who scrolling through a computer on her lap. "Let's warm up. You know the movements everyone, drop your arms, stretch up and hold and to the side and hold. Remember to breath, now head to the left and forward and drop your neck..."

"Okay shake it out for a minute," she told them after running through the series of exercises. "Fall into pairs. We're going to pick up where we left off last week, *Waltz of the Flowers* please, Mary."

Sam saw Betsy's delight as the music flooded the room and the group split into couples moving in harmonized rhythm. One two three, one two three, forward and back, circling their chairs around each other, arms poised, extended and then linked together. Eileen passed by each student straightening an elbow or tilting a head and emphasizing the beat with swings of her arm.

"Not bad," She told them as the music faded, "but you need to work a little harder on that forward push. Let's take it from the top again, and this time try to keep the space between each other consistent each time you move away. Try it tighter."

"Mary, again please. Take your places everyone I'll count you in."

As the music began again, Eileen pulled up alongside a girl who was struggling to get into position."

"Do your best, Moira," she told her, "I'll get Matt to have a look at that wheel for you."

The group went through their routines a second time.

"Much better, everyone. We're going in for the Tango next week...you've been warned," she said in mock menacing tones. "But today we have company, so we're going to boogie. Mary, could we have *You Wanna Bamba*, please."

A distinctive Nigerian beat filled the room, and the six dancers staccato-clapped, then formed a diagonal line. They turned in one coordinated movement before separating out, shunting forward and back in time with the rhythm. At a signal from Eileen, they formed a circle. A woman spun across to Betsy and took her hand. She stood up and began grooving with her, shaking her hips and hanging her arms above her head. Eileen nodded to Sam to join her. She shimmied over, arched her back, bent her knees and limboed lower and lower until their shoulders were parallel, and their arms were moving to the same beat.

"Bloody hell, Sam. Where did you learn to do that?" Betsy squealed as her friend's hands touched the ground behind her and she "crab walked" a few yards before lowering herself onto the floor as the music stopped.

Sam sat up and grinned at her. "One of my many hidden talents." She laughed.

"Thank you so much for letting me watch," Sam said to Eileen after the class had been dismissed. "That was so much fun."

"I'm pleased you were able to join us," she said. Then, turning to Sam, "When're you going back to London?"

"Not sure, exactly. Mum's moving in at the weekend, so we're helping her settle in."

"Great. See you soon then," she said spinning around to leave. "Have a good one."

"That was incredible," Betsy said. "I must have been living under a rock, but I never saw anything like it before. Those dances were so beautiful. It looked like proper ballet."

"It is proper ballet. You learn absolutely everything you would in a regular dance class, but then, depending on your muscle strength, you adapt the movement to your own body. The wheelchair becomes your legs."

"I'm totally blown away."

"I knew you would be. They bus down from all over for the classes. She was telling me she has a waiting list. They're raising money for a show in the autumn and fundraising like crazy. I thought you might like to run your marathon for them."

"I've been set up. You kill me."

"Yep." Sam grinned.

"It may take a while, but I will find a way to get you back." Betsy laughed. "You know I can't say 'no.' I wondered why you were so keen to get me here. I thought you were going to say you're getting a job teaching or something."

"Teaching? No. I'd never have the patience."

"Eileen's a great teacher, isn't she?"

"She is. She was a professional dancer with English National Ballet, so she really knows her stuff."

"What happened?"

"A car accident about seven years ago." Sam said. "She was quadriplegic for a long time, but I think her dance training helped a lot with the physio."

"How awful. She's incredible. I'll run several marathons for her. The thought of that makes me so grateful I can walk, let alone run."

"Well start with one," Sam laughed. "Okay. Let's grab some lunch and have a wander around the shops. Remind me I need to call into the bookshop on our way back."

DIERDRE

The doors clanked shut on the container truck.

Deirdre watched from the garden as it chuffed loudly in the driveway, then slowly maneuvered through the gates and picked up speed down the lane. She waited until it was a dot in the distance before turning and going back into the empty house. She stood a while at the kitchen window staring out at the mountain. Then, filling a water jug, she snipped the stems of the yellow roses on the draining board and placed the arrangement on the ledge. She propped up the welcome card next to it and glanced at her watch.

'I don't want to be here when they arrive,' she thought, running upstairs to make one last check to be sure that all the windows were closed, and the radiators turned off. She lingered at the view from the bedroom window one last time. A heavy mist was hanging over the pine trees. She glanced around. The room had lost its charm. The unfiltered light coming through bare windows was accentuating the cracks in the plasterwork and the paintwork looked tired. She had another long look and closed the door. Her footsteps echoed as she crossed the landing.

'It's only bricks and mortar,' she thought, 'And yet all that love and laughter must have surely sunk into the walls.' She stopped and said a little prayer that the house would wrap itself around this new family in the same way it had around hers.

Lifting her bags from the hall, she carried them across to the car, then she dashed back and turned the key in the lock. The wind was picking up, and the sky had turned ominously grey. It matched her mood. It would be harder to leave if the sun were shining.

She glanced back at the house before driving off. A few yards down the road, blinded by tears, she pulled over and switched off the engine. Grabbing the steering wheel with both hands, she lowered her head onto it and closed her eyes.

"You can do this," she said, grasping it more tightly. "You can get through this. You can. You have to. You have no choice."

She fired the ignition again and drove on, hooting the horn as she pulled up in front of Caroline's cottage. Struggling against the gale, Caroline came out and helped her in with the cases.

"I thought you were only staying the one night." She laughed. "Come on in, the kettle just boiled. You look wrecked. Are you okay? You should have let me help this morning."

"It was a wrench leaving alright," Deirdre said. "But I needed to be on my own to say 'goodbye' to it. Somhairlin walked the length and breadth of it the other day saying hers. She told me she feels okay about it now, that it's a new start for the both of us."

"It is. It really is, and you're here now, so let's have a cup of tea and I've a couple of iced buns. We can go for a walk later if that wind dies down, and if it doesn't,

I'll get the cards out and we'll have a game of Whist. When are you moving in?"

"Sunday or Monday. Somhairlin's going to call when they have the beds made up. The girls are going to stock up the fridge and unpack some of the boxes for me."

"Well, you know you can stay here as long as you like. Isn't it great they're doing that while we get to put our feet up. Talking of that...here Dee, have a pair of slippers."

She threw a couple of sheepskin mules in Deirdre's direction.

"Thanks," Deirdre said, sliding into them.

The rain had set in for the day. After a short walk with the dog as far as the village, they settled down for the evening. Caroline lit the fire and put a cottage pie into the oven.

"That'll be ready in half an hour." She said joining Deirdre on the couch in the sitting room. Deirdre looked up.

"This is so cozy. I'm going to miss having a fire in the flat."

"No bother. You can share this fire with me any time."

"Thank you, and you're welcome to drinks on my verandah anytime too."

"Best of both worlds." Caroline smiled. "How are you feeling about it all, Dee?"

Deirdre shifted in the armchair and curled her feet underneath her.

"I was just thinking about that," she said. "I was happy the family who've bought it are from these parts."

"Joan, at Mam's day care center, is related to an aunt of his from Drogheda. I heard the mother's one of the O' Malleys, the ones with the cafe in Dundalk. Nice family by all accounts."

"I met her just the once. She did seem nice. He's a solicitor. In Belfast, I think."

"I'll pop round with a few cakes and say 'Hello' once they've had a chance to settle in."

"Ah! That'd be lovely. Good idea. You can be my spy, tell me if they've paved my vegetable garden or built on one of those plastic conservatory things."

Caroline laughed.

"I think you'd be better off not knowing. So how're you feeling about the flat?"

"Not sure. It seemed a bit too modern for me the second time I went back. It was raining, and I wondered if I've done the right thing."

"Sure, if you change your mind, you're only renting."

"Yes. That's what I tell myself. I'm trying my best to think of it as an adventure, although I'm so tired."

"Moving house is a killer at the best of times."

"How long have you been here now? Remind me."

"Coming on fourteen years," Caroline said, shunting newspapers off the coffee table, and putting her legs across it. "Where does the time go?"

"You have it so comfortable, Caroline. It's so cozy. It feels safe. I was thinking this morning how houses all have a 'feel' to them, don't they? Mine felt safe too. I was thinking about how we need to nest, to have our own little corner of the world."

Deirdre had a faraway look.

"You'll have it again, Dee."

"I hope so. I was so glad when you came back. I missed you."

"Ah! London's grand, but I needed to come home. You can take the girl out of the country..."

"But you can't take the country out of the girl..." Deirdre agreed.

Caroline rarely talked about her time in London. From the odd remark here and there, Deirdre sensed it was a closed chapter.

"You know Caroline, I have to say something to say."

"Go on."

"I have to confess that until Niall died, I never appreciated how hard it is to live on your own. It never really sunk in with me that you come home every night to an empty house."

"Ssh!" Caroline laughed, putting her finger over her lips, gesturing to the dog stretched out by the hearth and the cat curled up next to him.

"Ha! Yes. Of course. My apologies, Sandy, and you too, Tipsy." She laughed.

"Seriously though Dee. I'm well used to it, and I have Mammy. I don't want to think what'll happen once she goes. Mind you, I think she'll grumble on for a good while yet."

"I suppose I'll get used to it too, then." Deirdre said, forcing a smile.

"One day at a time, remember?"

"You're right. It's the only way. I know that."

"Okay," Caroline said. "Dinner's on the timer. I'll set the table. You stay put, you'll be busy enough tomorrow. Would you like a glass of Chablis?"

"Just the one." Deirdre said, making to stand up.

"Stay there. Relax."

Deirdre picked up one of the books on the side table and stared at the image of the Eiffel Tower on the cover. She flicked through the first few pages.

'Paris...' She thought. 'Will I ever go back?'

She rested it down and watched the flames flicker.

"Here you go."

Caroline handed her a glass.

"I'll come in and help you," Deirdre said, sensing that if she sat on her own, even for a few minutes longer, she might fall apart. She followed her into the kitchen.

"Somhairlin's really taken to the dancing again."

"She was so talented. I remember her in *Sleeping Beauty*."

"Yes. Niall and I were so proud that night. I told her if she wants to train to be a dance teacher, I'll support her, but she said she doesn't want to teach."

"Ah! Well, she's young. She'll find her way," Caroline said, lifting a plate and handing it across the table. "Mind. It's hot. Help yourself."

She sat down opposite and shook out a napkin.

"From what she told me, that job was a nightmare."

"It was."

"Will she stay home for a while?"

"No. She's heading back to London."

"Do you want sauce with that?"

"No thanks."

Caroline caught her eye. "Are you okay about it? I know you were half hoping she'd stay a while longer."

"I just want her to be happy."

Deirdre was aware of a sudden hollow feeling in the pit of her stomach. She reached across for the wine bottle.

"They're staying on for a week. I'll be fine to be on my own by the time they leave."

"Well, I'll stay over with you whenever you want."

"Thank you. I may keep you to that." Deirdre put down her fork. "That was lovely Caroline. Sorry I can't do it more justice; my stomach's in a knot."

"No bother. At all. Would you like a slice of apple pie?

"Not right now, later please," she said, lifting their plates.

"Just leave them on the side. I'll get to them later."

Caroline stood up and stretched out her back. "Let's have that game of cards or we could watch something on Netflix, what do you fancy."

"Do you still have a Scrabble set?"

"I do indeed. Are you sure you're up for the challenge?" she asked, a glint in her eye.

A few hours later, Deirdre was snuggled in the tiny bed in Caroline's spare room. She pulled the patchwork quilt up around her shoulders, closed her eyes, and listened to the trees creaking against the wind and the rain lashing at the window. She heard Caroline moving around beneath her, the clink of dishes, the shunt of the latches on the door, her footsteps on the stairs and the rumble of the dog as he scurried up behind her. After the bedroom door closed, she heard Caroline talking to him. A chain was pulled and the sound of running water gurgled in the pipes for some time before the house fell deeply silent.

'Maybe I should get a dog,' she thought. 'But then I'd be tied.'

With that thought came another. She wasn't tied. She was free to do whatever she wanted. She thought about the painting and the photography, how she'd had the freedom to do those things for as many hours of the day and night she wanted. She thought about the opportunity to do a course in Ibiza or wherever she chose and the many things that could be possible. With each thought, the tears welled up and trickled down the side of her face. She wiped them away and stared at the shadows bouncing across the ceiling.

'Freedom,' she thought. 'I'm free to travel the world, I'm free to fantasize about making scarves. I'm free, but I don't want to be free. I'm scared. I have no home. I'm already homesick. I want to be back in my own bed. I was safe there. I've done the wrong thing and I can't undo it.'

She turned onto her side and flipped onto her back again, then sat up and checked the time. It was just after midnight. Switching on the bedside light, she lifted a book from the nightstand. The poetry anthology fell open at a page; *For Grief* by John O'Donohue. A couple of lines leapt from the page. '*Suddenly with no warning. You are ambushed by grief.*' She read on; '*And when the work of grief is done, the wound of loss will heal.*'

"When the work of grief is done," she murmured. "When the work of grief is done."

'I am nowhere near the end of this,' she thought. 'I need to slow down. I'm trying to rush. The world may think I'm all sorted out after a year, but I can't get over forty-four of them that quickly. I need to give myself more time. It's still baby steps. I'll get there. I have no choice."

She laid down the book, turned off the light and closed her eyes.

SAM

Betsy had dragged Sam into yet another vintage shop on their way home from The Academy. She'd been scouring the rails for the past half hour, getting more animated by the minute. Sam was starting to fade.

"Do these suit me?" Betsy asked her, positioning a pair of steel-framed glasses on her nose.

"In a weird kind of way they do, but I'd ditch the footwear."

Betsy yanked off the white pleather boots.

"They're too big for me anyhow," she said, lifting a yellow dress with black polka dots. "Ah! Now this is rather cute don't you think? Life was so much more fun in the fifties, wasn't it? I mean who invented skinny jeans? I'm absolutely serious Sam. Somebody's responsible for it."

"I think it was Kate Moss."

"Really? I'll never be able to think of her the same way again." She laughed. "I'm going to try all of these on."

"Okay. I'll meet you back here in fifteen minutes, I'm just going over the road to Gallagher's bookshop."

Betsy disappeared into a cubicle, her arm full of clothes. "No rush. I could spend the rest of the day here," she shouted.

Sam crossed over to the other side of the street and nipped down a side lane to the indie bookshop. The doorbell clinked as she opened it, and her old school friend looked up from behind the counter.

"Hi Sam. How's it going? Coffee?"

"I'd love one, Maureen."

"I'll put the kettle on."

Sam worked her way along the lower shelves and pulled out a copy of *The Wilde Anthology*. She flicked through the pages, checking that it included extracts from plays as well as poems and letters. She closed it over and took it to the counter.

"Ah! No better man than Oscar!" Maureen said, taking Sam's card and popping the book into a cloth bag.

"Housewarming present for Mum. She's moving into a flat just across from here. I'm sure you'll see plenty of her."

"Hope so. Here. I'll close up for fifteen minutes and join you. I've not stopped all day."

"Great. I've a friend over from London; she's down the road. Shall I text her? I'd like you two to meet."

"Dead on," Maureen said, flicking over the "Open" sign. "Tell her to push the door. I'll make the coffee. Back in a sec."

She disappeared behind a curtain. Sam surveyed the noticeboard crammed with cards and flyers, picked up a few, then sank into one of the battered leather armchairs.

"Here you go," Maureen said, handing her a mug. It's black. 'Sorry, the milk's off."

"No problem. Thanks. How's business?" Sam asked her. "You seemed pretty busy last week."

"Yes. Sorry I didn't get time to talk. Everyone's been so supportive, ordering through the shop a lot instead of using Amazon and the writers' evenings have taken off. You should come next Tuesday. We've a brilliant poet, Mel McMahon doing a reading."

"I'd definitely be up for that. What time? I'm sure Mum would love to come too."

"I'll save you a few seats. Get here around seven."

"Ah! This must be your friend," Maureen said as the door sprung open. "Cool dress," she greeted Betsy.

"Thanks. Four pounds. Just bought it over the road. Love it so much I didn't change out of it. I'm Betsy."

"Maureen. Nice to meet you. Sit down. Put your bags here. Looks like you got quite the trawl. That mug's for you, hope it's okay black."

"Fine for me, thanks. This place is awesome," she said, dropping her bags and gazing around at the antique mirrors, the oak dressers, and the books stacked in every possible nook and cranny as high as the ceiling alcoves.

"It's yours now, isn't it, Maureen?" Sam said proudly.

"It is! I've worked here ever since I left school Betsy."

"It was always her dream to have a bookstore of her own." Sam interjected.

"It was indeed. I rent the building, but the business is mine now."

"Maureen's always been a bookworm, haven't you? She won the literature prize at school for three years running."

"True, but you were brilliant at gymnastics."

"Fat lot of good that did me." Sam laughed.

"She was incredible today," Betsy said. "You should have seen her."

"We were at the Academy," Sam explained. "I treated Bets to my limbo shuffle."

"You can still do that?"

Sam grinned. "I'm not that old, Maureen."

"Fair play. Listen girls, I could chat all day but there's Mrs. Rafferty hovering outside the window. Are you around over the weekend? Up for a jar or two?"

"For sure. Tomorrow might work. I'll let you know."

The girls sauntered over to Deirdre's apartment, Betsy checking her phone and Sam thinking about how Maureen had known what she wanted to do since she'd been any age. She'd never left the town, rarely been out of the country. Books were her life, and she'd built a community around doing what she loved. Sam was happy for her, but it was hard not to feel a tad envious. Why hadn't she discovered what she wanted to do? You couldn't make a career out of the things she was good at. There were no signs on the notice board saying "Wanted: Thirty-four-year-old limbo dancer who can also do the splits."

Reaching the apartment, Betsy's phone rang.

"Have to take this." She mouthed, disappearing into the bedroom.

Sam took off her coat and went into the kitchen. Balancing on a crate, she flicked through the book she had bought her mother. A quotation leapt out; *To live is the rarest thing in the world. Most people exist, that is all.* It resonated. She didn't want to simply "exist." She could feel the stirrings of an energy she'd not had in ages, but where was she to direct it? She glanced through the flyers, tossing them with the tote onto the countertop and began unwrapping dishes from the packing cases. She scrunched up Kraft paper and aimed the balls at a box. Slicing open another carton she unwrapped a tannin-stained mug. She turned it around in her hands. "World's Best Dad" was emblazoned on the side.

'I so remember buying this...' she thought. I can't have been more than ten. I used all my pocket money on it. To think he kept it all this time.'

As the memory crashed in, her throat tightened. Fighting back tears, she put the mug on the sink and dashed for the door. Racing down the stairs and turning onto the towpath, she ran until she couldn't run any further. She stopped abruptly at a grass verge and leaned her arm against a tree to catch her breath, then seeing that the tide was out, she climbed down the watermen's stairs to the beach of sludge and water weeds.

She stepped along the riverbed, across the stones and pebbles, and sat down on a rock watching seagulls circling the bridge. Her brain felt as if it were on fire. Should she be going back to London? What was she going back to? Did she need to go back? Where did she belong? What was she going to do?

Her mother was moving on, and yet she was stuck. Something was very wrong with this picture. A tingle of fear ran through her,There was nobody, absolutely nobody coming to rescue her. With her father gone, her mother would need her differently now. She was an adult and yet she had been thinking like a child. It was time to grow up. All her friends here were taking charge of their lives. They weren't drifting. Eileen, against all those odds, was running dance classes. Bridget, at her age, was still working on expanding the reach of the Academy. Maureen's bookshop was an important fixture in the town. They were all committed to doing something that mattered. Their lives had meaning. Whatever she did next, whatever that turned out to be, she determined it would be something where she would give a hundred percent. It would be a lifestyle, a commitment, not just another dead-end job.

As the sun dropped behind the mountain and the wind changed direction, she stood up with a shiver. Wending her way back along the towpath, she felt calmer, and as she walked on towards the apartment, she had the strangest sensation that she wasn't walking alone.

DIERDRE

Caroline was loading up her hatchback with bric-a-brac when Deirdre came downstairs. She waved to her through the window as she was making a pot of tea. Caroline slammed down the lid of the trunk and came inside.

"Ah! Good morning. How'd you sleep? I was going to leave you to lie on."

"I got a good few hours, thank you. That bed's as comfortable as ever. What time are we leaving?"

Caroline glanced at the clock and took a mouthful of tea. "In about ten minutes. Are you still coming with me?"

"Of course," Deirdre said, buttering a bagel. "I forgot we were doing the market this morning, but I'm all set."

"Okay. Great. There's a spare pair of wellies and a jacket in the hall. Grab a scarf, it can get cold out on that field."

Caroline stuffed a couple more boxes onto the back seat. She drove them the few miles to the disused airfield and parked in her usual spot. Unfolding tables, they began setting out the jumble that Deirdre had given Caroline to sell when she'd been clearing out the house.

'Who on earth would want this?' she thought, jiggling one of her old coats onto a wire hanger.

A couple of punters were already circling, hoping for an early bargain.

Caroline finished arranging a collection of vintage dresses onto a rail and propped up a display case piled with costume jewelry. Leaving Deirdre to arrange the glassware, she wandered off to look around the other cars. She was back soon carrying a couple of large paintings.

"Here. Help me get these into the back of the car," she said.

"Really?"

Deirdre looked at the badly-drawn flowers and the gaudy backdrop. "Are you planning on bringing these home?"

"Two quid each and they're gorgeous."

Deirdre was stumped for words. Maybe she was missing something, but she was having a hard time believing they were worth anything at all."

"It's the frames, Dee. Just look at these frames. Can you not just see your collages in them?"

Deirdre looked at the mitred redwood frames. They were beautiful.

"You have such a good eye. I would never have spotted those in a million years," she said. "What a great idea. Thank you. Yes, I really can. Thank you."

As the morning went on, Deirdre was amazed by how much of her old "junk" sold and the amount of cash Caroline was accumulating to donate to the children's hospital.

"I can't believe someone actually bought that cheese grater and my old tea towels," she said. "And they didn't look like they wanted for anything, they were well dressed."

"It's the idea of getting something for nearly nothing," Caroline said. "You'd be amazed. That guy over there had an old toilet seat and it looks like it's gone."

"Shudder the thought." Deirdre laughed, savoring how much she was enjoying herself. It felt so good to be doing something completely different. After a few hours, they packed up the car and went to the food truck, where they sat at a plastic table with their mugs of tea and crispy bacon sandwiches.

"You know Dee, I love nothing more than a morning like this. I sometimes wonder if I shouldn't have opened a second-hand shop, you know, 'We buy junk and sell antiques' kind of a thing. I don't know what stopped me."

"I can see you with that." Deirdre said, "It'd be a little gold mine."

"I'm not sure about that, but it'd have turned over a bob or two and I do love a good barter."

"You're great at it too. You got a good price for that coal shuttle there today."

"I did indeed."

"I don't know why I've not been here with you before. It's worth coming just for these chips." Deirdre said, dipping one into brown sauce. "I've always had a fantasy of having a little café, you know just tea and scones, like Delaney's, only more of a place where you maybe have a bit of art on display and some jewelry for sale."

"If only we had our time over again, what would we do?" Caroline sighed. "But I'm glad I came back home. We haven't had such a bad old time of it, have we Dee?"

"I wouldn't change a thing for all the world. I was telling Sally, if I had my time over, I'd do it all again. Talking of Sally, she's going to be in Ibiza with her husband while I'm there. I hope we get to meet up. I've grown so fond of her. We only have one more session."

"She's lovely. I'm sure you'll be friends; it's not like she's your therapist. She's coaching you. It's different."

"I'm so grateful to her, Dee. She's helped me so much, and I can't thank you enough for the introduction."

"Happy I was able to help. I'm so impressed with all your art and your photographs. I'll come over to the flat when you've settled in, and we can decide which of your pictures to put in those frames."

"I'll give you one for your kitchen."

"I'll take you up on that." Caroline said. "And you have to sign it. It could be worth a fortune one day."

"Well," Deirdre laughed. "I wouldn't hold your breath."

SAM

Sam pushed away her plate. "Delaney's should have an award for the best breakfast in Ireland," she said.

"True," Betsy agreed, finishing off the last of her soda bread.

"Our work is done! "Sam announced. "The beds are made, the kitchen's set up and the freezer's stocked. We're off duty, Bets."

"So what's the plan?"

"Oh! I forgot to tell you. We're meeting Eileen this afternoon. She's looking at a space to rent and wants me to see it with her."

"Sounds good. What time? I want to get my nails done. Is there somewhere near?"

"There's a place down the road. I'd be up for that too. The appointment's not until two."

"Okay, great. Let's boogie on down."

"Okay." Sam laughed.

Later that afternoon, fresh from the salon and a tour of yet more charity shops, they walked over to the warehouse district. The agent was waiting with Eileen when they arrived.

"Hello. I'm Orla," she said with a smile. "This way." She opened the doors and waited for Eileen to drive up the ramp.

"I'm Sam and this is Betsy," Sam said, stepping behind her.

"This way," she said, leading them down a corridor. "The building was originally a linen mill, as you know. The renovations were finished only two years ago, so everything is state-of-the-art: new electrics, lighting and furnishings.",

She pushed open the door to the studio and held it open for them.

"It's so spacious," Eileen said, wheeling to the far end of the room. "I'm loving the floor-length windows."

"Yes, the ceiling height's incredible, isn't it. Let me show you the communal kitchen and break out area, they're just along here. You said you were interested to see the white box spaces too. We can take the lift to the first floor. The two we have available overlook the canal. You can also book meeting rooms. I'll show you those as well."

"So, what do you think?" Eileen asked when they were back out on the street and Orla had left them.

"I think it's perfect." Sam told her. "There's such a great atmosphere, everyone was really friendly."

"Great vibe." Betsy said. "I'd work here any day of the week."

"I'm going to take it." Eileen said. "I've been waiting for ages for something to come up in this building Oh! Sam, I've a friend in London, a dancer, who'd looking for a PA. She asked me if I knew anyone. Shall I send you the ad? Are you still looking for a job? She's based in London."

"I am. Yes, definitely, let me have a look."

"Okay. Will do. Have to dash, I've a class in half an hour. Thanks for looking around with me. Catch you later."

"She's awesome," Betsy said, watching Eileen turn the corner. "I don't think I'd be so positive if that happened to me."

"Me neither," Sam said, glancing at her phone. "Mum's texted to say she'll stay another night at Caroline's. What do you fancy doing?"

"We still haven't checked out Malone's."

"Okay. Malone's it is. I'll let Maureen know. We need to pick up some bread on the way back."

"Okay, and I'd like to buy your mum some flowers."

Eileen's email came through a while later while Betsy was in the shower. Sam opened the link and went out onto the verandah to look at it.

"A unique opportunity for a highly capable Personal Assistant with the ability to support our client, a principal dancer, in all aspects of their business."

'A principal dancer?' Sam perked up. 'Principal. What company, I wonder?'

"The position requires a self-motivated, hands- on individual who is able to work one-on-one as well as independently and who enjoys looking after everything from the small everyday tasks to more exciting and creative projects."

'That's definitely me.'

She read on. "There will be plenty of opportunity to accompany the principal to rehearsals, auditions, meetings, and events. The office is in a domestic setting with the principal's family, cat and, dog in Bloomsbury, London."

'I like the idea of working in a home office.' she mused.

She scanned the list of responsibilities. They ranged from handling social media and press enquiries to internet research on upcoming projects and diary management. It gave no further details about the dancer, only that she was "a powerhouse in the Arts."

Who was it? What ballet company was she with? Sam had a thrill of excitement at the thought of supporting someone whose work she could respect and understand. She texted Eileen to say she was interested and to find out more. When she learned that the dancer was Colette Ingram, Sam knew beyond a shadow of doubt that she wanted the job.

DIERDRE

Deirdre gave the girls one last wave as they reached the entrance to the airport, and the doors slid closed behind them. She sat for a few moments with her eyes tightly closed. Then, with a deep sigh, pulled away from the curb, switched on the radio, and picked up speed. Approaching her building an hour or so later, she felt a flutter of nerves negotiating the car into her underground parking space.

Taking the lift to her floor, she hesitated before opening the door to the apartment, knowing there would be nobody there to greet her. She hung up her keys and glanced into the spare bedroom. The girls had left it tidy, the bedding folded, and Betsy's futon stowed away.

Walking into the living room, she caught her breath. Across the river, the rays from the setting sun were bouncing off a glass atrium, intensifying the rich golden light and creating mirrors on the water. As she stepped out onto the verandah, a formation of Canada geese honked overhead, then circled back and skimmed the river.

In the resident's garden below, an elderly couple were sitting on a bench holding hands. A wave of tenderness and a deep yearning washed over her. She remembered the words of the poem. *"Suddenly with no warning you are ambushed by grief."* She looked away. She would not be ambushed. Not right now. This magnificent sunset had welcomed her home. It was a gift, and she would hang onto the sense of wonder. She watched the sun sink behind the mountain, leaving the sky a blaze of orange and reds, and stayed until it had faded to a pale pink in the twilight. Then, shivering slightly, she went back inside.

She glanced around, missing the atmosphere the girls created; their cardigans thrown across chairs, shoes randomly scattered, cups and glasses abandoned on the coffee table. The floral patterns on her cushions looked incongruous against the clean lines of the sectional couch. The lack of a focal point, of a fireplace, seemed odd. There were so many changes she would make if this place were her own. 'This grey carpet would be the first thing to go,' she thought.

She reminded herself it was temporary, a first step on the road to creating a new life. What did it matter that the furnishings weren't hers? It would be good not to have constant reminders of the past. She would pack away the cushions.

Already familiar with the kitchen, she quickly rustled up a pasta and chatted with Somhairlin, who checked in to say that they had arrived safely in London. How lucky she was to have her daughter, and one day she might even have grandchildren. The thought was bittersweet. She made her way to bed early. Tomorrow was a new day, and today had not been nearly as hard as she had expected it to be.

She opened her eyes next morning to a shaft of sunlight and dancing shadows on the wall. What was today? Ah! Yes. She remembered; the girls had gone home. She lay there for a while listening to the already familiar morning sounds; footsteps shuffling across the ceiling, the whistle from a dog walker on the towpath, the thrum of traffic through the town.

'What different worlds we inhabit,' she thought, padding to the bathroom, then across to the kitchen. She watched the now familiar scene of joggers running by and the seagulls feeding in the ravine as she filled the kettle. The mountain she loved so much was still visible in the distance. Waiting for the kettle to boil, she felt more connected to the world than she had in some time. Others were also starting their day. 'Every one of those people has a story too,' she thought.

She took her coffee to the small armchair facing the river and gazed out at her changed vista, struck by the thought that her morning routine would follow a new pattern. It felt good not to be on automatic pilot, to be looking out with fresh eyes. She would find new walks, starting today with one into the center of the town. She showered and began dressing. Then, as she pulled on her jeans, she stopped and wriggled out of them, lifting a pair of black pants and a cream sweater. She topped off the look with a beige tailored coat and appraised herself in a long mirror.

"Not bad. Not bad at all. You're still in there somewhere," she told her reflection.

Pulling her hair back in a clip, she picked up her bag and went across to the lift. Walking briskly, it took her only fifteen minutes to reach the cathedral in the middle of the town where she crossed the road and called into Rafferty's bakery.

"Ah! Good morning, Mrs. Macardle. How are you? I see you brought the sunshine with you today."

"Good morning, Siobhan," she said eyeing the pastries in the glass display case. "Beautiful morning indeed."

"So, what can I tempt you with?"

Deirdre picked out a chocolate croissant and ordered an Americano. She took it to a seat in the bay window. 'To say that I feel like I'm on my holidays would be overstating it,' she thought, but there was no denying that she was having a frisson of pleasure from arriving on foot and having her breakfast out. She stayed a while after she'd finished eating, debating where to go next, and settled on the department store where a navy leather jacket caught her eye as she browsed the racks of women's clothing. Pulling it from the rail, she slipped off her coat and tried it on. It kicked just at her waist and had a subtle 'biker' feel to it.

An assistant was at her side.

"That really suits you," she said.

Deirdre turned around. The girl had a warm open face, and Deirdre had the impression she genuinely meant the compliment. She looked at the price tag.

"I'll take it," she said.

Feeling a bounce in her step as she swung the cardboard bag over her shoulder, she took the escalator to the beauty department and wandered around the cosmetics counters, where she was persuaded to hop on a stool and have a lesson in applying blusher. She bought a coral lipstick and the blusher knowing she would never wear it, but happy for the girl to have the commission. Leaving the store, she knew exactly where she was headed next.

"Are you busy, Teresa?" she asked, poking her head around the door of the hair salon.

"Ah! Good to see you, Deirdre. Give me a minute."

The stylist put down the hairdryer and addressed her client through the mirror. "What do you think?" she asked, unclipping her nylon robe.

"Grand, Teresa. Thank you," the woman said, standing up and running her hand through her hair.

Teresa turned to Deirdre.

"I am here on an impulse," she said, unclipping her hair so it fell onto her shoulders. "This has got to go."

"Experience tells me that might not be a good idea."

"Yes. But you also know I've been talking about getting a bob for years."

"Donkey's years."

"Today is that day if you have any free time."

"I just had a cancellation, but you might want to give it a bit more thought? Are you sure you're sure?"

"Show me to the chair! I've made up my mind," Deirdre said. "Today's the day and if I don't like it, well, sure it'll grow back."

An hour later, she caught her reflection in a shop window. She flicked her chin length bob and walked on with a whole new confidence to 'Rive Brasserie' where she ordered steak frites and a lime and soda. She would save up the glass of wine for the evening.

It was late afternoon when she stopped at the Cancer Research Shop to have a browse through the books. A title sprung up at her. *All Along You Were Blooming... Thoughts for Boundless Living.* She flicked through the artwork, read a passage, then took it to the counter.

"How much is this?" she asked the volunteer.

"Ah! That was donated new. I'm afraid it's nine pounds."

"I'll take it," she said, happy to have contributed a little to the cause.

She stood outside the shop, about to turn left to the carpark, when she reoriented herself towards the flat. 'Old habits die hard,' she thought, surprised that she was happy enough to be going in a different direction.

SAM

Sam stared out at through the rain-streaked window of the cab.

"Thank you," she told the driver as he pulled over. "Keep the change."

Leaping over a puddle and side-stepping the curb in her new suede boots, she dashed toward the door of the Italian restaurant. A waiter shepherded her inside. She scanned the room and spotted Jon at the bar. He caught her eye and pushed through the crush towards her.

"You look really well," he said." Great to see you."

"You too," she said, running her hand through her hair. "It's wild out there."

"Let's go straight to the table. You can't hear yourself think here."

He turned to a man in an open necked shirt and apron.

"Giovanni, *Siamo pronti grazie.*"

'He speaks Italian,' Sam thought. 'As if he weren't enough already.'

"Sam, meet Giovanni, owner of the finest restaurant outside of Sicily."

"*Buona Sera Bellissimo,*" Giovanni said, taking her hand. "*Bella, Bella.*"

He led them up a couple of steps to a booth at the back of the restaurant and returned with two glasses of Prosecco.

"*Gratuita,*" he said.

"*Molte Grazie, Giovanni.*"

"*Prego.*"

"Do you come here often?" Sam asked. '...Did I actually say that?' she thought.

"How did you guess?" Jon grinned. "I do. The food's great and I like the old-fashioned vibe.

"It feels authentic," she said. "Like it could be in Italy, apart from the weather."

"Ah! The weather. There is that. Cin Cin," he said, raising his glass.

"Sláinte," she said.

"So tell me why you left the bureau. Alexandra came back on crutches. That left quite a lot to the imagination. Were you wounded?"

Sam threw her head back and laughed.

"I've no physical scars."

"Okay good, although I can imagine the mental damage working for Alex might have wrought." He grinned.

"The short version? She slipped on marble tiles in the bathroom. I found her, got her to the hospital, picked her up the next day and then... you know it doesn't sound all that dramatic as I'm telling it, but it was horrible at the time. She was in vile humor, and I was tired, and anyway, I ended up getting her on a flight, and there were all kinds of complications around me getting back. I'd just had enough of the auld fecker. So I left."

"You sound so Irish when you swear."

"Well, there'd be a reason for that," she quipped, realizing that she sounded just like her mother.

Giovanni had returned and was propping up a blackboard. He interrupted them to announce the specials. Deciding on the seafood linguini, Sam agreed on a bottle of Chianti.

"Your turn now. Why did you leave the bureau?"

"It's been coming for a while. I need a company that can handle more than speaking gigs. I've signed with CAA. I'd like more TV work. The circuit gets to be a treadmill; it's exhausting."

She nodded. "I can see how doing all those events must have been tiring, even a couple of long-haul flights wiped me out for a week. You seemed to enjoy it, though. Your talk in Kauai was…" she hesitated.

"Brilliant?' He offered.

"I wouldn't go that far, but I did have a compliment brewing." She laughed. 'If only you knew,' she thought. "So, will you stay in London now?"

"Yes. I'm about to start work on a book. That's another reason I want to get off the road."

"What's it about?"

"I'm still working on my 'elevator pitch'."

"Your what?"

"Oh! Where you describe something in the amount of time it takes to tell a person in an elevator."

"I love that."

"It's an L.A. expression. People have short attention spans there. Did you get a chance to see any of it on that trip?"

Sam paused for a moment while their wine was poured.

"Not a lot. Santa Monica and the hospital was about it. It felt surreal. I'm not sure if it was because of all that was going on, but I felt like I wasn't quite there."

"It's not you. It's definitely surreal."

"How was Vegas? Did you give the same talk?"

"Never. No. That one was about mental health."

"You never give the same talk?"

"I'd be bored rigid.

He waited as their plates were served.

"This looks good," he said, flapping open a napkin. "So, tell me, what does Samantha do next?"

"Somhairlin, if we're being formal." She laughed. "Irish for Samantha."

"That's a great name. I won't even begin to ask how you spell it. So, what does Somhairlin do next?"

"I'm not sure. I've applied for a new job. It's as a PA to a principal ballet dancer, Colette Ingram. I want to be around creative people. My dad died last year, and..." The words tumbled out before she had a chance to catch herself. She lifted her wineglass. 'Why did I say that?' she thought. 'What just possessed me?' "Sorry. That came from nowhere, not exactly a cheerful conversation for dinner, is it?"

"I'm so sorry," he said leaning forward. "I kind of sensed you were feeling sad in Kauai."

"Really?"

"Yes, when we talked about how there isn't a man in a white robe in the sky."

"I remember. You're right. I was thinking about my dad, wondering where he's gone."

"I know how that feels," he said.

"You do?"

"I do."

They said nothing for a few moments. Sam waited to see if he would explain, tell her about the person that he'd lost, but he didn't. He reached across the table and put his hand on top of hers.

"I'm glad you told me," he said. "And by the way..."

"Yes?"

"Your dinner's going cold."

Sam glanced at her plate and laughed. She picked up her fork and twirled the pasta.

"I'm not being facetious by the way, I hear you," he said. "Grief isn't funny."

"It really isn't, is it? I've been so intense since he passed away. It's thrown me completely. It's like I'm starting my life over again. I feel different."

"Losing someone changes you for sure."

"It's made me question pretty much everything," she said. "I'm sorry. I'm not exactly being a laugh a minute."

"You don't need to apologize. This is the most real conversation I've had in ages."

"I've my second interview on Tuesday. The first one was on Zoom in Ireland. It wasn't really an interview, I suppose, just a general chat, although I was really nervous. She's a huge name in the dance world. I have her on such a pedestal."

"So, you already knew who she was, then?"

"Absolutely. She's a legend. I saw her in *The Nutcracker* when I was fifteen. I was a 'balletomaniac' - I danced for years, and I've been taking classes again recently. I'm panicking a bit in case she wants a reference from AISB."

"You can give my name if you like, if it will help you avoid Alexandra. I was your client. I saw you in action. You were great."

"Really? That would be wonderful. Thank you. I already gave her Irish Heritage and a character reference from my old dance teacher; it's just if she asks for it. Two should have been enough really, and a friend of ours recommended me, so she knows I'm not a stalker. I'm just overthinking everything."

Giovanni was back at their table with a dessert menu.

"May I recommend our tiramisu?" he said.

"You may," Jon told him with a grin.

Sam smiled. "Yes, please."

"If this job is what you want, I really hope you get it, "Jon said, turning back to her.

"Thank you. I do want it badly. Do you remember that Confucius quote you used at the end of your talk? That's how I want to feel about work."

Jon nodded.

"It's a bit overused, but I couldn't think of a better way of putting it. I'd been having a drop of existential angst and wondering what I was a doing with my own life. Giving talks was never the plan."

"So, how did it happen? How did you get into it?"

"I was in practice for a few years, and then started working 'in house' with companies as their consultant psychologist. I gave a talk at a conference, it went down well, and I got invited to do more, then AISB approached me, and I signed with them."

"So how did you get to be on *Clue Time*?"

"I didn't plan that either; gave a talk at the BBC., one of the producers was in touch afterwards. I got a ton of invitations to speak after it aired, and I've been pretty much on the road ever since."

"How long ago was that?"

"About three years ."

He looked up as their dessert was served.

"Thank you," he said. "I was doing it for all the wrong reasons. Money, mostly. I was asking myself a lot of questions, thought I'd make a few people think about what they were doing, too. I bet at least half that group didn't want to be in the jobs they were in. I mean, who says to themselves when they're at school 'When I grow up, I want to be head of Human Resources in a pharmaceutical company'?"

Sam laughed.

"Very few, I imagine. You certainly got the message across to me."

"Really? That's good to hear."

"Kauai had exactly that effect on me too. I'd be out walking, and then I'd have to go back into the hotel to all those executives, and I didn't want to be there. I wanted to be part of what was outside. All I wanted was to walk around and breathe in all the plumeria. It was like I belonged to something bigger than myself and it was drawing me in. Does that sound mad? I'm not doing a very good job of explaining. It's hard to put into words."

Jon's eyes were warm as he looked at her. "I know exactly what you mean. I think we were tuned into the same thing when we went for that walk, asking the big questions."

Sam was surprised and thrilled he remembered. He drained the last of his wine and put down the glass.

"I didn't invite you for dinner just to talk about AISB, you know."

"You didn't?" Sam teased, knowing exactly what he meant from the way he was looking at her.

"I didn't. I've been thinking a lot about that evening."

"I have too," she heard herself say.

He motioned for the bill.

"There's a great bar in Spitalfields. Can I buy you a drink before you head home?"

"Yes. I'd love that," she said, finishing the last of her wine.

DEIRDRE

Deirdre pushed her dining table against the wall and pulled her desk next to it to form an L shape facing the river. She stacked several boxes of photographs, propped up a few collages, and plugged in the printer. It whirred reassuringly. She stood back, pleased with her efforts.

'Now I can watch the world go by as I work.' she thought. 'As I work? That's how it feels, my work.'

Sitting down at the desk, she looked around at what she'd brought with her for this new life; the framed Rodin prints, the black-and-white etchings of dancers they had found in Italy, the seascapes of Donegal and a few books. Even there, she had chosen carefully and only brought her Yeats and Shaw anthologies. The Oscar Wilde from Somhairlin had been a welcome addition.

There were jugs for flowers, lavender candles, and her collection of crystal vases. It was all so feminine; there was no male paraphernalia set out next to her own. No dish to collect Niall's change when he emptied his pockets, no horn-rimmed reading glasses, no heavy set of keys on a black leather fob. Her phone rang as she was fighting off this dip in her mood. It was Caroline.

"Hello missus. How're you getting on?"

"I'm okay. Still unpacking," she said.

"I'm going into town soon. Will you be there? I can't stay long, though."

"Of course. Come over. You'll be my first guest."

"Okay. I'll see you 'round eleven. Do you need anything?"

"Don't think so. Just bring yourself. See you soon."

The doorbell rang a few minutes after she finished the call. Deirdre opened the door to a woman of about her own age. Her red coat and purple scarf were set off with a violet cloche hat pinned with a peacock feather. She was holding a bunch of yellow tulips.

"Good morning," she said. "I'm Cara, your neighbor from over the way, number seven."

Deirdre took the flowers from her.

"I'm Deirdre," she said. "Lovely to meet you, too. Thank you so much. These are lovely, and I just this minute unpacked a vase."

"If you need anything, that's where I am." Cara said pointing across the hall. "Just me and Chanel. Chanel's my cat," she added. "Will you come 'round for a glass of wine one evening?"

Deirdre beamed.

"Yes. That'd be really nice," she said.

"Great. I'll see you soon, then."

Arranging the tulips in a vase, Deirdre mused on how much that simple act of kindness had lifted her spirits. The prospect of getting to know her neighbor was exciting. It had been so long since she'd met anyone new. 'I wonder what she does with her time?' She thought. 'She was very colorful. That was a lovely coat.'

"It makes you look ten years younger," Caroline greeted her a little while later.

"Do you think so?"

Deirdre ran her hands through her hair.

"I do," she said. "It really suits you. Here, I've a card and some chocolates from Mary. O'Rourke. She says she'll call you to invite herself over."

"Ah! How lovely."

"And here's a little housewarming present from me," she said, handing her a brown parcel. "That view is stunning Dee and you've so much space. I'm half-ways jealous. It's all so uncluttered, makes me wonder if I shouldn't be getting rid of some of junk."

Deirdre wasn't listening. Clicking open the brass hinges on a deep wooden box she was admiring the rainbow of acrylic paints laid out by color. She slid out a tray lined with different sized brushes and another with pastels. So much love and thought had gone into picking out this present that she was quite lost for words. Her eyes were shining as she looked at Caroline.

"Aw come on now Dee. It's just some auld paints. Here give us a hug."

Deirdre put her arms around her friend.

"Thank you," she said. "Thank you so much. That's so kind. You couldn't have got me anything more perfect."

"Aw. I'm glad you like it. I know you'll put it to good use. Oh bugger. Look at the time. I can't stop for coffee." She said, checking her watch. "I've to collect my mam from the 'Over Eighties Bingo.' I was just looking in on you. I'm running late. Let's make a plan for a walk by the river. We can have lunch and a few jars in the The Loch Bar and stagger back here down the towpath."

"Sounds great," Deirdre said, escorting her to the door. "Let's do that soon. Caroline, thank you so much. This present has made my day."

"Well, enjoy the rest of it," she said, giving Deirdre's hand a squeeze. "We'll have to plan a little housewarming. Leave that with me."

Deirdre was glad to have some shape to the day. It had been lovely so far and there was a call booked with Sally early afternoon. So much had happened since they'd spoken a few weeks ago. Given her breakthrough with the collages and how busy she was, Sally had suggested she prioritize her sessions with Isabelle while she was moving house.

After a salad lunch, she picked up the book she had found in the charity shop. *All Along You Were Blooming....* 'What a wonderful title,' she thought. As she turned the pages, something sparked a memory. She put the book down and scrolled through her photographs until she found the one she'd snapped a few hours after she'd heard the news that Niall had died. She studied the bleak sepia image of a weeping willow dragging its lower branches through a stream and recalled the howling wind and the sense of utter desolation that had enveloped her in that moment.

She sat questioning why she had taken the photograph and then it hit her. She had found something that captured her emotions so perfectly that she had taken a picture of it, to show to Niall. She had been out of her mind, deranged with shock. Her brain had not caught up with the reality of what had happened.

Each picture was evocative. She relived something of the months spent trudging through the woods, climbing the mountain, watching the sun rise and watching it set. She saw how the year had passed, the lilac of springtime, the rains of summer, the showtime colors of autumn, the bare black branches, the snow of winter, and the full-circle renewal in the photographs she had taken last week. They showed the beauty that could be found in the most unlikely places; in the water weeds of the river and the stones in the walls. It made a story from when everything had fallen apart to the flickering sense of hope she was experiencing now.

She remembered the music she had played on repeat, the poetry that had guided and lifted her, the art that had channeled her pain. Her mind exploded with ideas for a book she could create. It would be filled with photographs, collages, poetry, and lines from songs.

"But where do I even start?' she wondered, giving in for a moment to the voice clamoring in her head. 'You're not clever enough. You've no idea how to go about this. Who'd be interested?' Then from somewhere came another voice. It was Isabelle's.

"When you're on the right path, the universe steps in to support you in ways you never thought possible."

Deirdre always had a hard job picturing "the universe" but she had a sense of what Isabelle meant. She wanted to believe her. It was perfect timing; she had a call with Sally soon and would run the idea by her. She sifted through the photographs and marked some with a little heart. Then, setting up the computer by the window, she dialed in for the call.

"Hello. That looks like a lovely day where you are," Sally greeted her.

"It is. Look at my view."

Deirdre lifted her laptop and swiveled it to face the river.

"It looks so beautiful, Deirdre. How do you like being there?"

"It's early days, but I think it was the right decision."

"That's so good to hear. Where shall we start this afternoon? We've not spoken for a while. I know you've been busy with the house move and Somhairlin being home. Is she still with you?"

"No. She left the other day. Her friend came over from London. They helped me move in and then went back together. She's applied for a new job. She has an interview lined up."

"Fingers crossed for her. How are your classes with Isabelle going?"

"Really well. I must get back to her. She's sent me through some dates for Ibiza. I'm looking forward to learning how to silkscreen and to work on an idea for a photography project I've had. I want to tell you about it. The idea came out of the blue this afternoon."

"It's so good to see your enthusiasm for all these new things. I know it's still not easy."

"It's not, but I do feel stronger. I've gone from not being able to imagine doing anything, to having a head full of ideas...mind you, having the ideas and the strength to do them are two different things. My energy's back some days, then others it's like wading through treacle."

"I can understand that," Sally said, pausing for a moment.

"So tell me about your ideas for a new project."

Deirdre glanced out across the river and hesitated. She had been cogitating on her plans for the last hour, and suddenly she felt strangely protective of them. Where to start?

"I think I must have told you, that after Niall died, I devoured any books on grief I could lay hands on." She began. "I couldn't retain much at the time but reading mechanically filled up some of the hours. Most of them were too autobiographical for me. I was locked in my own world, couldn't think outside of myself. I wasn't ready to hear other people's stories. It's why I didn't try to find a grief group."

"I can understand that, especially now I know you a little better."

"The thing is, nothing prepares you for grief. It blindsides you and one of the hardest parts is getting back a sense of hope. That's what deserts you in the early days. Hope. I didn't find any books that really gave me that in the way I needed it, and then yesterday I came across one."

She stopped speaking. Sally's face had frozen.

"Shite. Of all the moments," Deirdre muttered, trying to reboot. There was no signal. She stared helplessly at the blank screen, then slammed down the lid in frustration.

Flopping back in the chair, she put her head back, grimaced at the ceiling, and closed her eyes. She was about to text Somhairlin to ask what she should do, when the doorbell chimed. She answered it to find Clara leaning against the jamb, resplendent in an orange kaftan and a pair of pink furry slippers.

"Fecking WiFi's out again," she announced. "Thought I'd better let you know it's the building, not you. Happens all the time."

"Ah! Thank you. That'll explain why my Zoom just froze. Come in. I was about to make a pot of tea."

Cara followed her down the hallway. "So, what part of the country are you from? I was reared in Derry, moved down here a few years back to be near my sister after my husband died. God rest him."

"I'm so sorry for your loss," Deirdre said, registering that she and her new neighbor had more in common than a love of oversized furry slippers.

Cara's visit helped Deirdre to shake off the feeling of anticlimax after the interrupted session with Sally, but she found the small talk exhausting. Once Cara left, she took the lift down to the communal gardens. Wandering along the symmetrical paths and manicured hedges, she became increasingly aware that she was overlooked by the other tenants' balconies. She longed for the privacy of her own garden, to be clipping the lavender she had planted the previous summer and trimming back her rosemary bushes. Turning back to the building, she struggled with the door code, relieved when she was able to follow someone indoors, but frustrated by her inability to recall the numbers.

Over the next few days, technology seemed to wage war on her. The electric stove was innately hostile; the slightest spill, and it shut off. The heating system with its 'smart' console and symbols was unfathomable. The digital thermostat for the hot water system was equally baffling. There were three remote controls for the television, and the range of options and buttons was daunting. The daily aggravations were relentless.

She became lethargic, aching to be back in her home and the comfort of curling up in front of a fire. She missed having space; the walls were closing in. Her sleep had become fitful, and the exhaustion overwhelming. Finding it impossible to establish a routine, she lost track of time. A dark mist was enveloping her, and she couldn't find her way out.

Over the last year, she had believed Niall's spirit was with her; she had talked to him often, sensing that he was watching over her. Now, from seemingly nowhere, she had lost that connection. She no longer knew what she believed. She couldn't visualize him or feel his presence. It was as if she had lost him all over again.

This morning, she'd dragged herself out of bed, determined to fight the onslaught of depression. She had journaled, spilled her thoughts onto the page, written how her loss was insignificant in the context of world suffering and made a gratitude list. It simply added a layer of guilt to her pain. Unable to muster the energy for anything more, she climbed back under the bed covers and stared at the wall. There was no fight left in her. She lay there until the doorbell shattered the silence. Pulling on her dressing gown, she trundled to the door.

"What's going on, missus?" Caroline greeted her, her voice gentle.

Deirdre's face crumpled. Caroline put her arms around her shoulders and held her tightly as she wept.

"Cry away Dee, sob your heart out. It's okay. It's okay."

Deirdre pulled back.

"I've destroyed your shirt." She mumbled, wiping away the tears.

"I'll send you the cleaning bill." Caroline smiled.

"Come in..."

Caroline surveyed the room, the half-drawn curtains and the disarray on the desk.

"I'm sorry for the state of the place," Deirdre mumbled.

"I'm more worried about the state of you," Caroline said, leading her over to the couch. "You had me worried there when you didn't get back to me."

"Sorry?"

"I've been calling you for two days. Here sit down. I'll make us a cup of tea. Have you eaten anything?" she asked, heading for the kitchen.

Deirdre shook her head.

Caroline opened the bread bin, wrapped a stale loaf in paper and tossed it into the bin. She found a packet of biscuits and carried the packet and tea tray into the living room. Deirdre was sitting motionless, staring at the blank television screen. Caroline lifted the accumulation of used plates and cups from the coffee table, came back, and sat down next to her. She poured tea into two mugs and handed one across.

"Here," she said.

Deirdre took the mug and set it back down on the table with trembling hands.

"I'm sorry. I'm just not doing well at all."

"Did something happen?"

Deirdre's shoulders began to heave. Folding her arms across herself, she rocked back and forth until the wave passed. Caroline handed her a tissue.

"I'm sorry... I'm so sorry. Nothing in particular," she said, blowing her nose. "It's just the reality of it all is hitting me more now I'm here. I've lost all the optimism I was feeling and I don't know why, but it's crashing in on me all over again and all I want is to be with Niall. I can't believe how he can just have gone. Why didn't I go with him? We were never meant to be separated like this, and I don't want to live here. I've made a terrible mistake, Caroline. I'm so homesick. I don't know what got into me, selling the place like that."

She blew her nose noisily, then picked up the mug of tea.

"Do you think I could buy it back? I'm half serious, Caroline."

"Well, I don't know about that, but what I do know is that you're not thinking straight right now. Moving house is stressful the best of times and you did it on your own. You're stronger than you know, but you're only human, and it's going to take longer than a few weeks here to settle in."

"I feel pathetic, really pathetic."

"Well, you can stop that right now. This is perfectly normal. You had Somhairlin home, you had company, and of course you'd be really feeling lonely right now. Anybody would Dee. Anybody."

"I had all these ideas, but I think I was fooling myself."

"What ideas?"

"It'll probably sound mad, but I was thinking of writing a book. Well, not exactly writing, more pulling it together with my photographs and quotes from poems and songs. A book to help other people struggling with grief. Not everyone has the luxury of a Sally or an Isabelle."

"That's so true."

"I thought maybe I could set out some of the photographs I took and match them with poetry and lyrics, and maybe that would be a comfort to someone who didn't know what to do with themselves or where to put the pain."

"That doesn't sound mad to me at all."

"You think I could?"

"I think you can do anything you set your mind to."

"It seems like a good idea one minute, and then when I go to the desk all the memories flood in on me when I look at the photographs."

"It may be too soon, then. You might need to give yourself more time, go to Ibiza like you were talking about and come back to it. You're tired. You're expecting too much of yourself. You can't help anyone else while you still need to get yourself strong."

"But I was feeling so good. How is this happening? I sound like a broken record."

"I think this is just all part of it, you know, and I think you should let me clear up a bit in the kitchen and go and have a shower and get dressed. Do that and then let's talk some more. I have all the time in the world."

Deirdre smiled weakly and stood up.

"Okay, if the water's not cold. That thermostat has a will of its own. I can't work it out at all."

"The water was hot when I rinsed the mugs just now, so go on ahead. I'll take a look at the dial for you."

Caroline had the table set when Deirdre reappeared.

"I'm boiling us some spuds. You've feck all fresh in the cupboard, but I've grated some cheese to go on them," she said. "I'm going to stay over tonight whether you want me to or not."

Deirdre heaved a sigh of relief.

"Thank you," she said. "I'd really like that.

SAM

Sam had spent the week preparing for the interview, searching for everything she could find about Colette Ingram, her early background, her businessman husband, her interests, and board memberships. She watched her on chat shows and scoured articles about her in *Vanity Fair* and *Vogue*. She also genned up on the artistic direction of the company and the other members of the troupe. Putting together her resume, she had been amazed to see that her career, which had felt so haphazard and unplanned, now looked perfect "on paper."

She'd listed her background in dance and gymnastics, the events she'd managed, her social media experience at Irish Heritage, the travel schedules she had organized at AISB. The exercise had given her a whole new level of confidence. She "did" have broad experience, and it actually "was" all relevant to the job description.

A text from Jon arrived as she was leaving the flat, and she smiled reading it.

You'll be great. You've got this. I'll call you later.

She found the Edwardian villa fifteen minutes before the interview and waited at the corner of the tree-lined street, checking the time obsessively. At exactly the hour she rang the bell. The door was answered by a housekeeper who greeted her warmly.

"Hello. You must be Sam," she said, going ahead down a chequer-floored hallway.

"I'm Silvia. Ms. Ingram asked me to show you to her study. She'll be with you in a few minutes; she's just on the phone. She asked me to show you the office."

Leading her through a sitting room, Silvia took her to an annex connected with the main part of the house. Art posters, photographs, and framed awards lined the walls. Two sofas faced each other across a large coffee table next to an antique desk with an array of silver-framed photographs. French doors opened onto a patio and walled garden.

"The office is through here," Silvia told her, indicating a room to the side.

Sam peeked in at the spacious office, which also led out onto the garden. It felt homely with its fitted wooden cabinetry and clean lines. 'Would this be hers, if she were offered the job?' she wondered.

"If you would like to take a seat in here, Ms. Ingram will be with you soon."

Sam thanked her and perched on the edge of the sofa. The minutes ticked by agonizingly slowly until the door finally opened. She jumped up as Colette, a vision of perfect minimalism in a black shift dress and flats, came across and shook her hand. A Pomeranian trotted behind her.

"I'm so sorry I kept you waiting," she said. Lovely to meet you. Do make yourself comfortable. This is Oleg." She said, indicating the ball of white fluff scuttling under her feet."

"He's adorable," Sam said.

"He's no trouble apart from attachment issues; he follows me everywhere." Colette laughed. "So... I already gave you a sense of what I will need when we spoke on the phone last week."

"You did."

"And I didn't scare you away?"

"Not at all," she said, returning her smile. "Quite the opposite, in fact."

"Good. How about we look at my diary and I'll take you through what the role entails. Please don't hold back. Ask me any questions you like."

Sam felt her shoulders relax, and the hour passed quickly.

Back at her flat,she paced the sitting room. It felt cramped. If she got this job, she would move.

'If, if, if...' she thought.

It was barely an hour since she'd left the house in Bloomsbury, but she was already telling herself she should prepare for bad news. Not that the interview had gone badly, not at all, but maybe there was some-one else in the frame, someone better qualified; a gourmet cook who spoke ten languages and typed a thousand words a second?

The more Colette explained what she needed; the more excited Sam had become. Had she come across too strongly? Had she gushed? She hadn't gushed, had she? Had she hesitated when Colette asked would she be able to accompany her on tour? Possibly, even though she'd leap at the chance. Had she made that clear enough or too clear?

Her phone rang as she was making her umpteenth circle of the bedroom; a robot call. She declined it and tossed the phone on the bed where it rang again instantly. She grabbed it.

"Hi there. How did you get on?"

"Oh! Who is this? Sorry. Hi Eileen. Sorry...it took me a moment there. I think it went well. I mean, I hope so. I'm waiting to hear.

"Fingers crossed. I've just signed the contract on the studio. It's a bit terrifying, but it's done. I've also snapped up the white box spaces. I'll be based there from the end of the month. Bridget has all sorts of plans for working with me. Won't bother you with it now but would love to brainstorm some ideas we're having."

"Congratulations. That's great news. I'm happy to brainstorm the minute I have my brain back, I'm on tenterhooks here."

"I can imagine. Okay I'll let you go. I'm gunning for you. Let me know."

Sam started clearing out bedroom drawers in an effort to stay distracted, flinging out sweaters and tossing old tee shirts. When her phone finally lit up and she saw Colette's number, she stepped over the heap of clothes and stood by the window hardly daring to breath.

"Sam? Hello. This is Colette Ingram."

"Hello Colette," she managed.

"I'm so sorry I didn't get back to you earlier today. A few things came up. This is the first moment I've had to myself."

Sam's chest was pounding. Her throat had gone dry. There was a pause. She waited.

"I would like to offer you the position."

"Really? Really?" Sam said, "Really?"

"From your reaction,. I take it you will accept?" Colette laughed.

"Yes. Yes. Of course. Sorry. Yes. I'm delighted. Thank you."

"Good. Are you available to come over Tuesday morning, and we can sort out the formalities?"

"I am. Yes."

"Good. Let's make it for nine, shall we?"

"Perfect. Yes. Thank you."

"Okay. See you then."

"Yes. Thank you." Sam said hopping madly on one foot and punching the air. Running down the stairs she flew onto the street, raced across the road to the park, made a lap of the lawn, then speed-dialed Betsy.

"I got it! I got it!" she yelled. "Betsy I got the job!!! Whoop! Whoop!!

Betsy whooped along with her, and they arranged to meet up after Betsy finished work that evening.

Sam headed back inside. Too adrenalin pumped to sit down, she put on Queen and bopped around the sitting room. "Don't stop me now!... I'm a shooting star..."

As the music faded, she collapsed onto the couch. She would call her mother, tell her the news. She had a feeling that her dad already knew.

DEIRDRE

"Good morning," Caroline said, drawing back the curtains.

"Thought I'd check in on you. It's ten o' clock."

Deirdre lifted her head and sat up groggily.

"Is it really?"

"It is indeed. Here," she said, handing her a mug and a plate of toast. "How did you sleep?"

"I think I passed out."

"Good. I'll leave you to come to. I've had a few ideas about what we should do today. Take your time and I'll be out on the verandah; well, that's if it stops raining."

Sipping her coffee, Deirdre sank back on the pillows, gazing out of the window and fighting back the familiar feeling of dread she had woken up with lately. Today was a new day. She had to rally, if only so that Caroline would feel she was doing her some good. Hauling out of bed, she washed her hair for the first time in days, and stepping out of the shower, began to feel more positive. She would make an effort, put on a dress and some lipstick. She owed her friend that much, even if she fell apart, which was highly likely as the tears were welling up already.

"That's more like it," Caroline said when she appeared outside. "You look like a new woman. How're you feeling?"

"Not so bad."

"I've been giving some thought to what you told me yesterday evening."

"What was that exactly? I don't remember."

"Your project. The idea for making a book from the photographs. I thought it might be too soon, then I got to thinking maybe I could help you sort through them, so you don't have to re-live it all on your own."

"Really? Would you be interested to do that?"

"I can see how it would bring you down doing it by yourself. I've plenty of time, and you know I enjoy organizing things. I can help you catalogue them, do the practical part, and you can get all creative. How does that sound?"

"It sounds wonderful," she said, sitting down next to her.

"I was also thinking that what you don't have yet is a routine. So, what if we said I'd come over around at ten a few days this week? That way you can plan around it."

"You're right. I do need some shape to the week. I've been feeling like I'm staring into an abyss."

"You need some fixed points, some days where you have a bit of company. That way you can get on with your collages when you're on your own. When are you going to Ibiza?"

"Early next month, I think. I'm not sure. Isabelle said she'd tell me this week."

"Okay. That'll give you something to look forward to, and in the meantime does this sound like a plan? I know it won't make the pain go away, but you shouldn't be on your own too much when you're feeling low and when you're finding your feet here."

"You're so wise. Thank you."

"Ah! It's easy to be wise when you're telling someone else. I'm in awe of you, missus. If it was me, I don't think I'd have been doing the half of what you've done. Go easy on yourself. You're doing fine, and there's no time frame on it. This will all go at its own pace. You'll have your good days and your bad ones."

"I know. I'll try my best to make this a good one."

"Great. I need to go over and see Mum," Caroline said, standing up and lifting her coffee mug. Will you be okay on your own for a few hours?"

"Of course. How's she doing?"

"Not much change. She sleeps a lot, but her appetite's good and she's happy."

"Give her my love."

"I will. Be back around two."

Deirdre looked out across the river. The sun had disappeared behind threatening grey clouds and the air felt heavy and damp. It would be good to get a few weeks of sunshine. She had that to look forward to and an incredible friend; she must be grateful. A few leaves swirled around her feet. She watched as the rain darkened the gardens and the river view disappear under the mist. Closing her eyes, she listened to it hammering relentlessly. As it gently eased, she opened them again. The outline of the mountains had become visible and the air smelled fresh. She stood up.

Going indoors and over to her desk, she lifted a well-worn poetry anthology and found the line *'around a blind corner, across hills, you must climb without know-*

ing what's on the other side..." It perfectly captured the symbolism of the new path you were forced to take when loss shattered your world.

She opened a photograph of the track leading up to the mountain. Bare tree branches formed an arch that drew the eye beyond to infinity. Its starkness captured something of the loneliness of her long walks in the early days and the distance there was still to go. She played around to find the right place to overlay the words. Lost in the process, she jumped when her phone rang.

"You are talking to Colette Ingram's PA, Mum. I got the job! I got it!"

Startled out of her trance, Deirdre sat up.

"Well done. Really? That's brilliant. Great news. Congratulations. I couldn't be happier for you. Tell me all."

Sam regaled her with every detail of the interview, tripping over her words in excitement. Deirdre listened. This was the girl she remembered. This was such good news. Her heart leapt.

"So, when do you start?"

"Next week. I can't wait. Mum, they're in the middle of a run of Manon. Can you believe it? Colette said I'm to go with her to rehearsal next week. I imagine I'll be flying around like a scalded cat, but I don't mind at all."

Deirdre remembered the performance she had seen with Somhairlin years before on their first trip to London together, how her daughter had talked about nothing else for months. They'd listened to the haunting melodies of *Elegy* on repeat in the car to her classes in Dublin. It had been the beginning of Deirdre's interest in classical music.

"I can only imagine," she said. "I'm thrilled for you. Congratulations."

"Thank you. I knew you would be. I couldn't wait to get telling you. So Mum, what about you? How're you feeling? You sounded so low the other day. Are you okay?"

"I'm fine, a lot better for hearing your news, that's for sure. It's given me a real lift; had a bad run of it there for a few days but I'm back on track, in fact I was knee-deep sorting through some of my photographs just now. Don't worry about me at all."

"Okay. If you're sure."

"I am. Caroline and I are going to work on a project together. I've all these pictures and journal entries and poems, and I'm planning on making a book, and then I've the collages to do and the work with Isabelle and the trip coming up. It's all going to be just great," she gabbled.

"Okay. Good," Sam said hesitantly. "Just making sure."

"Of course. Well done again. Go and enjoy yourself. Go celebrate. I'm so proud of you."

Caroline arrived back as Deirdre was ending the call. She told her the news as they sat outside chatting.

"I didn't realize how much I was worrying about Somhairlin until that call." Deirdre said.

"She's such a breath of fresh air, that girl. I'm so happy for her. It'll be a whole new start."

"It will. Talking of new starts, I found the photograph I think I'll use to open the book. Want to see it? I've a poem to go with it too. I'll not use the whole of it. I want the picture to do the work."

"Show me," Caroline said, standing up and following her inside to her desk.

"It's beautiful." She said. "I love the way your eye's drawn through the trees to all those rays of sunshine at the end."

"Oh! Good. That's exactly what I want people to see, that they're walking a new path and feeling lost, but there's a kind of guiding light there too,"

"You're 'cooking with gas now' missus. Let's get down to work. Where's the poem you want to use with it?"

By the end of the afternoon, Caroline had collated Deirdre's photographs and collages into chronological order and opened new files for the poetry. Deirdre picked out more to mark with the little hearts so they could go into a shortlist file. She was in awe of Caroline's ability to pull down templates and the speed at which it was all coming together.

"Where on earth did you learn to do all this?" she asked.

"A boarding house doesn't sell itself," Caroline said. "It's not rocket science. I resisted the auld technology at first, but I came round to it in the end. It makes life easier, not harder. I took a course in London, put everything to do with the business online. You'll get the hang of it. Anything a Millennial can do, we can do too. They just do it much faster," she added with a chuckle.

"I couldn't be more grateful. It'd have taken me months to get to this point. It looks like a proper project."

"That's because it IS a proper project. The more I see of your photographs, the more impressed I am. You've a real eye for it. Let's print some of these off and call it a day. I bought a bottle of Chablis on the way over. I'd have got Champagne if I'd known the news earlier. Let's get a takeaway and toast the new job, maybe Face-Time Somhairlin so I can say 'Congratulations'."

241

SAM

Sam was thoughtful after the conversation. She hadn't registered quite how alone her mother would be after she and Betsy left. Her voice had sounded forced towards the end of the call. Caroline was a wonderful friend, but she couldn't be there all the time. There was that course in Ibiza, but she would need more than that long-term. Winter wasn't far away; the dark nights would soon be drawing in.

She checked the time. Eileen should have finished work by now. She called her back.

"Eileen, I can't thank you enough. I have the job!"

"I know! You are so welcome. Colette rang to say she thinks you'll be a great fit and to thank me too. I'm getting a lot of 'thank you's' today."

"She did? That's wonderful!"

"I think you'll like working for her. I've known her for ten years or more. You know the type; she's driven, disciplined, demanding, but in a kick-ass way. She's very well respected in the company. Her last assistant adored her. was with her for about eight years until she got pregnant. That tells you a lot."

"It does."

"I didn't want to say too much before, knowing the both of you, but I think it's a perfect fit."

"I hope so. I'm really charged about it. So now I've calmed down a bit, tell me about The Mill."

"It's coming along well. Bridget's going to use the hall for some of the community events, and now I won't have to limit my numbers. I'll be able to expand, do some work with kids with special needs. I'm using the white box space as my office, and long-term, I'm thinking about having a podcast based in the other. This show is a hell of a job to co-ordinate, but Bridget's seconding me a manager."

"That's great. I'm so pleased."

"When you come down to earth, I'd like your ideas on some of the social media stuff. I know you're good at that."

"I'll help anyway I can. I'm so happy for you."

As Eileen was talking, Sam made a connection.

"Eileen, you said just now you had long-term plans for the other white box space."

"The podcast? Further down the line for sure. I want to give a platform for inclusive dance, but it'll take a bit of planning."

"Is it going to be empty for a while?"

"Probably, but that's okay I'm sure it will come in handy in the meantime. I didn't want to risk not getting the one next to mine."

"Would you be up for subletting it for a while?"

"I haven't given that any thought. Why?"

"Well, say for example it was my Mum. Would you be up for that?"

Eileen giggled.

"I'd hardly be able to say 'no' to your mum, now would I?"

"I've only thought of it while we're talking, but she's doing all these art and photography projects and I think it would be good for her to be in a creative space around other people. It might help her get a few things off the ground. As I said, I just had the idea a minute ago. I imagine it'd only be for a while, and she could rent one herself if it worked out for her, or whenever you'd need it back. It'd be extra money to put towards your work, too."

"It's a no-brainer for me. Of course, she could have it and forget about subletting, she'd be welcome to use it."

"I'm sure she would want to pay you for it. I might be getting ahead of myself here, but could I suggest it to her?"

"Of course. Talk to her and let me know."

Sam thanked Eileen again and clicked off, glancing at the time. She would call her mother back in the morning.

After showering and putting on her favorite red silk dress and denim jacket, she studied her reflection. Her eyes were shining. She couldn't remember the last time she had felt so alive. Making her way across Clapham Common, she joined the rush hour commuters crowding the path. Side-stepping some kids whizzing past on bikes, she dodged around a dog walker and cut across the grass. The air was thick with the drone of peak-hour traffic, distant sirens and planes overhead. She sensed the pulse of the city in a new way, feeling part of it, knowing that she was exactly where she was meant to be.

Weaving through the circles of happy hour drinkers, she pushed through the swing doors of the pub and spotted Betsy waving at her.

"Well done, you." She beamed, leaping up and hugging her. "I'm so proud of you."

A barman with a bottle of Prosecco and two tall glasses appeared at the table.

"We're celebrating!" Betsy told him.

"Birthday?"

"Job!"

"Cheers to you then." He smiled.

"Thank you."

Sam put her jacket on the back of the chair and sat down. Betsy leaned across and poured them each a glass of bubbly.

"To the new job! I'm so happy for you. When d'you start?"

"Middle of next week, which is great, gives me a few days to get my head around it. I could do with getting a bag and some new Converses. I want to look the part."

"You always look great. We can go on Saturday. I need new runners. I've signed up for the marathon. Let me know how much you're in for."

"Will do.

"So why couldn't you come to Soho House the other night? You said something about a work thing."

"I went out for dinner."

"With Sandra? You said she'd left there, too. Good for her."

"No. With Jon Porter."

"Jon Porter?"

"Yes. I thought it was just a leftover work thing from AISB and..."

"And?"

"And... it wasn't!"

Betsy knocked back her Prosecco, topped up their glasses and shifted her chair closer to Sam.

"Okay. Spill."

Sam threw her head back and laughed.

"Okay... So yes. Thing is, I did tell myself it was only a work thing. He's left the bureau too, but anyway, we talked about work a bit. I told him about what happened in L.A., but after a while we got onto other things and..."

"...and?"

"We went to a bar, hung out for a bit. Then he dropped me off in an Uber."

"That's all I'm getting?"

"That's all there is." Sam smiled. "Well, except that he texted me next day and we met up for coffee. I'd told him I had the interview coming up, and he offered to help with my resume."

"That's a whole new pick-up line." Sam grinned. "I'll have to remember that one."

Sam giggled. "It does sound a bit naff when you put it like that, but he really did want to help. I hadn't a clue where to start."

"So, did he offer to help you with anything else? Just asking."

"Very funny. No. Seriously, I didn't tell you about it, but the talk he gave in Kauai kind of changed my life. I mean, he doesn't know that, obviously, but it did. It was all about how we shouldn't waste our time in crappy jobs and how short life is, and I know I knew that already, but it was something in the way he explained it, and maybe because I was feeling lost, you know, since my dad died."

"This last year's been so rough for you. I'm sorry I was being flip."

"It's okay. I love how you pull me out of myself, but I've been taking this really seriously, trying to work out if maybe I was looking for someone to replace my dad. It's so hard to explain. I didn't want to talk about it until I'd worked it out a bit myself."

"I can see that."

"I don't want to risk getting hurt. I'm only starting to get myself together, and he's so different from anyone I met before... I'm going to take it slowly."

"So, when are you seeing him again?"

"He's taking me out to celebrate tomorrow night."

" That's 'going slowly'?"

"You know what I mean, Bets. Emotionally slowly. I'm not going to build up some wild fantasy where we sail into the sunset."

"I get it, but you know what, Sam, as they say, life's short, and for what it's worth, I think you have good instincts. I'm happy for you. I really am."

She refilled their glasses. "Shall we stay here to eat or find somewhere else? Your shout."

Sam was relieved that the conversation seemed to have moved on from Jon. She was counting the hours until she would see him again.

The next evening, when she walked into the snug library of the NoMad Hotel and Jon jumped up to hug her, she abandoned all thoughts of taking things slowly.

"How lovely is this," she said, sinking into the plush velvet couch.

"It is, isn't it? It's not been open long. I thought you'd like it. As you can see, there's a ballet theme."

Sam glanced admiringly at the gilt framed series of dancers above the book lined shelves, the prints of The Royal Opera House, and the tasseled luxe curtains.

"I love it. It's like a stage set."

"You'll be coming to Covent Garden a lot now. I thought you should know about this place. Ah! Here's our Champagne now."

They waited while their flutes were filled.

"Cheers." Jon grinned, raising his glass to hers.

"Cheers."

She took a sip.

"Congratulations. I'm so pleased for you."

"Thank you. I still can't quite believe it," she said, setting down her glass.

"You look so happy. "He said. "You're lighting up the room with that smile. Here..."

He handed her a small box wrapped with a black ribbon.

She untied it carefully and pulled out a glass candle. Lifting the silver lid, she tilted it to her nose.

"Plumeria!" she said. "This takes me right back to Kauai."

"I knew you'd like it...it's just a little something to say, 'Well done.'"

"I love it," she said, her eyes dancing. "Thank you."

DEIRDRE

Deirdre had deliberated for some time over what to wear to meet Eileen at The Mill. Somhairlin had told her it was a "Creative Hub." She'd explained that although they were technically offices, the people there were in the "creative industries." Deirdre wasn't entirely sure what that meant but was interested to find out. She settled on blue jeans, a white shirt, and her new leather jacket.

"Hmm," she told her reflection. "Not half bad at all."

Eileen met her at the door with a huge smile.

"Hi Deirdre. Come on in. Can't wait to show you around. How are you? Excuse the state of me, am only now finishing up class. Studio's this way."

She wheeled ahead of her, chatting and nodding hellos to everyone who passed.

"So here we are. My studio! " she said, turning on the lights. The performance is in six weeks. We'll have raked seating at that end and create a circular 'stage' over there."

She pointed to the far end of the room.

"Brilliant." Deirdre said. 'What size of an audience can you have here?"

"About sixty."

"Really? That's great. If you need anything at all by the way, I'm more than happy to help."

"Thank you! I will most certainly take you up on that. It's all hands-on deck. We've incredible resources on tap into; lighting crews, video producers, tech guys. The support for what we're doing is fantastic. If you decide to take the space, I'll introduce you to every-one."

"That'd be lovely."

Deirdre followed her down the corridor.

"Sam told me you're writing a book "she said over her shoulder.

"I am, although it's not so much writing, I'm using a lot of quotes from people and photographs. It's more visual. I can't really explain." 'I need to be able to explain,' she thought.

"Really? An anthology? Very cool."

Deirdre nodded. That didn't quite nail it, but she'd store it up as a quick answer if anyone asked her.

"Hold the button please," Eileen said at the lift. "I'll come in after you."

As the doors opened onto the first floor, a guy stood back while she reversed her chair.

"Hi, Peter,Just the man I need to see." she said. "Can you drop by later, I've a few questions for you."

"Sure," he said. "

"Great. Thanks. This is Deirdre. She's a writer. She's looking at taking the room next to mine."

Deirdre returned Peter's smile. It was a surprise to hear herself introduced as a writer. For a second, she felt vaguely fraudulent.

"Good Luck Deirdre. Catch you later Eileen." He said.

"Peter's one of the lighting technicians." Eileen told her. "We're just 'round the corner now."

The room was spacious and light with two long windows and a view across to the canal. Deirdre immediately knew it would be perfect.

"I love it," she told her. "If you're certain, I'd like to take it."

"You're very welcome. It'll be great having you here. You can bring your own furniture, but you should check out the storeroom first. They've pretty much anything you'd need, and it's all good stuff. I'll show you what I have when you come back next week."

"That's great. I'll make a list before then."

"Will next Tuesday work for you? If you come in at ten, I can introduce you to people and help you get set up."

"Wonderful. Tuesday it is. I'll let you get on. I know you're busy."

"Can you remember how to get out again?"

"I can. Have a good weekend. Thanks so much Eileen."

Deirdre hovered outside on the steps to the building feeling a rush of excitement. She'd liked the atmosphere and could see the potential for making it her own. She strolled along the quayside, planning how she would arrange a table under the window and put up a cork board the length of one wall. As she approached the flat, her heart grew heavy. Niall would not be waiting to hear her ideas, help her move in, or meet her at lunchtimes for a walk.

She slumped down on a bench, fighting back tears and swallowing hard against the constriction in her throat. All the optimism of the last hour was ebbing away. She stared at the ground, feeling increasingly invisible and alone. Getting up wearily, she passed a group of young mothers with prams chatting by a play area.

'Life goes by so fast.' She sighed. "It seems like five minutes ago since that was me.'

Turning back, she began doubting herself. Weren't there a ton of uplifting books out there already? Was it madness to think she had something new to offer? Who would publish hers? If only she could talk about it with Niall. What would he have said? She could almost hear him.

"Och, Dee. Why are you worrying about getting it published when you haven't even written it yet?"

He would have teased her, made her laugh, reminded her that nobody was holding a gun to her head to do it. She determined to snap out of her mood, the way she knew she would if the conversation with Niall had been real.

Within a week, Deirdre was settled into her new space. A trestle stacked with paints and brushes ran one length of wall under a cork board festooned with swatches and collages. On the other side of the room, under the window, was her desk, ink jet printer, and filing cabinet.

As her book took shape, it became clear that pulling it together wasn't a simple matter of compiling images and quotes. There had to be a theme weaving through it, some connective tissue, an introduction, a guiding voice - her voice. She was sitting cogitating on this when she heard a tap on the side of her door and a head appeared from behind it.

"Have you got a minute?"

Deirdre looked up and rested her pen.

'Come on in." She smiled.

"Thanks. Hi. I'm Sinead McCloughlin. I'm with the production team across the hall."

"Lovely to meet you, Sinead," she said, noticing the girl was heavily into the punk aesthetic.

"We're making a promotional video for The Mill. I'll be speaking to people who work here for it. Can I interview you? It'd only take a few minutes next week. I've a prep sheet if you're interested."

She handed Deirdre a sheet of paper.

"They're only pointers. You can change them if you like."

Deirdre was distracted for a moment by the sleeve tattoo on Sinead's arm.

"Thank you," she said. "Could you let me think about it, give me time to look it over?"

"Of course. Awesome. Not a problem."

"When would you need to know?"

"Deadline's Monday, I think. Shoot me a text. My number's there."

"Thank you."

"Are those yours?"

Sinead was peering at the line of black-and-white collages on the cork board.

"They are, yes. I made them last year."

"Cool," she said. "They'd make cute tee graphics. "Bye."

"'Tee graphics?" Deirdre wondered; she'd have to ask Somhairlin what that meant. 'How nice to be included. Why not? I can tell them what a lovely place it is to work and give a plug for Eileen's show.'

She looked at the sheet: "What are your preferred pronouns? What company are you with? What's your job title? What's your Tik Tok/Instagram handle? How many followers have you got? Who are you following? Your top three bands? Where have you worked before? Where do you see yourself a year from now? What are three words your friends would use to describe you?"

She read it again, running a gamut of emotions ranging from mild amusement to cultural displacement. Out of all these questions, the first was the only one she felt equipped to answer. She looked up as Caroline landed in.

"Bloody Hell!" Caroline muttered, shaking off her raincoat and propping up a dripping umbrella. "Brass monkeys out there today."

"You look frozen! I'll get you a coffee. I could do with one myself."

"Thank you. What's that?" she said, picking up Sinead's sheet from the top of her desk where Deirdre had tossed it.

"They want to interview me about working here. It's for a promotional video they're making. They're some of the questions they might ask."

Caroline looked down them.

"Hmm. How things have changed."

"Quite! As you can see, I don't exactly fit the demographic. I suppose to be PC, they have to include everyone these days."

"Why wouldn't you do it, though? You'd have to come at it from a different angle, but I'm sure they'd be flexible about that."

"Caroline. If the whole idea is to promote The Mill. I don't think I'd be doing them any favors. I'm a dinosaur."

"What?" Caroline's eyebrows furrowed and she shook her head. "That's not like you at all, Dee. I know you're not young, but you're doing something very creative. It doesn't have to be all over Tik Tok or whatever. You should do it, let people know us Boomers are still here, part of the scene, shaking our tail feathers. You do still have a tail feather, don't you?"

"I think I might have misplaced it."

"I think you might, but you'd better locate it fast missus. You need to do the interview."

"Really? You think?"

"I do. When this book comes out, you'll be doing lots of them."

Deirdre's eyes widened.

"Why will I be doing interviews?"

"Promotion. Marketing. I've been researching it. There's a lot to do down the line. You'll need a blog for starters."

"A blog? I will? Why?"

"Don't bother your head with it for now. Just saying, you may as well get a bit of practice in."

Deirdre plonked down in the chair."

"I haven't even thought about what happens if it gets published," she said. "I mean, I fantasize about seeing it on the shelf in Gallagher's, but that's as far as I've got."

"You should stop thinking 'if.' It's about 'how.' It'll either get published by a professional publisher or we'll do it ourselves. Either way it's getting published, and either way, you're going to need a blog and be on social media. The world has changed, and you if you don't keep up, then you really will become a dinosaur."

Deirdre sighed. "I was on Facebook there for a while. I'm not completely out of touch. But a blog?"

"The good news is you don't have to think about any of it yet, and the other good news is that it'll be fun when you get to that point. You can hire some young wiz kid here."

"You're really taking this seriously, aren't you?"

"I am. This book will help people who are going through some of the worst times of their lives. That's why you started it. One day, probably when my mum goes, it'll be the first thing I'll want to pick up. I know that. I'm not working on it to keep you company. I believe in it. I can see it..."

"I can too, and it seems to have taken on a life of its own, like it's getting bigger than I imagined. I feel out of my depth. I need to write an introduction and find a way to guide people through the pictures. It's not easy; I'm not a writer."

Caroline smiled. "Halfway through is when things get hard, and that's when most people give up...and that, missus, is when you, Deirdre Macardle, are not going to give up."

"I'm not giving up," Deirdre assured her. "I'm stuck. That's all. Thank you for what you just said. Thank you for the reminder. I needed it.

'Okay, well, you can thank me by getting that nice cup of coffee you were promising." Caroline smiled. "I'll have that first photo up on the screen when you get back."

That evening, Deirdre looked again at the questions and found them surprisingly easy to answer. First off, her preferred pronouns were 'she/her.' Second, she was self-employed. Third, she was writing an "anthology." Number four, she did indeed have an Instagram "handle"; that was simply jargon for "name." How this had come about was a complete mystery until she remembered that she and Somhairlin had played around on it a few years back. By some miracle, it turned out that she had fifty-four followers and was following a hundred and ninety-six people.

The fifth was easy. Her top three bands were The Stones, Eagles, and Queen. Six was a long time ago when she had worked before, in Niall's office and in the primary school, and finally, the three words her friends might use to describe her: "Pain-in-Arse" was Caroline's contribution when she called her. She settled on "Loyal, Honest, Reliable."

Of all the questions, the one that pulled her up short was where she could see herself a year from now. Since Niall had passed away, her vision of the future had been blurry. Would she still be in the flat? Would she still be feeling so lonely? Of course, the question was specific to work. A year from now she would have finished her book. That was all she needed to say.

When Caroline asked how the interview had gone, she couldn't remember the detail. Sinead and her assistant had put her so much at ease, she'd forgotten she was being filmed. All she could clearly recall was talking about the book, and how happy she was to be working at The Mill.

"They weren't in here for more than ten minutes." She told her. "I don't know why I got myself in such a state. I enjoyed it."

"You see?" Caroline said. "I told you it'd be fun."

Over the next week, frustrated with her failed attempts to write the introduction, Deirdre took Isabelle's advice.

"You're doing too much left-brain work,"she'd said. "Let go a little. Get back in flow. Paint. Walk. The words will come in their own good time. Stop pushing."

She took it on board. She would be going to Ibiza in a few weeks and had all the time in.the world. Why come in every day as if there were some urgent deadline? She started to take walks again and pulled out her watercolor box.

Somhairlin checked in regularly, texting pictures of her office, of Colette's dog, and a few she had promised not to share with anyone, not even Caroline, of backstage at the Opera House in Covent Garden. She was in her element, and Deirdre could not have been happier for her.

The day before she was due to leave for Ibiza, Sinead dropped by.

"Hi," she said, "Have you got a minute?"

"I do. Come in. How's your video coming along?"

"Good. We're about to start editing."

She glanced across at the wall.

"I was wondering. Could I use that? I really like it."

Deirdre glanced up at her collage.

"You mean that one? The one with the trailing branches?"

"Yes, for a tee shirt. To screen print."

"Of course." Deirdre's face lit up. "I'd be honored."

"Thanks," she said, taking out her phone.

"Cheers. I'll get you to sign them when they're printed. You could be the new Vivienne Westwood."

Deirdre stood up and unpinned it from the board.

"You do screen printing?"

"Yeh! It's my thing. I sell shirts at the market. I can give you something for using it if you like."

"No. Please, not at all, though do let me have one. No, I want to ask you. Do you know how to go about printing a pattern onto silk?"

"Sure."

"Would you be able to show me one day?"

"Of course," Sinead said. "No problem."

DEIRDRE – ONE MONTH LATER

The sun was high in the sky as Deirdre's taxi drove up the unmade lane to Isabelle's house, leaving clouds of dust in its wake. She climbed out and ducked under an archway spilling with bougainvillea. The front door was open.

"Hello Deirdre, come through," a voice called out. She followed it into a spacious studio where a faint scent of jasmine filled the air. Every surface was covered with artwork on trestle tables, walls, free-standing installations, and sculptures, all under a ceiling of parachute-silk.

Isabelle uncurled from a low futon. She was more slender than she'd appeared in their Zoom sessions and had an air of fragility. Her yoga pants and shirt were stained with paint. Her feet were bare.

"Hello Deirdre." She smiled, crossing the room and giving her a gentle hug. "It's so lovely to meet you in person. Welcome to my little corner of the world."

"It's beautiful," Deirdre said, glancing around again." Is this all your own work?"

"Part of it,"she said. "I have so much more in my workshop in Santa Eularia. That's where I take the group classes. You must come over one day while you're here."

"I'm blown away. It's wonderful."

Deirdre sauntered around the canvasses and instal-lations. The work was of such a high standard that it forcefully reminded her how far she had to go on her own artistic journey.

"Let's start today with a few moments' meditation," Isabelle said, gesturing to a space underneath the window where a water jug and glasses had been set out on a low table. "When we calm our minds and come to our work from a place of stillness, we can connect with our creative selves more easily."

Deirdre eased down opposite her onto one of the large Andalusian cushions. She closed her eyes and inhaled deeply.

After the first afternoon, Deirdre quickly fell into a routine. In the early mornings, she clambered down the cliff at the side of the hotel and swam for an hour or so before coming back up for breakfast. The owner would nod the occasional "Ola" to her as he came to and fro, but that was the extent of their exchange. It suited her well. It was her first trip alone, and she had no desire for small talk.

The classes with Isabelle gave a shape to the after-noon and left her with a feeling of connection. When the heat of the day had passed, she spent the evenings wandering the narrow roads overlooking the sea and watching the spectacular sunsets throw bolts of scarlet onto the crumbling edges of the cliffs.

Each session with Isabelle was different. Her approach to art therapy was not at all as Deirdre had imagined. She took her for hikes through the canyons, encouraging her to take photographs of "attractors," which, she explained, were anything that drew Deirdre's eye - the texture on the stump of a fallen tree trunk, the mushroom clinging to bark, the shadows of branches on a crumbling stone wall. Deirdre took pictures of drift-wood and shells on their beach rambles and snapped leaves, pinecones, and olives as they wandered through the woodlands. She had never looked so closely at what was around her. They meandered in silence and Deirdre found the quiet space between them calming.

Back in the studio, Isabelle would print off some of the photographs and teach her new ways of using them to collage with colored tissue and chalks. She showed her how to create a book from beautiful handmade paper and suggested she use it as a prototype for her own. They worked on abstractions for the cover, trying out different effects using acrylics and stencils. Deirdre loved the idea of creating an original version that she would always have for herself.

A day or two before the end of her stay, they drove to the north of the island and followed a stony path to the rocky promontory overlooking a wild bay. They perched on the wide rocks, breathlessly recovering from the effort of the climb and gazing out at the spar-kling sea. The landscape reminded Deirdre of Donegal, of the craggy bluffs and beaches at the Cliffs of Moher. 'This is beautiful, ' she thought, 'but Ireland is home,'

Next day, on her way into Santa Eularia she called Caroline.

"Can't stay on long; I'm in a taxi, on my way to meet up with Sally." She said. "Wish you could join us for lunch. It seems weird to be meeting her without you."

"How' bout I come with you later in the year and we can celebrate finishing the book? I bet Sally would be up for that too."

"That's a brilliant idea." 'And it'll be a great way for me to thank you,' she thought, but didn't say.

"How are you? How's the rest of the week been?"

"Good. I'm as brown as a berry."

"I'm so jealous." Caroline laughed. "Glad to hear it's still going well. Take lots of selfies. Give my love to Sally. Can't wait to hear all on Tuesday."

Deirdre tucked her phone away and sat back as the cab swung through winding roads, past olive groves and open fields to the edge of the town, to the port, where she jumped out and stood for a moment to take in the view from the bay. The sailing boats far in the distance seemed painted against the background of cliffs and the cloudless blue sky. She breathed in the salt air, then with a flutter of excitement, saw Sally waving to her from a sidewalk cafe. She crossed over the street.

"Here," Sally said, "Come round this side so you get the view, It's so wonderful to finally meet you properly. "

"You too." Deirdre smiled, squeezing in next to her at the slatted table." It's great we managed to get our trips to overlap like this.

"It is."

"And I wouldn't be here without you. I can't thank you enough for making the connection with Isabelle. She's incredible."

"I'm so pleased." Sally said, yanking at her skirt which had caught under the leg of her chair. "I think I may have gone a bit too far with this floaty look." She said. "I'm releasing my inner hippy."

"Go for it. It's lovely." Deirdre laughed.

" Okay, tell me what you've been up to. Have you seen much of the island?"

"It's probably an overshare." Deirdre said, "but I've been swimming in the buff every morning."

"Which bluff?"

"No." Deirdre giggled. "The 'buff'…with no clothes on! The Spanish don't care if you're naked at all! I found this beautiful beach really close to where I'm staying. It's a bit of a hike to get there from your hotel, but it'd be worth it."

"It sounds incredible."

"It really is. Shall we get coffee?"

"Good idea. I'll get the girl's attention." Sally said, flagging down the waitress and placing their order.

"You know Deirdre, not everybody in your circumstances would be off swimming in Ibiza, with or without their clothes on." She said, turning back to her. "Seriously, I mean it. You're an absolute inspiration. It takes a lot of strength to build a whole new life like you're doing. I want you to know it's been a privilege to be a part of your journey."

Deirdre's eyes were misty. She took a moment to reply.

"Thank you, Sally. You've been a very important part of it. I haven't felt strong at all, and I'm not sure how I'm an inspiration, but you know… I suppose that I am proud of myself. I think Niall would be too… I found the fighter in me, and I like her. Thank you for saying that Sally. It means a lot."

The waitress had arrived with their coffees. Deirdre tore open a sugar sachet.

"I'm still very much a work in process, but there again, aren't we all? We just have to deal with whatever life throws at us as best we can."

She stirred her latte slowly.

"Niall and I had a wonderful life together; losing him is harder than I could have ever imagined, but life must go on. I'm so grateful for what we had."

"...and you've been a great reminder for me to appreciate what I have, too."

"That's lovely to hear, Sally. Thank you."

"So tell me, what you're up to at the Mill. Are you still enjoying it?"

"Very much." Deirdre said. "I enjoy going. It's done me so much good to be part of something. Everyone's years younger, but it doesn't seem to matter at all. I love being around their energy. You'll have to come over and see us."

"Try stopping me." Sally grinned. "...and your book? How's that coming on?"

"Good, I think. I had absolutely no idea what I was getting into when I started. I couldn't be doing the half of it without Caroline... She..."

Her voice was drowned out by the boom of a ferry boat pulling in. "Shall we walk?"

"Let's." Sally nodded, pushing away the half empty cup, and counting some euros into a dish.

They weaved their way down the bustling promenade, past the line of restaurant tables and ice cream parlors until the path became quieter and they found a seat overlooking the beach.

"Before I forget, I meant to ask, how's Somhairlin enjoying her new job?"

"She's absolutely loving it. She sounds like her old self since she went back, and I don't think that's just because of the job."

"Has she met someone?"

"She has. She says it's early days, doesn't want to jinx it by talking too much about it, but I get the impression it's serious."

"Oh! To be young." Sally smiled. "I'm happy for her."

"You're still incredibly young."

"Well, they do say forty is the new thirty, I suppose."

"You look wonderful," Deirdre told her. "I wouldn't mind being your age again, for sure."

Later, over a dish of shared paella and a few glasses of sangria, Deirdre told Sally where she was up to with her book and how full her days were now that the project was coming together. It had been an age since she'd been out for a lunch like this, and she relished every minute. They parted late in the afternoon with promises to be in touch again soon.

The next morning, knowing it was her last day on the island, Deirdre made her way down the path to the beach early. The sun was rising over a glimmering mirror of calm sea. She left her clothes on a rock and waded up to her waist. The water was warm and felt silky against her skin. She stretched out her arms and bounced her feet on the seabed, looking across to the circular horizon. The skyline and water were ablaze with a deep golden light. Her heart lifted with sheer joy at the incredible beauty that was hers alone to see. She carved into the water and began to swim.

Later that day, as the plane gained height and the island disappeared under a layer of cloud, Deirdre opened her notepad and began to write. The words came easily.

"I'm so sorry you're reading this book. I know you are reading it because you have lost someone you loved very much. Although you think you might never smile again, I believe you will, and you will find a way of keeping your person in your heart. Grief is a path none of us has chosen. It is indescribably lonely, but I want you to know that you are not alone. There are so many of us living our lives after loss. When my husband died, I found some relief from walking in nature and from these poems and songs. I've pulled them together here for you in the hope that..."

She paused. It was only a first draft, but she had discovered her voice.

DIERDRE - SIX MONTHS LATER

Deirdre dashed in from the wind that was whipping around the corner of the building. She shook the rain from her shoulders and looked in on the studio.

"Good morning," she said, "I'm on my way up. Can I get you anything? Coffee?"

"No thanks. I'm still speeding from the espresso I had earlier," Eileen shouted from behind a screen.

"Okay. I'll catch you later."

Deirdre took the lift and felt a frisson of delight, as she often did, opening the door to her own creative space. She threw down her bag, hung her coat on the back of the door, and set up her laptop. Lifting one of her handmade silk scarves, she spread it out on the table and took a series of photographs from different angles. Allowing it to drape over the edge, she took a couple more shots. It was closer to what she needed; the silk pooled softly in intense violet and yellow swirls. This image would create the background for the last page of her book.

What words would she overlay? On the previous pages, she had shared some of the songs and poetry that had helped her to navigate the terrain of early grief.

Her reader would be someone searching for hope, for a sense of direction as they came to the last page. What could she give that person? What was it that she had clung to that had given her strength?

She thought back to the early months, how she had tried to make sense out of her loss and struggled to find a new purpose. She remembered those desolate days and endless nights. What would have consoled her?

Glancing down to the crowded pavement, she saw people going about their day, people who, just like herself, had their own struggles and their own stories to tell. She had her answer. What had given her hope, what continued to give her hope, was the certainty that she still had something to give to the world.

She held the scarf in her hands and closed her eyes. An image floated in front of them of Somhairlin as a little girl in the back seat of the car, her eyes sparkling as they sang an old gospel song on their way to The Academy. She could hear it now:

This little light of mine.
I'm gonna let it shine.
This little light of mine,
I'm gonna let it shine.
This little light of mine,
I'm gonna let it shine.
Let it shine. Let it shine... Let it shine.

She had found the words for the last page. She had also found her title.

THE END

AUTHOR'S AFTERWORD

In March 2020, my husband and I flew from California to London. We were relocating, planning our third act, buying a house in Oxford where we would run courses, write books, and maybe even slow down a little. Within a few days of arriving at our rental apartment, the UK went into 'lockdown.' Nothing had prepared us for what lay ahead, and nothing had prepared me for losing the love of my life, my partner of forty-four years, and my anchor.

After Ken died, the apartment fell silent. Our possessions were still in containers, the Oxford house a lost dream. I craved my piano, books, desk, fire, garden, kitchen - all the comforts of home. I longed to sort through our memorabilia and photographs, to make sense of a lifetime of love and connection, to lose myself in memories. I ached for the freedom to travel, for the companionship of friends. In the absence of it all, I walked...and I walked. The apartment overlooked the river, and I was grateful for the empty towpath and the uncanny silence of a world that, like mine, had stopped turning.

One morning when the tide was far out, I spotted a heron perched on a rock, pulled out my phone, and took a snap. What I captured surprised me. The photograph had a stillness about it, an ethereal quality and a sense of composition. That evening, I printed it off and tacked it to a wall. Over the next few weeks, I set out on the walks with a new sense of purpose, phone in hand.

I saw the ordinary with a new intensity; the texture of fallen bark, the water weeds, the algae, the riverbed. Snatching these images connected me to something outside of myself and to something deep within. Over those months, I took hundreds of pictures, playing around with them on Apps, turning them into collage. I learned that even in the midst of intense pain, it was still possible to find beauty, to be absorbed and in flow. I started to write *Let it Shine* around the time of the first anniversary soon after I had taken an art therapy course in Ibiza. This is not my story, although it is my path.

Of course, not everyone wants to paint or dance or make music, but we all have something, some creative spark that we can kindle to see us through the darkest times. Grief is isolating. It is relentless, but I believe that finding a form of creative expression for it gives us the strength not only to move forward, but to shine our light for others as we do.

Here are a few of the books that have lit my way:

> *Seven Choices: Finding Daylight After Loss Shatters Your World* – Elizabeth Harper Neeld.
> This is the one that I still keep on my bedside table. It is the most comprehensive, practical, and uplifting book on grief and mourning that I've found. It also has a comprehensive Directory of Resources.

Finding Your Element: How to Discover Your Talents and Passions and Transform Your Life – Ken Robinson with Lou Aronica.
This is the sequel to *The Element*. I helped birth the book but had not read it in some time. One day, coming across it, I flicked through the chapter headings. A few leapt out - 'Where are you now?' 'Where's your tribe?' and 'What's Next?' I had no clue, but I took great comfort in the idea that my husband had left me a road map.

All Along You Were Blooming: Thoughts for Boundless Living – Morgan Harper Nichols.
I reference this in *Let it Shine*. The author is a well-known Instagram poet and artist. I found her words to be an incredible source of comfort. I've bought several copies for friends.

The Poetry Pharmacy: Tried-and-True Prescriptions for the Heart, Mind and Soul – William Sieghart
You can dip in and out for a poem depending on your mood. It's "medicine" for the heart.

A Thousand Mornings: Poems – Mary Oliver

Anam Cara – John O'Donohue

And here are some resources for anyone dealing with grief:

> *Surviving Grief* by Gary Sturgis is a wise and authentic guide. I follow Gary on social media and find his daily posts always lift and reassure.

> Mira Simone is a grief coach specialising in healing from trauma. Find her at newmoonmira.com

ABOUT Thérèse

After several years teaching the arts in schools, Marie-Thérèse Robinson started a high-profile publicity and events company specialising in cause related marketing. She launched and managed her husband's career and continues to promote his legacy and the importance of creativity. She is currently designing creative workshops, renovating a cottage in Ireland, and learning how to laugh again. She is the author of two previous novels, *India's Summer* and *Letter from Paris*.

ACKNOWLEDGMENTS

Thank you, Lou Aronica, for making this book possible. Writing it has been an absolute lifeline for me. Thank you for your encouragement, your guidance, and your belief in my work.

Thank you, Ursula McHugh, for spurring me on to write another book and for lighting my creative path.

Thank you, Roseline de Thélin, my "real" creative arts therapist. Your formidable talent as both artist and teacher is a gift.

Thank you Anthony Dunn for helping me to navigate the high-tech world.

Thank you, Lena Byrn, for suggesting the heart-shaped Lough Ouler for the cover. It is beautiful.

Thank you Julie Epstein for the American fine-tuning.

Thank you, Bernadette McMahon, for your feedback on the drafts and your endless patience with me. Your love means the world. Thank you also for the potatoes, the robins, the houses, the roses and the many occasions when I came for a few days and stayed for many weeks.

Thank you, Mel McMahon, for taking time off from much more important work to read the drafts and for the videos, rainy walks to ancient cairns and an ever-open door.

Thank you, Jane Arnell for keeping me on track, and for a lifetime of laughter, manifestation and friendship.

It has taken a village. My heartfelt thanks to my family and friends for always being there when I needed you most; Herb Alpert, Graham Barcus, Tony Barton, Fabienne Barault, Anita Boyle, Zoë Camp, Kath Desforges, Paul Desforges, Ann Dickson, Bryn Freedman, Matt Goldman, Lani Hall, Bronagh Hillan, Sheran James, Carol King, Beryl Lowe, Dee Lakhan, Donna Luskin, Diane McCarter, Noelle Mc Alinden, Rory Mc Shane, Angela Mc Shane, Avril More, Sybille Palmer, Mimi Peak, Ron Pompeii, Lyn Oddo, Christine Ranck, Renee Rolleri, Mark Shelmerdine, Tim Smit, Niki Wheeler, Sheelagh Woods.

Thank you, James and Kate, for always encouraging my writing and for the love and support you have given me while navigating your own grief. Your dad would be incredibly proud of you, as am I.

Thank you to the love of my life, my partner and soulmate Ken (Robinson). This book would not have been written if you were still here, but like so many things in my life, it is only here because of you.